Dedicated to
my wonderful Mom,
and my incredible sister, Laura Baker,
who were both by my side every step of the way,

and to

Luz, My Love,
You are my happily ever after.

Acknowledgments

I would like to thank my family for all their love and support.

I would also like to thank all my friends who supported me throughout the writing of this book.

Finally, a special thank you to Mike Butler, for teaching me so much about the business of thrift stores. I Love You.

Cassie's junior year in high school started out with a bang. Not only did she have the usual first-day-of-school jitters, but she was looking around the crowd for a familiar face – preferably her best friend, Abby, and couldn't find her. Cassie wasn't paying attention to what, or who, was in front of her and, boom, she walked right into the most popular guy at Pueblo Valley High School – Peter Tennison!

Peter was a senior, a jock and every girl in school had a huge crush on him. Cassie was no exception. She was quite certain that Peter didn't even know she existed. After all, last year, she was a mere sophomore and certainly not one of the popular girls at school. This year, Cassie was a junior, and up until the collision, she felt rather mature and excited about being a junior.

Her new-found confidence was helped by the fact that over the summer, she finally, *thank you God in heaven,* started to fill out. She now had boobs and no longer looked like a twelve-year old boy with long hair. Cassie's new breasts and curves still amazed her.

When Cassie collided with Peter, he touched her elbow gently, but then added a cocky sounding "Watch out there, sister." Peter and his friends laughed as they strode down the hallway. With their laughter lingering in Cassie's ears, her newfound confidence was crushed.

Over the next several days, Cassie often passed Peter in the hallway and he never referred to her as "sister" again, but she felt so awkward about the incident, that she imagined each time that he passed her in the hallway, that he assumed that she was just an unbearable klutz and he couldn't possibly notice her for any other reason.

To Cassie's surprise, during the third week of school, she was putting her books away in her locker and Peter walked up to her.

"Hi," Peter casually leaned one arm on the locker next to Cassie's and looked down at her face, "so that body-to-body contact was a cool way to start the first day of school."

"Ah, ah," Cassie stuttered and stammered. Startled, no words would come out of her mouth. Body to body contact! Was he flirting with me? It wasn't possible, was it? With Cassie's inexperience, she truly did not know. Her mind raced and she quickly concluded that more than likely, he was just trying out a line, like he probably did to every girl in the school. Peter was athletic, handsome, had a quick smile and Cassie suspected he wasn't used to sitting home alone on Friday or Saturday nights.

"I'm sorry," Peter chuckled. "Cat got you by the tongue? Let's start over. My name is Peter Tennison and you are…?" A lazy grin formed on his face. Of course, she knew who he was. Who didn't? He was like a God to all the girls at school.

"You didn't startle me." *Liar.* "Hi, I'm Cassie, Cassie Reed." Peter arched a single eyebrow, took a look around to see who was close by and lowered his head to look into Cassie's eyes. "Pretty name, pretty girl." Cassie couldn't believe her ears.

"Some of us are hanging out after school on Friday at Hank's Diner. We're gonna grab some sodas and fries. Do you want to come with me?"

And that was Cassie's beginning with Peter. They ended up becoming high school sweethearts. Cassie never dated another guy. After Peter graduated from high school, he worked part-time at his father's auto parts store and attended the local community college in town while Cassie was a senior year of high school. Peter's desire was to become a commercial airline pilot. In fact, much to Cassie's dismay, Peter had just told her that he was planning on telling his parents that he wanted to enlist in the Air Force right after his upcoming nineteenth birthday.

When Peter told Cassie his news, she couldn't hide her disappointment. Peter hurriedly reassured her that he still wanted her in his life and that he couldn't leave if he didn't think that she would be here waiting for him when he returned home. Still worried, but feeling somewhat appeased, Cassie tried to accept Peter's life plan with some tentative confidence that she would be part of the picture. As a doe-eyed young girl, Cassie couldn't see her future without Peter Tennison in it.

A few weeks later, Cassie was in her bedroom with Abby. She was fidgeting and couldn't hold still. Abby watched her closely as she nervously bit her nails, sighed and finally jumped up from the bed.

Abby was concerned. "Cassie, is something wrong?"

Cassie hesitated in her movements but then sat back down on the bed next to Abby.

Abby continued. "You've been acting kind of funny for a few days now."

Cassie did have something on her mind. She had been worried for a week and just couldn't keep it to herself anymore. It was unbelievable that she hadn't already told Abby what was on her mind.

Cassie exhaled a deep breath and then blurted out, "I think I might be pregnant!"

Abby gasped and clasped Cassie's hands into hers. "Cassie! Oh my God!" Abby gasped out loud again.

"Have you taken a pregnancy test yet? I can't believe it! I mean, yes, I can. I thought you were on the pill. Oh God. Wow!" Abby was rambling.

Abby pulled Cassie into a hug. "I'm a blithering idiot, I'm sorry. Are you okay? What can I do to help?" Abby pulled her back into an even longer hug and Cassie felt a moment of comfort for the first time in several days.

Tears sprang from Cassie's eyes. "I'm not on the pill," she explained. "I was paranoid about my parents finding out. You know how strict they are. Peter's been using condoms, although he hates them. I think he got too excited and forgot to put it on once," she sighed, "maybe twice."

Cassie took in another big breath. "I haven't taken a pregnancy test yet, but I'm never, *ever* late Abby."

Abby was the strong voice of reason that Cassie needed at that moment. "Okay, here's what we're going to do. We're going to go to Don's Drugstore right now and buy a pregnancy kit. If it's negative, then this is just a false alarm and there's nothing to worry about."

Abby gave Cassie a reassuring look. "Being late can happen, but if it's positive…" she paused and Cassie added "then what?"

It was Abby's turn to take a deep breath. "We'll figure it out." They were clutching hands and Abby finished her thought. "Just like we always do. Together!"

They hugged tightly. Somehow, somewhere inside Cassie, she had to believe that Abby was right. Suddenly Cassie could wait no longer and she needed to know now if she was pregnant. Yes or no.

A half-hour later, they were back from the drugstore and in the bedroom again. They had both read the packaging of the pregnancy test a dozen times. There was nothing new to learn. Cassie was just trying to get up the courage to pee on a stick. Abby watched as Cassie nervously twirled her long chestnut colored hair in her fingers. Cassie chewed on her bottom lip, but then sucked in her breath.

"Here goes." Cassie grabbed the pregnancy test kit and headed to the bathroom.

Two minutes later, they stood outside the closed bathroom door. The stick they were so anxiously waiting to see was lying on the bathroom counter. It would have a negative sign or a positive sign. Cassie looked into Abby's eyes for reassurance and she nodded. Cassie pushed aside her worries about what a pregnancy might mean to her and Peter. Cassie squeezed Abby's hand into her own.

Cassie tried to build up her own confidence. "If it's positive, I know I'm not the first girl to get pregnant in high school and there are lots of young Moms, but it's just a little…" she searched for the words, "just a little scary."

Abby agreed. "Okay, count of three and we'll open the door together and look in. One, two, three…"

Cassie opened the door quickly and they simultaneously looked at the stick on the counter. *Positive.* A lump immediately formed in Cassie's throat. Tears came to her eyes and Abby encircled her in a hug. *I'm eighteen years old, pregnant and Peter's planning on leaving soon. What now?*

Chapter One

Present Day

Bright and early Monday morning, Cassie was feeling more refreshed and relaxed now that the emotionally charged weekend was over. She unlocked the front door and let herself into the quiet of her business, Cassie's Closet. With steaming coffee in one hand, she was ready to start the day.

It *really* had been an emotional weekend. Cassie had taken her only child, Brett, to college in Southern California. After Brett graduated from high school and as the lazy, warm summer months in Northern California unfolded, every day Cassie could feel that the time was quickly approaching when she would have to make the long drive, so that Brett could start his journey as a college freshman.

Throughout the summer, Cassie had an odd, unexplainable feeling that it would be the start of a new journey for her too, just as it did when she discovered she was pregnant while in high school. She couldn't explain where the feeling was coming from, but she could intuitively feel it.

Cassie blew on her coffee and glanced down at her to-do list. It was extensive as usual, especially after being away for an extra day, but before she forgot, and the day got too busy, she remembered to add at the bottom of the list, *'Ask Colleen for the name of her contractor.'*

One of the things she had been delaying for months now was the construction project that she'd had in mind for Cassie's Closet. After jotting down a few more items on the to-do list, Cassie sighed and realized that it felt good to be back to the routine of work.

Cassie took another sip of her coffee and relished the quiet before she opened for business. Cassie's Closet was the lone thrift store in the heart of Pueblo Valley, just on the outskirts of Napa Valley, California. This beautiful and serene valley was famous for its lush vineyards and proximity to San Francisco, or you could drive a couple of hours in the opposite direction to reach the gigantic redwood trees of Mendocino County. Cassie had always considered it God's Country. You had the serenity of the sea or the country close by, or the excitement and activity of San Francisco just a short drive away. It was stunningly beautiful here no matter what the season, but fortunately, in this part of California, there were mild temperatures most months of the year, so it wasn't uncommon at all to see the locals and visitors wearing flip-flops and shorts as early as March, and all the way through late October.

Cassie's Closet was a haven for Cassie and always had been. Some days, like today, when it was quiet before anyone arrived, Cassie looked around the building and still couldn't believe that it was hers. Her good luck in acquiring this business arrived, literally, on the heels of Peter asking for a divorce. It gave Cassie so much, then and now. It offered her a certain financial security, a place where she was needed and the pride in knowing that it had prospered under her care.

Cassie had worked at the store part-time, throughout Brett's childhood. When she first started working there, it was called the "Old Town Thrift Store" and it was owned by Margo and Sean O'Connell. Cassie loved going to work each morning. The customers were always kind and she enjoyed listening to their stories. Oftentimes, they were struggling to make ends meet and this store allowed them to clothe their children or pick up small household items or furniture at a reasonable cost. Other times, the customers were serious collectors and looking for whatever treasure might be discovered. The last several years, other people were interested in going "green" and wanted to reuse and recycle as much as possible. The reasons for shopping there varied and it made for a lot of different customers with various interests and needs.

Near the time of Cassie's divorce, the O'Connell's were getting close to retirement age. They had been relying on Cassie more heavily, trusted her with their store and were eager to teach her the ropes in the hope that she could manage the business for them as they eased into retirement.

Their only son, Kevin, had no interest in this business. He owned 'Pueblo Valley Playhouse,' the local theater, in town, with his wife, Colleen. Kevin O'Connell had two loves in his life; one was for his wife, and the next was the theater. His passions were in that order and that order only. His passion did not include the thrift store.

Cassie, on the other hand, enjoyed every second of it. Cassie often threw out suggestions to the senior O'Connell's. "What if we had quarterly sales where absolutely everything was fifty percent off? We'd have customers lining up the door." Sean O'Connell would just mumble under his breath that they couldn't reduce the stock to that level and replenish it overnight. Even though Mr. O'Connell didn't agree with all Cassie's suggestions, she knew that with the right marketing, they could have a ton of customers in the store, move out the old, stale items and have new, fresh stock ready within days.

Cassie suspected that both Mr. and Mrs. O'Connell liked her ideas and drive, and could certainly see the value in them, but those ideas required a great deal of energy and it was something neither one of them had the stamina for. Cassie noticed they were talking about retiring much more frequently.

Just days after Peter told Cassie that he wanted a divorce, Cassie was not only hurt, but frightened. Among all the worries and concerns, one of the biggest was what was she going to do financially? When she became pregnant during her senior year in high school, she graduated, but never attended college. She was a new Mom and focused all her time and energy on being the best Mom that she could be.

Now Cassie was sick with worry about her lack of education and not having any skills in the real world. The thought of going back to school was a possibility, albeit a very scary one.

It was during this difficult time, when Cassie was at work sorting inventory and tears rolled down her face. She hadn't noticed that Margo O'Connell had entered the inventory room. She sat down next to Cassie and pulled a tissue from her shirt pocket and gently started to wipe Cassie's tears away.

"Child, what on earth is wrong?" Margo touched Cassie's face softly with her hand.

Cassie felt like she had been carrying a burden so heavy and so daunting that more tears came when Mrs. O'Connell touched her cheek. Cassie sobbed out the words. "Peter wants a divorce."

Mrs. O'Connell pulled Cassie close to her and held her tight as Cassie sobbed. At one point, Cassie noticed that Mr. O'Connell walked into the room, but Mrs. O'Connell silently shooed him out and he closed the door quietly.

"Now, now, child, everything will be okay." Mrs. O'Connell handed Cassie another tissue, as the other one had practically disintegrated.

"Mrs. O'Connell, what am I going to do? Peter wants to sit down with Brett in the next few days and tell him that we're getting a divorce. How am I supposed to explain this to Brett?"

Cassie took another gasping breath with the thought of her most pressing worry. "How am I going to support my son?"

In frustration, Cassie exhaled out a huge breath. She slumped her shoulders. "I know I'll find a way. Maybe I should go back to school – I don't know. I just don't know what to do."

The tears that never really stopped running down Cassie's cheeks started flowing again. Mrs. O'Connell held Cassie as she stroked her hair and whispered softly over and over again, "everything will be just fine, dear." Cassie wanted to believe her, but at that moment, she believed that nothing would ever be fine again.

A few days later, Cassie was once again sorting through inventory in a back room. Mrs. O'Connell had graciously allowed her to stay behind the scenes for now and away from the customers. Cassie was eternally grateful to her. Normally she loved chatting with the customers and being up front at the store, but her heart and soul just wasn't into casual conversations and the tears still arrived on an unexpected and random basis.

Mrs. O'Connell popped her head into the room. "Dear, do you think you could stay a little late tonight?"

Cassie had nothing else to do and Brett was at a friend's house working on a school project. "Sure, what's up?"

"The mister and I would like to have a few words with you before you leave. Could you come into the office about 7:00 p.m.?"

Cassie wondered if perhaps the O'Connell's were going to offer her some additional hours. "Sure, I'll be there."

At promptly 7:00 p.m., Cassie walked into the small office. Both Mr. and Mrs. O'Connell were already there and waiting. The office was crammed with a desk and two small chairs parallel to it. Next to the desk was a large four-drawer filing cabinet and a credenza that held a computer, printer, fax machine and dozens of unorganized files. Mr. O'Connell motioned for Cassie to sit down as he finished writing on a legal pad. He considered the computer some new-fangled gadget and he had no use for it. It was only there because their son, Kevin, bought it for them as a gift and Kevin promised them great rewards of organization beyond their wildest dream. Mr. O'Connell had his doubts about that.

Cassie had often eyed that office and thought herself efficient enough to one day get it in order. Cassie wondered if she offered to organize the office now, if it could be a way to get more hours and help the O'Connell's. Cassie knew they could use the help and it became even more obvious as she looked at Mr. O'Connell's swollen, arthritic knuckles, as he painfully struggled to finish writing his notes.

Mrs. O'Connell had been leaning against the filing cabinet and she pulled a chair next to her husband's chair. "Come on, now, Sean, Cassie here would like to go home at some point this evening."

Mr. O'Connell looked up and smiled at his wife. She could always get him to do what she wanted. It had been that way for over forty-five years now and he wouldn't have it any other way. He then turned his attention to Cassie and motioned for her to close the door.

After she did so, she watched as the O'Connell's looked at each other. Mrs. O'Connell nodded to him and with a smile said, "Go on, Love, let's have our talk with Cassie and then we can all head home for the evening."

Mr. O'Connell began, "Cassie, I want to start off by saying that my lovely wife here told me about your troubles with your husband." Softly he looked into Cassie's eyes. "She wasn't trying to betray your trust by sharing your secrets,"

Cassie eagerly jumped in when he paused. "Oh, I know that!" It never occurred to Cassie that Margo wouldn't tell her husband what was going on with Cassie. "I'm glad you know what's going on."

Mr. O'Connell smiled at Cassie sweetly and continued, "Cassie, dear, let me finish."

Then Mr. O'Connell began, "As you know, dear, we've been considering retiring for quite some time now." Mr. O'Connell looked at his wife and there was a twinkle in his eye.

"I would like to spend my remaining days with my beautiful Bride." Cassie caught the blush along Mrs. O'Connell's cheeks. It wasn't the first time that she'd witnessed them flirting. She found it very sweet and charming. That's what she always imagined growing up and it was still something she secretly longed for, even in the face of Peter's demand for a divorce. To have the kind of love the O'Connell's shared for a lifetime, would be such a gift to Cassie's way of thinking.

Mr. O'Connell spoke and brought Cassie back to the present. "For a time there, we thought that Kevin might like to take over this business, but his love is at the performing arts center and we could never ask him to give up something he loves so much." Once again they looked at each other. There was a silent, mutual understanding of what was to be said next.

"As you know from your years of working here, this business certainly isn't glamorous, but it's provided a steady and decent income to us for many years now."

Mrs. O'Connell could no longer contain herself and she jumped in as soon as her husband paused to take a breath. "Cassie, dear, we want you to buy the business from us!"

What! Buy their business! Cassie's mind suddenly raced and she scooted to the edge of the chair.

"I would love too, I mean, I love this place. You know that, but with the divorce," Cassie slowly shook her head in doubt, "I don't know how I could possibly afford it and I have to think about Brett, and…"

Mr. O'Connell held up his hands to interrupt. Then he slid his handwritten notes from the legal pad to Cassie. As she glanced at the figures and words on the rough outline, he continued.

"We don't expect you to fork over a fortune right now. We know you don't have it, but we think we've come up with a way to have a win-win situation for everyone."

Cassie was listening with every fiber of her being and she was just short of sliding off the edge of her chair now.

"Not only do we own the business, but we own the building. The missus and I are proposing that you lease the building from us. We'll see about renewing the lease, or perhaps you can buy us out, in say, five or ten years. We think that will give you time to get on your feet."

Mr. O'Connell looked to his wife and she once again nodded in reassurance. "Of course, we would receive a small percentage of the store sales, and a portion of the lease payments would go towards the purchase price. This arrangement helps to pad our retirement too. Hopefully, at the end of that five or ten year period, you will have put all your great ideas into this place and make it even more profitable."

A smile grew on both of the O'Connell's faces. "The missus and I believe you will have great success in this business."

Cassie was absolutely flabbergasted and thrilled, but she was stunned into silence. Not an easy feat for her. Mrs. O'Connell jumped in, "We'll let the lawyers take a look and make it all legal," she paused, "that is, if you're interested."

Mrs. O'Connell drove her piercing blue eyes into Cassie's, as if to break her from the stunned silence. "Assuming it's something you would want to do, dear?"

Cassie immediately jumped up from her seat. "Oh yes! Absolutely! I have so many ideas." Her thoughts raced wildly, "I really think I could make a great success of it." Cassie briefly hesitated, suddenly feeling insecure. "Are you sure?"

Mr. and Mrs. O'Connell laughed together before Mr. O'Connell answered her. "We're no dummies and you don't think we'd sell our business to someone who would make a mess of it, now do you?" Cassie raced around the desk to hug them. At that moment, they weren't her future landlords or business partners, but her dear, sweet friends and in the most unprofessional manner possible, Cassie gave them each a big, fat, juicy kiss on both their cheeks. They all laughed. Cassie realized that in that moment, it was the first time that she had laughed or felt hopeful since Peter told her he wanted a divorce.

Later that night, Cassie sat on the sofa, holding a glass of chardonnay in one hand and the O'Connell's proposal in the other hand. Brett was in bed and asleep, blissfully unaware that his parents were going to turn his world upside down in a matter of days. Cassie couldn't think about that in this second though. Her mind was awhirl with the possibility of buying the thrift store.

It wouldn't be easy and it would require a ton of work, but she wasn't afraid of hard work. In studying the O'Connell's proposal, Cassie started to think of ways to assemble potential sources of cash to buy an ownership of this business. The O'Connell's had been very generous and kind, certainly much kinder to Cassie than they would have been to a stranger proposing to buy their business.

Cassie knew that selling her current home was an option for a larger chunk of cash. It was an option she realized she would need to consider after Peter's big announcement anyway. Peter would get his share of the house proceeds, of course, but she and Brett didn't need such a large home. Cassie could use some of the proceeds from the sale of this house to purchase a smaller home for the two of them and the rest could be invested into the business. On top of that, she and Peter had some savings and when her grandfather passed away, Cassie was granted some stock. Perhaps it could be sold and liquidated?

The more Cassie thought about it, the more she believed this could be a viable way to support herself and Brett. Additionally, this business allowed her to have some flexibility with the hours if she needed to be home for Brett, and continue to hone her developing business skills. Cassie also wanted to pursue the idea she had to create a partnership with various local charities to receive some of their unused donated items. Another idea dancing around her head was the idea of buying out estate sales of fully furnished homes.

Mr. O'Connell was right, this wasn't a glamorous business, but it was much needed and valuable to the community. With the opportunities Cassie envisioned in working with the larger charities, it would allow her to keep a larger volume of inventory on hand. The extra inventory would help her to actually advertise and have those quarterly sales events that could be quite prosperous. Cassie saw that alone as an opportunity ripe for success.

After talking it over with Peter and the lawyers, Cassie met the O'Connell's and their attorney three weeks later to sign final papers. It took major scrambling, including Peter signing off his interest in the business, since they were still married, but the attorneys took care of that and the details had finally been sorted out. Peter was quick to sign off on the business once it was confirmed that he'd have no liability for any loss. He probably believed that there would be no gain either, but Cassie believed it could and would be profitable and she made it clear that Peter wouldn't have any interest in the gains either.

It *was* hard work to build-up the business. Fortunately, all that hard work was rewarded and Cassie had the incredible opportunity to buy-out the rest of the O'Connell's interest in the business several years later. Shortly before she paid off the O'Connell's, she knew it was time to really make it her own. With the blessing and support of the O'Connell's, the name of the business was formally and legally changed to 'Cassie's Closet.'

Now that Brett was away at college, there were some more changes Cassie wanted to make; this time to the interior. Cassie had grand ideas for showcasing her biggest sellers. Before she got lost in thought again, she picked up the phone and left a message for Colleen to call her with the name and number of the contractor she had used recently for the remodeling project at the Pueblo Valley Playhouse.

Chapter Two

"Colleen, just the person I wanted to see." Cassie smiled at her friend's unexpected appearance.

"Hello, Cassie, darling, I noticed that you left a message on my voice mail, so I thought I would just stop by instead of calling." Colleen looked around and waved to a few people in the store that she knew.

Colleen approached Cassie for a hug. "You mentioned to me last week that you have a box of accessories that we can use for this season's production of "Dig It, Dudley" so I thought I'd pick those up while I'm here *and* check in with you."

'Dig It, Dudley' was the next production to be held at Pueblo Valley Playhouse. It was going to be a fun, funky musical romp through the 70's and Colleen and Kevin were expecting mostly sold out crowds for each performance. Cassie had found some pieces in her store that she thought would work great for this production.

Cassie smiled at Colleen warmly. "I'm so glad you stopped by. The accessories are in a box in my office. Do you have time for a cup of tea?"

Colleen responded by placing her arm around Cassie's back and led her towards Cassie's office. "I always have time for tea with friends."

In walking back towards Cassie's office, Cassie thought to herself, that it was somewhat surprising that they were such good friends, because on the surface, there were far more differences between them than similarities, but they just clicked instantly when they met all those years ago and their friendship had grown stronger over time.

Colleen is fifteen years older than Cassie and her life is so different from Cassie's. She's been married to Kevin O'Connell for almost thirty years and they are still ridiculously happy. They never had children, but the theater, the cast members and crew became their children. It was their life and they lived it and loved it to the fullest.

Colleen is colorful, feisty and gregarious. In running the performing arts center with Kevin, it reflected her personality perfectly. She's bold, funny and every word that she said is meant to be heard by whatever audience is present. That was in sharp contrast to Cassie's much more introverted, quiet personality.

Colleen had been coming to Cassie's Closet for as long as Cassie had worked here. As the daughter-in-law of the O'Connell's, the prior owners, Colleen had been a regular and frequent visitor. As Colleen and Cassie got to know each other, especially more so after Cassie purchased the business, they became very close and each counted the other as one of their closest friends.

In addition to that, Cassie helped out Colleen and Kevin at their theater. Having Cassie's Closet allowed her to provide some of the much needed clothing and accessories for their various theater productions.

As Cassie poured hot water into their cups, Colleen inspected the contents of the box. "Oh Cassie, these are just wonderful. These funky, colorful scarves will be amazing for the show. Oh, and look at the platforms on these shoes!" Cassie smiled at Colleen's excitement.

Cassie nodded towards the box. "With the 70's theme of the production, I suspected those would be perfect. Did you notice the wide, white belts that are in there too?"

Colleen practically purred. "Oh, very nice! If you happen to come across any shirts or blouses that have a psychedelic-type pattern, those would be perfect too."

Cassie made a mental note of her request. "I'll keep it on the list."

Then she thought of something else. "If we don't find something in stock that works, you can always come by and get some of the silk sheets and have the seamstress cut swatches from them and design matching shirts."

Colleen's eyes tinkled. "You're such a smart girl!" Cassie had to laugh. "Well, I'm certainly glad you think so."

As they sipped their tea, Colleen continued to inspect the contents of the box. Once she was finished with her inspection, she sat back in the chair more comfortably but then remembered to pull out a business card out from her purse.

She handed the card to Cassie. "On your phone message, you said you wanted the name of the person I used for the renovations at the theater. His name is Jack Shaw from 'Shaw Brother's Construction Company.' He and his crew did a fabulous job!"

Cassie took the business card from Colleen's hand and looked at it. "I remember being impressed with their work when it was done. The "before and after" work was amazing and really made the theater look sophisticated."

Cassie looked at Colleen. "I recall you saying that they were pretty reasonably priced too, yes?"

Colleen waved her hand in response. "Absolutely! You know Kevin. He had a very strict budget and Jack's company never went over budget *and* they finished ahead of schedule, which is amazing for a construction company."

Colleen continued. "I had checked with several friends that used Jack and they were all very pleased, so it's not just my recommendation."

Even if it was just Colleen's recommendation, Cassie trusted her friend and knew she wouldn't mislead her. If Colleen was happy with their work, then that was all the recommendation Cassie needed.

Suddenly, Colleen was smiling at Cassie. Cassie recognized a very familiar, devilish look in her friend's bright blue eyes. Cassie wondered what was going through Colleen's wicked little mind this time?

"Colleen…what is that mischievous look for?" Colleen threw her head back and laughed. Her soft red hair framed her pale Irish skin and a soft pink color was coming to her cheeks.

"What?" Impatience was getting the best of Cassie only because she knew her friend and she was clearly up to something.

Colleen took another sip of her tea before elaborating, "I just remembered what a handsome, hunk of a man Jack Shaw is. If I remember correctly, and I'm sure I do, he's divorced and about your age."

Cassie shook her head, no. "No, no, don't go there." Cassie lifted her hands up in mock frustration. "Remember me. I'm the one who's not good dating material. My last few dates haven't gone so well." With her eyebrows cocked, Cassie tried to drive her point home. "Don't we remember?"

Cassie felt like her statement was entirely true. The couple of dates she had gone on since the divorce were agonizingly boring and she wasn't in a hurry to travel down that road again. However, on occasion, in quiet moments, she allowed herself to think that if she ever started dating again, that that man would need to be a very special man; otherwise, it wasn't worth the effort to date or consider risking her heart with another man, not after her ex-husband's infidelity.

Colleen disagreed completely with Cassie reference to dating. "No, dear, it wasn't you. You're a doll, simply a gorgeous doll and I've watched dozens of men in here, turn their head to take another look at you. The last few guys you dated were just losers and not worthy of you anyway."

Cassie sighed a little and thought to herself that she just needed a contractor, not a date, yet she appreciated her friend's support. "You're just saying that because you're my friend, but I love you for it anyway."

If the truth be told, Cassie did think about enjoying male companionship from time to time. Her friends had all been pressuring her a bit more lately, now that Brett was flying from the proverbial nest, to at least activate an online dating account.

It was a scary thought for Cassie. On the one hand, of course, she would love to have a great dinner conversation with a gorgeous man who couldn't take his eyes off her, followed by a slow, sexy dance or two, followed by an even slower, sexier romp afterwards, but the reality of it was that it never flowed quite that easily and history had confirmed for her that that kind of relationship didn't seem to be in the playbook for her.

On top of that, Cassie was a bit old-fashioned, at least in some ways. In her heart, she knew what she really wanted was a *real romance* that was more than just sex. Cassie was doubtful of it happening for her now. She wasn't willing to put herself out into the dating world right now. But there were other times when Cassie wishfully allowed herself to consider that, maybe, just maybe, someday, it would be wonderful to meet an attentive, caring man who wanted the same kind of relationship that she desired.

Of all the great romances Cassie had known in her life, such as both sets of the O'Connell's, and her parents, all of them were genuinely best friends first and foremost, and they each knew that they could count on their spouse for life, no matter what life brought them. To Cassie, everything else, the intimate dances, stolen glances and the sexy romps, were all just the icing on the cake to the kind of commitment they shared.

Colleen nudged Cassie from her brief fantasy, when she reminded Cassie that she had urged her to "casually stop by" when Jack Shaw was working for her at the playhouse. Cassie remembered that she was slightly intrigued by the idea at the time, but she let her nerves get the best of her then. Besides, Cassie was pretty certain that Colleen wouldn't be subtle about it. Knowing her friend's well-intentioned ways, Colleen would probably throw Cassie on top of Jack Shaw, tell him that Cassie was the one for him and walk away with a satisfied smile on her face.

Colleen continued. "Wait until you see Jack, there's something sort of rugged and sexy about him. I'm telling' you, if it wasn't for the fact that Kevin can still curl my toes, I would have thrown myself at Jack's feet and offered to be his sex slave for life."

Cassie feigned shock at Colleen's declaration, "Colleen! What would Kevin say if he heard you say that?"

Colleen swatted at the air, "Pashaw, I told him that myself and more than once too."

"And what did that sweet husband of yours say to that?"

Colleen chuckled and a blush crossed her checks. "Oh darlin', it's not so much what he said, but what he did!"

Cassie laughed out loud. Knowing Kevin the way she did, he would have taken it in stride, but made sure that Colleen wouldn't be thinking about another man anytime soon. No doubt, ultimately that was Colleen's ulterior motive.

"Colleen O'Connell, you're a trouble maker." They chuckled together and Colleen nodded. "Yes, I am, and proud of it!"

Cassie teased her sweet, charming friend, "You know one of these days, I'm going to whisper in Kevin's ear that he's been making a mistake for thirty years and that I'm really the one for him. I'll suggest that we run away together and live out our days in Ireland."

"Darlin', if you told him that, he'd be floating on Cloud Nine for weeks and his head would be so puffed up, there'd be no living' with him."

At that moment, Abby, Cassie's best friend, popped her head in the office door. "Hey, are you two having a party without me?"

Cassie walked over to give Abby a hug. "Thank God you arrived and saved me from ruining Colleen's marriage and running away with Kevin."

Abby jumped in on the teasing. "Oh no you don't, I'm next in line if Kevin ever leaves Colleen. I'd fight you to the death in a duel."

Colleen just shook her head while listening to the two of them tease her about Kevin and giggled under her breath. It wasn't the first time that Cassie or Abby had threatened to steal Kevin away. It was a fun, harmless running joke that they all shared.

But the truth of it was, and everyone knew it, Kevin thought the sun rose and set on Colleen and vice versa. For all her declarations of willingness to become someone's sex slave for life, she still looked at Kevin like they were newlyweds. More than once, Cassie had witnessed tender, loving looks between the two of them. It made her certain that the honeymoon certainly wasn't over for them, even though they had stood at the altar thirty years ago.

Cassie thought many times that it must be the most amazing and wonderful feeling to find your true love, your soul-mate and know with absolute certainty that you had found your life's partner.

Probably one of the things that intimidated Cassie most about dating and looking for love, was simply not knowing where or how to start. She met Peter when she was a teenager. She had never dated another guy before him and never learned the technique of flirting or showing someone that you were interested in them. Nor did she learn to recognize when someone appeared to be interested in her. It seemed to Cassie that some women just knew how to flirt, be suggestive and feel sexy instinctively, but Cassie certainly wasn't one of those women.

After Abby and Colleen left Cassie's Closet, Cassie placed a call to Shaw Brother's Construction Company and spoke with Jeremy Shaw, who is one of the co-owners. Cassie gave him a brief description of what she was interested in having done at Cassie's Closet and they agreed that his brother, Jack, would stop by the following afternoon to meet with her, do a walk-thru of the area and take some measurements.

As Cassie wrote the appointment in her calendar, she tried to ignore the memory of Colleen teasing her about Jack Shaw being a good-looking, sexy, divorced man.

Chapter Three

Jack Shaw pulled his work truck up in front of "Trebbiano's Restaurant." His crew had just finished working there after four weeks of some pretty serious renovations. Jack was planning to meet with the owner, Doug. Jack had heard through his brother, and business partner, Jeremy, that Doug was angry over the final bill. Apparently he had a dispute about time and costs versus what was in the contract. Jack had a copy of the signed contract in his shirt pocket.

Dealing with the contracts and bills wasn't normally Jack's forte, as Jeremy usually handled that, but since Jack had known Doug since high school, both he and Jeremy were hoping that Jack could resolve the billing issue quickly. Jack wasn't looking forward to dealing with the financial aspects of a dispute. He was the doer, the worker and the skilled carpenter – Jeremy was the dollar and cents guy, although Jeremy could still swing a hammer when he needed too. Still, Jack didn't want to have a dispute with any customer, friend or not, so he had every intention of leaving with both sides feeling satisfied with the outcome.

Today Jack had been working almost non-stop since 7:00 a.m. at his latest project at one of the picturesque vineyards in Napa Valley. He was hot, sweaty and thirsty and the liquid gold of the thirst-quenching beer from the tap was calling his name. No beer yet, Jack told himself. First, deal with this money dispute, do an estimate for someone over at Cassie's Closet, and then you can treat yourself to a hot shower, a big, fat medium-rare burger and a cool, satisfying beer.

Jack walked up to the newly refinished bar and stroked the smooth surface. It now had a deep, rich mahogany color to it that was reflected by the dim, low-hanging pen lights. He took another look around and was proud of the work that he and his team had done in the restaurant. Before the remodeling was done, the restaurant hadn't been refurbished in probably twenty years and it looked tired and dated. Now it looked and felt renewed. Several patrons sat along the bar, sipping beer or cocktails. Jack knew several of the locals and nodded to them in greeting.

Nicki, the very pretty, and sexy, young bartender sashayed up to the counter. "Hey, Jack, what can I do you for?"

Doug was a smart business man and he hired Nicki for a reason. With her long blonde hair, low-cut black vest and rockin' body, she was very easy on the eyes. The regular patrons of the restaurant weren't coming in just to look at Jack's handiwork, that's for sure.

Nicki had been flirting with Jack throughout the renovations, but Jack didn't take it too seriously. In fact, he never took any woman too seriously these days. Jack returned Nicki's smile, but he wasn't interested in her, although this tired, thirsty man sure did appreciate that she threw him a come-on glance once in a while.

Instead of teasing back, he gave Nicki a quick smile and nodded to the back door, "Is Doug here?"

"No, not yet. He called a few minutes ago and he's stuck in traffic. He asked if you'd wait for him. He'll be here soon." She leaned over so that more of her cleavage was showing. "Can I pour you a cool one while you wait?"

"Unfortunately," Jack stated, and he genuinely felt that way at the moment, "I still have an estimate to do. How about a glass of ice water instead?"

Nicki reached for the dispenser and filled it with cold water. "I owe you a rain check then." She winked at Jack as she handed him the cool glass of water. Jack took another glance at some much-appreciated cleavage before she straightened up, turned and sashayed away.

Jack thought he had noticed his youngest brother, Jon's, car in the parking lot, which wouldn't be surprising. He headed towards the back room where the pool table was and there was Jon. He was bent over the table ready to sink the eight ball in as his opponent watched and readied to pull some money out of his wallet. Jon sank it in the right corner pocket, just as he called out. "Pay up suck-errrr!" Jon's latest victim plopped a twenty on the table and stormed out of the room.

Jon realized Jack was watching and leaned over to give his brother a high-five. "Pretty sweet shot, huh?"

"It was a pretty sweet shot, but don't get too cocky little brother, because I can still kick your ass at pool on any day of the week that ends in 'y.'"

Jon, Jeremy and Jack had a long history of good natured brotherly competition. They all claimed they could out-do the other at anything the other claimed to do better. Not so gently, Jack reminded Jon that he was still the undefeated champion of the pool table in their family.

Jack noticed Jon looking Nicki's way. The corner of Jon's mouth was turned up into a partial grin as he watched Nicki glide towards some new customers who entered the bar area. Now, Jack understood why Jon was here in the middle of the afternoon. That, and he was a cop and his days' off were mid-week.

"So little brother, are you going to go for it?" Jack asked, nodding his head in Nicki's direction.

Jon took his eyes away from the buxom bartender for a split second. "I'm trying! I'm telling you Jack, she's every man's dream come true. Look at her. She's the perfect woman! That honey blonde hair, those blue eyes, the sexy tan – she's the total package!"

Jon looked at Nicki dreamily." I swear to God, the buttons on that vest are ready to give way any second and I don't want to miss a second of it when it happens!"

Jack couldn't disagree about Jon's description of her, but with one major exception -- she wasn't his dream come true. Nicki was perfect for his flirtatious, long-confirmed bachelor of a brother. Jack enjoyed the view, but he stopped believing in perfect women or dreams coming true when Stacey left him and the divorce followed.

Divorce, he still struggled over the definition of that one little word. How could you call it a 'divorce' when total abandonment was more like it? How could it be a divorce when you walk into your house after work and it's completely empty? All the furniture—even the dishes and towels were gone, and Stacey was nowhere to be found. His entire life had been stripped completely bare.

But much more important to Jack was that Stacey had taken his sweet little Charlie with her. Charlie! An innocent two-year old toddler! To this day, it created such a pain in Jack that he didn't think he could ever be whole again. No, Jack didn't give a damn about the furniture or anything else that was taken from the house, *except for Charlie*. That was the daily nightmare that never ended for Jack.

To be so betrayed by your wife! It left Jack a tormented man for the better part of two years now. Even remembering it now, the shock; the utter disbelief; the terror and panic of a missing toddler, made the bile raise in his throat and he could feel the intense burn from it lace his throat.

The memories were still powerful and disturbing, even now. Thinking about that terrible day, and all the rage-filled days that followed, Jack could still feel the internal turmoil in his soul. Never in his life, did he think it was possible that one person, much less a person that you thought you could believe in, could betray another human being in the horrible, vicious way that Stacey had betrayed him.

Charlie and Stacey had vanished into thin air. Jack hadn't seen, or heard from Stacey since that fateful day. After several months, and much searching, when Stacey couldn't be located for personal service of the divorce papers, the divorce had to be handled publicly, by way of announcements through various newspapers. Legally that was all he could do since he couldn't find her. But at least that part of it was done and Jack acknowledged several times since then, that he didn't want to be legally tied to Stacey, but the emotional ties he had to Charlie, still clung to his heart.

Jack spent that first awful year searching high and low for Stacey and Charlie. It would have been easy for him to let Stacey go; that's not who he wanted to find. It was Charlie. His search had *everything* to do with Charlie.

Jack had long since quit caring about Stacey. What Jack couldn't face then, but what he understood as the veil of pain lifted, was that Stacey was too young, restless, selfish and immature to be married, or to be a parent. Unfortunately, Jack realized it too late.

An actual marriage meant nothing to Stacey, but she just wasn't the type to be without a man in her life. Soon enough Jack would discover that it wasn't just one man that she needed, but several.

Jack was ashamed of it now, but he chose to ignore it when he caught Stacey flirting with his friends, his brothers or any male that was in her immediate vicinity. He had his reasons for staying with her, and again, they all had to do with Charlie.

After Stacey left, he was forced to face all the inner demons and listen to the voices that he tried to quiet while they were together. Stacey wasn't just a harmless flirt, like Jon. The odds were more than pretty good that she had cheated on Jack, and more than once. His strong intuition never misled him, but he couldn't face breaking up his family then.

Although he couldn't imagine life without Charlie, he'd been forced to live with it since Charlie had vanished with Stacey two years ago. He missed the child that he thought of as his son, even if the evidence Stacey left implied something contrary to that.

Now Jack was trying to move on and pick up the pieces. He had no other choice.

Jack shook off the memories. For now, he had to stop remembering. He needed to resolve the contract issue with Doug and then go and do that one final bid at Cassie's Closet. After that, he'd treat himself to a cold beer that sounded even more appealing now that he had let himself remember Charlie's disappearance once again.

Jack nodded to Jon. "Good luck with Nicki, little bro. I'll see you at Mom and Dad's on Sunday for dinner." With a swat across Jon's back, Jack headed towards Doug's office.

Chapter Four

Jack pulled up in his truck in front of Cassie's Closet. It was a much larger building than he had anticipated, very industrial in style and warehouse like, surrounded by several other businesses – a Chinese restaurant, a jewelry store, a party supply store and a drug store. Actually, it was at a great location, with an easy route to another mini-mall and access to the highway nearby. He had driven by this area many times while working or running errands, but he had never paid much attention to what was specifically in this location.

As he walked through the parking lot towards the door, he breathed in deeply. His earlier trip down memory lane, remembering Charlie, had taken the wind out of his sails, but this was the end of the day and afterwards he would go home and grab that hot shower and cold beer that he had been thinking about for the last hour.

With his old-school notebook in hand and tape measure attached to his belt, he walked in and was surprised by the number of people still wandering around Cassie's Closet. It was a huge space, probably 20,000 square feet. Inside, there was a vast area of clothing; another area of furnishings; another with kitchen appliances and dishes; yet another area with shoes, purses, belts and even a decent size jewelry counter. Next to it was an area that was total mish-mash with toys, books, glassware and anything else you could imagine. It seemed to be organized chaos and a place that he was sure his mother would absolutely love. In fact, now that he thought about it, he had some recollection of his Mom talking about this place before.

Jack approached the main cashier area and was met by a quick, friendly smile from a teenage boy.

"Hi, can I help you?"

"I have an appointment with Cassie Reed. My name is Jack Shaw."

"I'll go get her." He left with a bouncy step after telling the other cashier that he was leaving but would be right back. Jack watched him walk towards a back office door and poke his head in.

A moment later, Jack spotted who he assumed was Cassie Reed walking out of the office and towards him. Something caught in his throat or his chest, he wasn't sure which, maybe both, but the feeling surprised him and he quickly tried to push it aside.

Cassie had long, chestnut colored hair; it was shiny and hit mid-way down her back. She was wearing a colorful, multi-patterned skirt that flowed down her legs. The fabric highlighted the outline of her long legs as she walked towards him. On top of the skirt, she wore a brown, three-quarter length sleeve blouse that clung to her body, along with a wide belt that sat at her hip. A large turquoise necklace and matching turquoise earrings swung gently as she walked towards Jack.

As she approached him, her hazel-colored eyes caught with Jack's eyes and she had a warm, friendly smile. A catch in his throat tightened.

"Hi, Mr. Shaw," she reached her hand out to shake his hand, "I'm Cassie Reed. Thank you for coming over to meet with me."

Jack cleared his throat a bit, returned both the smile and the handshake. *I'd gladly meet you anywhere, he thought to himself.* "Call me Jack."

Cassie released his hand from their handshake. "Jack, it is. Please call me Cassie." With a nod of agreement, Jack bowed his head slightly. He realized that he hadn't taken his eyes off her since she walked out of her office. He looked away then and looked towards the store.

"My brother didn't give me too many specifics about the type of work you're interested in. Do you want to walk around and give me some of your thoughts, or maybe talk first in your office?"

"Why don't we go into my office and talk first?" She turned towards the office. With Jack behind her, Cassie raised her eyebrows and let out a silent whistle once her face had turned away from Jack's. Cassie reprimanded herself. Maybe she should have let Colleen throw her onto Jack when he was working at the theater; he was absolutely gorgeous!

When they got to Cassie's office, she signaled for him to sit down in the chair across from her desk.

"Would you like something to drink?"

Since Jack could feel the now, ever present, lump in his throat, he responded, "some water would be great, thanks." Cassie retrieved two bottles of chilled water from the mini fridge in her office and handed one to Jack.

Cassie observed Jack from across the desk. She was pleasantly surprised at how handsome he was. When she spotted him at the cashier's counter, she noticed immediately that he had wispy, black hair, with just a hint of gray along the temple. He had gorgeous dark eyes that looked almost black. His dark eyes were complimented by his tanned complexion. She suspected it was more from working outdoors than heritage, and Jack was very appealing to look at. She felt a strange something stirring in her belly and the realization of it caught her off guard.

Jack was wearing jeans and a light cotton flannel shirt, unbuttoned at the neck, with the sleeves rolled up to his elbows. Underneath was a deep, blue t-shirt that matched the color in the flannel shirt. She guessed that he was about her age, maybe a couple of years older. As she handed him the water, she noticed that she could smell the sweet scent of wood on his skin, which was also oddly appealing to her.

Cassie began to talk and Jack reached for his notepad. "I don't know if it's possible, but there are certain items in the store that sell really well and I'd like to somehow showcase the areas where they're located." Jack could hear the excitement in her voice growing, as she started to speak.

"I have this idea, that along the perimeter of the store, I would like to set up a few different areas to highlight different sections of the store. The first one is the children and baby section. That area has a lot of customer traffic, so if it's possible to design a space that looked like a kid's room, I think people would gravitate towards it."

At Cassie's pause, Jack jumped in. "It wouldn't be a problem to design an area that looks like a children's bedroom." He went on, "I noticed a huge amount of children's clothing that was hanging up. Do you still want to do that?"

Cassie shook her head no. "My biggest seller is the clothing for adults and there's no way that I could create a space where they weren't all hanging up, but for the kids' area, I would really like to soften it up and have shelves or maybe open-faced dressers to act as shelving units, so that a lot of the kids' clothing could be folded."

Jack nodded in agreement and he was starting to catch on to her vision. "We could even do something that looks like a crib, but without the front railing, and shelves that look like bunk beds, although obviously, lower."

Cassie clasped her hands together and smiled with glee. "Oh, I love that idea."

Jack started to take notes feverishly and Cassie continued. "I know I'll never get away from the industrial look, and I don't want to actually, but I would like the store to feel more welcoming and warm." Jack bowed his head as he took notes, but thought to himself that he felt very warm suddenly and suspected that it may have something to do with the lovely lady that was sitting across the desk from him, versus the temperature of the office.

Jack realized that he wasn't paying close attention, as he caught the last part of Cassie's comment. "...making the perimeter walls act as more valuable space, then it gives me more room within the store to showcase other items."

Jack could see the pride in her eyes and it was obvious that she really cared about her store.

Cassie looked down at her notes, so that she wouldn't forget anything.

"The next area that I want to highlight is the kitchen area. I was thinking that if we had an area that looked like a kitchen; it would be a place to keep a large number of the plates, cups, platters and the like. I would also want some shelving for the small appliances and electrical outlets available so that the customers could try out the appliance before they purchased it."

Cassie's vision was starting to form in Jack's mind and he felt like a similar approach to the toddler and baby area could be used for the kitchen area.

"I think it would be nice to have a designated kitchen area. I can give you estimates for different types of wood for the cabinets, but I see the kitchen area as having all open cabinets, top and bottom, to add storage in both areas."

Jack paused as he thought about it. "But not too deep so that your customers can't access the items." Cassie's eyes shone brightly and told Jack that she agreed with him. "The counters could hold the small appliances and I could create an overflow shelving area for anything that the kitchen shelving couldn't hold."

Jack looked into her eyes to see if his comments continued to hit home and represented to Cassie what she envisioned. She smiled at him and he could see the twinkle in her eyes. He was excited too, that their visions were now merging in each other's head. He grinned back at Cassie in response to her smile.

Jack noticed that she had a beautiful smile and one, single dimple on the left side of her cheek – not on the right side, just that one, single dimple on the left side. It was very charming and when Jack looked at it, it caused an unexpected stirring from within once again. Jack thought it was such an ironic twist and a far cry from thirty minutes ago when his spirits were so low, that he seriously considered calling it a day and rescheduling this estimate.

Cassie thought about his ideas for the kitchen. "Oh, Jack, that's a great idea. I like it very much." Her smile grew and Jack felt a surge of pride pounding within him. "I'm so glad you like it. Is there anything else you have in mind?"

Cassie laughed, "You betcha," Jack found himself chuckling along with her.

"The next area is probably more basic, but again, I'd like to feature items that we sell that are normally in a living room area. I want a space that has shelves for books, maybe even pictures and frames and then a place where we can place various chairs, couches, end tables and the like in a kind of living room setting. I know it will be crowded with furniture and won't have the same homey feeling, but again, it would showcase that specific area."

After considering Cassie's comments for a moment, Jack looked up from his sketch and suggested that she simply do a slightly raised platform of approximately 15 feet by 15 feet in dimension to display that area.

"This would give you some of the space you need for the furniture. If you like the sound of it, we could even fabricate what looks like a front door and a non-working fireplace on one standalone wall that is anchored from the ceiling."

Cassie's eyes sparkled. "Oh, that would give it more of the feel I'm going for and really make it look like a living room." She did a mini drum roll on the desk with her hands. "I like it."

Jack continued. "I'll need to take a look at the area and do some measurements, but when I walked in I noticed the furnishings area now. I think we would be able to construct something like you want and also have some storage behind the standalone wall, that wouldn't be accessible to your customers. Then you could store extra furniture, mattresses and bed frames behind it, so that it wouldn't look so cluttered."

Cassie couldn't contain her excitement and clapped her hands together. "I was wondering how to handle that aspect of it. I'm really looking forward to seeing your drawings for that space."

Cassie carried on with her ideas. Jack listened as Cassie talked about expanding the dressing rooms and a few other projects she had in mind.

Jack made notes on the notepad and then looked up at Cassie when it appeared that she was done talking. He put his note pad and pencil down on the desk and for the first time, looked beyond Cassie and noticed the pictures of an older teenage boy on her desk tacked to the billboard behind her desk. Jack nodded towards one of the pictures. "Is that your son?"

Cassie looked to the picture and immediately felt the warmth of both motherly love and pride. "Yes, that's Brett." She exhaled slowly. "He just left for college in southern California last week and I'm trying not to miss him," she hesitated and smiled weakly, "well, at least not too much."

Jack understood all too well about missing the child you love. It was something he could relate to all too well.

"He's a good lookin' boy," Jack paused slightly, "you and your husband must be very proud of him." Jack could kick himself. Why did he say something about her husband? It sounded so obvious, even to his ears. Besides, he'd casually glanced at her left hand and it was bare of a wedding ring, although that often meant nothing these days.

"We are very proud of him. He's a good kid and he has his head straight on his shoulders." Cassie laughed. "At least until he discovers all the gorgeous girls at college. I hope he keeps his head on straight then."

Jack nodded in agreement, but felt an unexpected sinking feeling in the pit of his stomach. She's married. She had specifically used a plural term when saying 'we are very proud of him.' Jack quickly told himself that it's just as well considering everything else in his life. Besides, since Stacey left, trusting women wasn't high on his list of priorities. In fact, he didn't think he could ever trust a woman again.

Cassie's eyes were drawn back down to a different picture of Brett from when he was five years old. He was getting ready to start kindergarten and it was the first day of school. He looked excited and a little nervous at the same time. The effect in the photograph was a charming picture of perfection of sweet little boy. It had always been one of her favorites and she kept it on her desk always.

Cassie remembered how Brett looked as he bounded away from her car last week and ran up towards his dorm room. No longer a scared little boy, but a confident, young man ready to tackle the world.

Cassie started to feel a twinge of sadness, but told herself to shake it off. This was a day to enjoy new growth at Cassie's Closet. She had waited for a long time to make the changes to Cassie's Closet and now it was the start of that dream and it felt good. She wasn't going to let missing Brett interfere with the excitement of today's new beginning.

Cassie looked away from Brett's picture and towards Jack. "I'm trying to accept that Brett is really living hundreds of miles away from home and has gone and grown up on me."

Cassie was reflective, but then continued. "I guess I need a few more days to adjust to the idea. My ex-husband," she paused, "Brett's father, and his wife, probably had the right idea to vacation for a few days after dropping off Brett at school." Cassie wondered why she made a point to say 'my ex-husband?' It certainly wasn't necessary, but oddly, she felt the need to clarify that she was no longer married. She tried to tell herself that she would do that in any situation. *Right*?

The sinking feeling that Jack felt in his stomach earlier, lifted just as quickly as it arrived. He was oddly cheered by the fact that Cassie was divorced. Then again, so what, he reminded himself, she could have a hundred guys that she's dating. After all, she's beautiful, seems nice and she has that dimple and... *stop*! Jack berated himself.

Suddenly needing to move around, Jack suggested, "Why don't we take a look around and we can talk about some potential spots for the areas you're suggesting. It will also give me a better lay of the land."

Jack stood and held open the door for Cassie.

They walked around together and Cassie gave him ideas about where she would like the dressing rooms and the perimeter areas she was considering for the spotlight sections. They discussed timing for the project and ways in which Cassie could keep the business running while construction was ongoing. That fact alone was critical for Cassie. She couldn't shut down for a month or more while construction went on. Jack reassured her that her business would be able to continue and that they could partition off the areas that they would be working on.

Jack looked into her eyes again and could see relief at his comments. He teased her a little. "However, I can't make any guarantees about the noise, but we'll do our very best to keep it at a minimum."

Cassie appreciated the effort; after all, she expected some noise. She knew Jack wouldn't be putting together the project with glue guns and tape.

After a while, Cassie returned to her office and Jack went about taking measurements and to take a good look around the store. He liked this place. He thought to himself that a person could get lost in the stories here. Every piece of furniture used to be owned by another person or family, every piece of clothing had been worn on a date, or to work or on a picnic. He correctly perceived that it suited Cassie well. She didn't strike him as the kind of woman that was drawn in to new and fancy items, but he could see her having passion for what once was, and making it special again.

In her office, Cassie thought to herself that she really hoped that they could work together, that is, if his estimate fell within her budget. She told herself that it had nothing to do with the fact that he was a good looking man, but she liked his ideas and they seemed to meld with her vision so nicely. Jack immediately thought of things that had been stumbling blocks in her head. It wasn't often that just anyone could listen to her and then come up with a plan that was just perfect.

Later, as Cassie was deep into work in her office, she heard a light knock on the door. She looked up to see Jack standing there. "I wanted to let you know that I've finished up with all the measurements. I'll take everything back to the office and we should have our estimate to you within twenty-four hours. Does that work for you?"

Cassie stood up and reached out to shake Jack's hand. "That would be perfect. As soon as I make my decision, I'll contact your office." Jack realized that he hadn't released her hand yet.

"It was nice meeting you Cassie. I hope that we can work together." Cassie smiled at him as they released their hands. "I do too, Jack."

Chapter Five

Cassie stretched out her legs in front of her and leaned back slightly in her chair, looking upwards at the sky. She was sitting at the outdoor section of the restaurant, waiting for Abby to arrive for lunch. The sun felt glorious on her skin and she could feel the heat penetrating her body with its blessed warmth. She could smell the slight fragrance of honeysuckle in the air. The scent wasn't overpowering and added a certain ambiance to the outdoor patio area. The restaurant patio was lined with pretty, colorful flowers and several round tables with white tablecloths and mint green cloth napkins. Cassie breathed it all in.

"Hi there, I'm sorry I'm late." Abby walked towards Cassie and gave her a quick hug before sitting down.

Cassie smiled at her friend. "No worries at all, I was just basking in all this warmth." Abby nodded to Cassie in agreement. In just a few seconds she could already feel the refreshing warm embrace of the sun on her skin too.

Cassie was happy to see her closest and dearest friend. "I wasn't sure if you'd be able to make lunch today with your patient going into labor yesterday."

Abby settled herself into her chair. "I wasn't sure either, especially when her labor lasted about seventeen hours."

Cassie winced as memories of a long labor with Brett came rushing back to her. Yet it was true what everyone said, you forgot about the pain of childbirth once you are holding your child. For her, that had absolutely been the case.

Cassie thanked the waiter as he refilled her iced-tea and handed a glass of the same to Abby. After dining there frequently, they both knew their choices for lunch and placed their order quickly, so they could get to the business of girl-talk. "So tell me about your patient. You know I love to hear all about them."

Abby was a midwife. One aspect of her job was to provide physical and emotional support to the mother during labor and to provide information before the birth to the expectant family. It's a centuries old occupation. Really, when has it ever been the case that women haven't been at the side of a laboring woman to guide them through the birth of their child?

Abby was extremely proud of her profession. Being in labor for the women is usually painful and oftentimes frightening, so to have a knowledgeable midwife present, allowed the laboring mothers to focus on transitioning their body through labor until their child's birth. Abby is also able to work much more closely with the other parent to assist them with ways to help the mother through labor and it was a very rewarding experience for that person too.

In all the hundreds of births that Abby has attended, even after being woken in the middle of the night, or standing on her feet for hours and hours, she had never felt anything but pure joy as the baby, or babies, were handed to the waiting arms of their new family.

"Oh, Cass, it was such a fun birth experience." Abby continued on with the eager prodding of Cassie's wide eyes.

"This was Mom's second birth, but also her second marriage and it had been over ten years since she'd given birth." Abby paused and took a sip of the iced tea.

"This was Dad's first child *and* first birth and he was just a nervous wreck. The poor guy had never been in a hospital room for a birth. He doesn't have any sisters and he'd never been a part of anything like this."

Cassie chuckled. "Oh, poor Dad is right! He was certainly in for a rude awakening if he didn't know what to expect at all."

"You know I had coached them as much as I could before labor and Dad had read all the books. He really thought he was fully informed, prepared and ready to deal with it all, but..."

Curiosity got the best of Cassie. "What? He couldn't deal with it? What happened?"

Abby laughed. "Ultimately he did deal with it, but he forgot one important element in all of this -- his wife being in pain! When she was in active labor and had reached five or six centimeters, she was clearly in a great deal of pain and Dad was struggling to keep it together."

Abby stopped talking while the waiter brought a bread basket. "Dad just looked pale, scared, and like he was completely at a loss as what to do or what to say. At first, he alternated between frantic rocking in the rocking chair, to pacing in front of the window, and finally to rubbing Mom's feet and legs as she labored?"

Cassie was sympathetic. "It really is so hard to watch someone you love be in pain." Abby couldn't agree more. "I know. I was finally able to show them some different positions to facilitate Mom's labor progress that Dad could help with. Dad was able to rock with her and massaged her lower back, while she gently rolled on a labor ball."

Abby sighed in silent pride at Dad and how he pulled himself together. "Near the end of labor, he got in the birthing tub with her and that was special for both of them. Mom wanted to have a water birth and Dad was able to help guide the baby out during the last push and lift the baby up on to Mom's chest."

Cassie didn't even know this couple, but she had a soft spot for stories about babies and she could feel the lump in her throat.

Cassie gently touched her hand to her heart. "Oh, that's a great story. I think a water birth would kind of freak me out, but so many people love it and what a great way to have Dad involved too."

Abby nodded in agreement. "Absolutely, plus Mom's son from her first marriage was there. Because the water birth was more serene for Mom, he didn't seem quite so frightened," she paused, "well, not too frightened. He was certainly concerned for his Mom, but he was excited to have a new baby brother."

"Oh Abby, you're so lucky to be able to see a new baby being born all the time."

Abby bobbed her head in agreement as she chewed a piece of bread. "It's all because of you too." The memories of nineteen years ago and Cassie's labor came flooding back to her.

"After watching you in labor with Brett, I knew then and there that I wanted to work in some field that dealt with babies."

Cassie had been so excited when Abby first told her that. "I know. Isn't it amazing how sometimes in one little moment, our lives can change so unexpectedly?"

Abby concurred. "For a long time after Brett was born, I was still trying to find out exactly what it was in the 'baby field' that I wanted to do. I didn't want to be a medical doctor, although a very admirable field," Cassie agreed and swallowed a bite of bread, "I just knew that wasn't quite the right fit for me."

They both knew the rest of the story. It wasn't until years later, after Abby married a horrible, evil man, who sent her to the hospital, after he treated her like his own personal punching bag. It was during that hospitalization when Abby happened to meet a midwife in the hallway of the hospital. After talking to her, Abby knew then and there, that that was what she was meant to do with her life. That hospitalization was the catalyst for Abby finding her inner strength, divorcing her ex-husband and going to school to become a midwife.

It seemed as if Cassie and Abby were both remembering that terrible time and they both shook simultaneously as if to ward off any more evil thoughts.

With perfect timing, the waiter came to the table and delivered their lunch. Abby realized then that she hadn't had a decent meal in about twenty-four hours and she was suddenly famished and took a too-big-of-a-bite out of her turkey and avocado sandwich.

Cassie quickly changed the subject back to the baby. "So what is the new little guy's name?"

Abby smiled at the memory. "Mom and Dad chose his first name, which is Thomas and then they let big brother chose his middle name."

"Oh, that was sweet." Then Cassie had a terrible thought. "Oh, but wait, did he come up with something horrible?"

Abby shook her head no. "This kid was so thoughtful about it. It was a toss-up between his best friend 'Christopher,' his favorite baseball player, as in 'Derek Jeter' and his grandpa Max, so 'Thomas Maxwell' it is!"

Cassie really did love hearing the stories about the new babies and their births. If she had her way, she would have had three or four kids, but it wasn't meant to be. After trying to get pregnant again, ultimately, she was diagnosed with 'undiagnosed fertility,' which seemed like such a contradictory diagnosis when she'd already had a child, but apparently, her irregular menstrual schedule was the culprit. She had Brett though and there were so many women that desperately wanted children and couldn't have them, so she felt blessed to have him in her life.

With Abby's mouth still full, but chewing, she motioned to Cassie, "I want to hear how you're doing. Have you heard from Brett?"

Cassie swallowed her bite. "Brett's doing well. I got an email from him yesterday. He's enjoying his classes but already feels overwhelmed by the amount of studying he needs to do."

Abby couldn't help but laugh. "If I know Brett, and we both know that I do," she said with a mischievous smile, "he's overwhelmed because he thought college was going to be about girls, parties, girls, getting laid, hanging out with friends," she took another bite, "oh and did I mention girls?"

Cassie couldn't help but to laugh. There's no doubt there was some truth to that, but her Mama Bear bias still wanted to believe that he'd be the exception to the rule and that if she called him anytime day or night, he'd be studying, with nary a female in sight.

Abby also knew her best friend very well, "I see that disbelieving look in your eyes, my friend."

"Well, no, I…" Abby interrupted her, "You have to face it Cassie, studying is going to be low on his list of priorities, especially at first. He's got his freedom now and he's going to play."

One thing about having a best friend is that they can say absolutely anything to you and ninety-nine percent of the time, it's dead-on right. *Dammit!*

They also both knew, without having to say it, that Cassie didn't want Brett to become a young parent, like she had. Ironically, Brett's life was now at the point where his parents' lives had changed so drastically.

"Yeah, yeah, smarty pants, I know. I also know that girls and good times are going to be what he wants for a while too." Abby just grinned. Score! She was right. She loves Cassie and sometimes it was fun to watch her squirm just a little bit.

"Okay, since you can't think about your son having a good time," she paused for the desired dramatic effect, "tell me what else is going on in your life."

Cassie did the only thing a mature, respectable woman would do in the same circumstance and she threw a cherry tomato at Abby. Abby just laughed, picked it up from her lap and popped it in her mouth.

"Let's see, first of all, I've decided to go ahead with the project at Cassie's Closet. I know it seems sort of financially irresponsible to make those kinds of changes with Brett in college now," Cassie paused, "and the project is certainly a good amount of money, but something tells me it's the right thing to do."

"Cass, I'm so glad. You've talked about those plans for a long time now and I think they're great ideas."

Cassie slapped at the table in defiance. "You know what? I do too! It's certainly not anything that I've seen before in this business and I think it's unique and it will make my store a better place, a smarter way to shop and it's going to look amazing when it's done!"

Abby's ravenous stomach was now starting to feel the effects of the food and she was no longer shoveling food in at break-neck speeds.

"You know I've spent tons of time at the store and I think your customers are going to really appreciate the changes and enjoy the ease of shopping for certain items."

Cassie smiled in agreement. "I do too. Some store owners would probably say that's the last thing you would want to do, especially in a thrift store. You want people to meander and wander and end up buying things they didn't expect too, but I think they still will. It will just make it easier to target certain items; then it gives them time to really just wander."

Cassie took another bite and then a long drink. "I also believe that it will benefit the people who are running in just for certain items and they don't have a lot of time. They can go to a particular area, get what they need and go. I don't want them to go someplace else because they think it will take too much time at my store."

Abby pushed her plate away, although she was still eyeballing the french fries left over on the plate. Not being able to resist one more, she reached over, grabbed it and popped it into her mouth. She silently wondered why french fries weren't a healthy food. She tried so hard to only eat them occasionally, but they were sure hard to resist when they were on the plate.

"So are you going to use the contractor that Colleen recommended?"

"I am. I met with Jack Shaw earlier this week and he had some great ideas that will work perfectly with my plans. His office faxed over the estimate a few days ago. I've reviewed it a dozen times and it's a reasonable price for what they are going to do, although God help me, it's still expensive. However, I think the work they did at the performing arts center was flawless, so I have a great example of their work to go by."

"Oh Cass, I'm so happy for you. I really am. It's going to be wonderful."

Cassie clasped her hands together in response. "I *am* excited. It's going to be chaos for several weeks in the store while construction is going on and trying to keep business running smoothly, but it feels like a really good decision to me."

Abby smiled and was thrilled for her best friend, but then remembered their impromptu meeting in Cassie's office with Colleen last week.

"So, Colleen said the contractor is a hunk, huh?" Cassie looked away briefly, unaware that a blush was coming to her cheeks, "Jack seems like a nice man and he was immediately clicking with everything I want to do in the store."

Abby interrupted once again. "And, he's a hunk, yes?"

Knowing she would have to answer her persistent friend, Cassie relented, "He's definitely a looker, Colleen's right about that. But I don't know how often he'll be around, I mean, he's got a crew that works for him and I don't know how hands-on he'll be with this project."

Funny, Cassie had wondered that same thing when she was going over the estimate. Of course it wasn't a factor in her signing it, but it did cross her mind that it wouldn't be the worst thing in the world to have Jack around from time to time. He was good looking and quick to pick up on her needs for the store's remodeling project. She then shook her head as if to remove the thought. No, besides, even if he's around, he'll likely be behind the heavy plastic partitions and Cassie wouldn't see him much. Would she?

Abby's sly grin crossed her face, "So he's a looker, huh? Any potential for less looking and more touching?"

Cassie laughed, "Abigail Santos, you, my friend, have been hanging around Colleen for too long and she's turned you into a trouble maker too."

Abby teased. "I'm just saying, a little more touching wouldn't be a bad thing, right?"

Would it be a bad thing, Cassie wondered? Her last few efforts at romance hadn't been very successful, not to mention the collapse of her marriage, which was the ultimate in failure.

Cassie's mind had wandered and Abby knew exactly what she was thinking about – Peter's infidelities and his desire to get out of their marriage. Cassie had been reminded of it all again when she took Brett to college last week. Naturally, Peter, helped take Brett to school, but his wife, Nora, also joined them.

While setting up Brett's dorm room, Cassie couldn't help but to reflect on her own life. Ten years after Brett's birth, Peter asked for a divorce. Once Cassie was over the shock, she was able to see that the choices they made early on contributed to the demise of their marriage. Peter never wanted to get married, at least not at that point in his life, but he felt forced into it – by Cassie's pregnancy and their parents.

When Peter asked for the divorce, in her heart, Cassie knew that she wasn't in love with him and hadn't been for a long time. After all, it's too difficult, if not impossible, to be in love with someone when they had chosen other women over you. Nora wasn't the first person that Peter had been with since their divorce.

Trying to shake Cassie from her trip down memory lane, Abby leaned over and touched her friends' leg. She spoke softly. "Cass, you know that not every man is like Peter?"

Cassie felt herself leaving the sad memories and she shook them off. "I know that." Cassie took in a deep breath. "I do see all these great relationships around me and I know they've remained true to each other."

Abby patted Cassie's leg again, but then pulled her hand away. "That's right. Just because Peter was, *well Peter,* is no reason not to give another man a chance."

Cassie looked closely at her friend and spoke softly. "I'm just a little scared, Abs. What if I let myself start falling for another man, any man, and he decides that he just can't be faithful. Being unfaithful is the ultimate cut."

Abby looked at her sternly. "Come on now! There are some great men out in the world that are just dying for the love of a woman like you."

Abby continued. "Has it ever occurred to you that there might be a man out there who wants to give himself to a woman who *he* can believe in?"

Cassie grinned. "I guess I never really thought of it that way." Cassie's brief sadness with thoughts of Peter's infidelity left her and she felt uplifted by Abby's comment.

Abby knew that her friend's mood had lightened once again. "So, if Mr. Carpenter guy is such a hunk, maybe you should let yourself see what happens?"

Cassie feigned annoyance at Abby's suggestion. "Even if I was interested in Jack," as she put up her hands defensively, "which I'm not, I'm sure he probably has a wife or a girlfriend."

Abby just shrugged her shoulders. "Or maybe he doesn't."

Cassie gave up. Her friend was right, at least to the extent that if someone who seemed special came along, she shouldn't automatically assume that he would be like Peter and cheat on her.

Cassie eyed Abby with a stern look. "Ok, all this talk of dating has made me hungry again. I'm ordering a slice of cheesecake and you're sharing it with me."

The two chuckled and Cassie signaled for the waiter. It was wonderful to spend time with her best friend and relax. The next several weeks would be chaotic, so enjoying the sunshine, the cheesecake, and Abby, was a welcome treat.

Chapter Six

It was early in the morning and Cassie's Closet wasn't open yet. Cassie had been there for hours getting ready for construction to begin. She stayed late last night and asked a couple of her employees to help clear out what would soon be the new kitchen area. So far this morning, she was alone, but she knew that these last few minutes of quiet would be the only ones she'd know for several weeks to come.

She took a look around and once again felt a great deal of pride in what she had accomplished. She was so worried when Peter first asked for the divorce and then this wonderful business fell into her lap. It had been such a Godsend when it allowed her to find her own self-worth, her independence and her ability to support both herself and her son. To continue to feel such pride, even after all these years, was a blessing and one that she didn't take for granted.

Cassie could feel the adrenaline coursing through her veins, especially surprising since she had only about two hours of sleep after tossing and turning all night with thoughts of construction *and* Jack's possible presence in her store. She thought her excitement was more about the start of her remodel, but she wasn't a hundred perfect sure about that. Maybe it was realizing a dream that she had been envisioning for so long? Maybe it was because of her conversation with Abby over lunch about letting herself be open to possibilities?

She didn't have time to wonder anymore, because there was a light tap-tap at the front, glass door. She turned and looked. Her heart beat an extra beat. There stood Jack. He had a slight grin on his face and nervously he used his hand to push back the hair that had fallen close to his dark eyes.

"Good morning," Cassie said as she unlocked the door.

"Good morning, Cassie." Jack took a look around and could see that the area where construction was to start had been completely cleared.

"Wow, did you do all this by yourself?"

Cassie held up her arms and flexed her muscles in the same way that Popeye would, but then giggled. "No, I bribed a couple of my strong, teenage employees with pizza last night and we all jumped in and cleared the area."

Jack was impressed as he expected to have his crew clear the area when they arrived.

"Would you like some coffee?" Cassie nodded towards the steaming coffee pot.

"I would love some." Jack followed Cassie towards the freshly brewed pot of coffee.

Jack, too, had been awake for hours. For the first time in a long time, he woke up from dreams that weren't about Charlie; the terrible ones that left his heart pounding in his chest and sweat dripping from his body. This morning, he felt surprisingly refreshed, ready to start the day and eager to get to work on the project at Cassie's Closet.

He had arrived early and expected to wait out in his truck and make some notes about the project, but he noticed a car. When he walked up to the glass door, he could see Cassie by the cashier's area and was pleasantly surprised to see her there already. Before any other thought entered his head, he quickly reminded himself that he just wanted to touch base with Cassie before all the chaos started.

As they walked towards the coffee pot, Jack noticed that Cassie smelled so nice. It definitely wasn't a strong perfume scent, just a hint of lavender or lilac. Whatever the scent was, he liked it. He despised the strong perfume that some women wore. It would get in his throat and make him cough and choke. He could inhale a ton of sawdust and survive it, but the floral, flowery scent of strong perfume left him coughing and with running eyes.

Jack raised his now steaming mug in toast towards the empty area where work was to be done. "To having the final result be everything that you're hoping for, and more."

Cassie was so touched by such a sincere toast that she rewarded him with a sweet smile as she gently touched her coffee cup to his. Jack looked at her genuine, dimpled smile and realized that his knees wobbled for a split second. It struck him as somewhat odd and surprising, how one little dimpled smile from Cassie could trigger any kind of reaction from him.

Jack quickly changed the subject. "I left samples of the wood stain with your clerk a few days ago. There's no hurry, but did you have a chance to look at them?"

"Actually, I did. I'll be right back." Cassie headed to her office to retrieve the samples. She realized that she felt a little like a school girl when she was around Jack. She was so aware of everything about him; his quick smile, the intense dark eyes that quickly looked away from her, after locking eyes for the briefest moment, and the wave in his shiny black hair.

Granted, they only met recently, but there didn't seem to be any pretense about Jack and Cassie liked that. He struck her as the "what-you-see-is-what-you-get" kind of guy. He seemed to feel comfortable in his own skin and had a confident air about him, but not cocky in the least. Any cockiness would have been a major turn-off for Cassie. His quiet confidence was refreshing and, Cassie realized, very appealing to her.

Cassie walked towards Jack holding two wood samples and a small piece of the granite they would be using for the kitchen counters. She stood close to him and laid all three on a nearby table.

"Initially, I was thinking about this color." She pointed to the ebony colored stain. "I thought it would work really well with the overall color of the granite, but then, my eyes kept going back to this one." She pointed towards the cherry-colored wood sample and her hand slightly touched his forearm. Cassie noticed the tingle, but silently told herself that it was probably just her imagination.

"The more I think about the overall look that I want, the more I think I want this one." Jack noticed that her eyes were twinkling with delight.

Jack looked at the granite, the cherry-colored wood sample and then back to her eyes. "You've made an excellent choice! I think you nailed it."

It wasn't his decision, but it's the same choice he would have made. He was silently hoping she would select this one. He was starting to have a real vision in his head for how her store would look and he wanted it to be just perfect. Simply perfect for Cassie.

As they discussed more details about the work for the kitchen, there was another tap-tap at the door. Cassie looked to see both Colleen and some of Jack's crew waiting. Cassie looked at all of them and then to Jack, "I think the party is about to start."

Once Cassie unlocked the door again and everyone headed in, Colleen made a quick beeline for Jack. She put both her hands on each side of his shoulders and kissed each cheek like he was her long-lost friend.

"Hey there handsome, how are you?" Colleen practically glowed as she held Jack's shoulders in her hands.

Jack seemed genuinely pleased to see her too. "Colleen, you look beautiful, as always." With that he gave her a genuine smile of his own. He lowered his voice slightly. "I'm great, and thanks for the referral for this job. I appreciate it."

Colleen released his shoulders and patted his chest. "Of course, darling, you do the finest work in town and I wouldn't want anyone but the very best for my dearest friend." Colleen realized that she hadn't acknowledged Cassie's presence.

"Speaking of which, Cassie, I haven't even said hello to you." Colleen turned from Jack and towards Cassie with both arms ready to embrace Cassie in a full-on hug.

Cassie teased Colleen. "I did feel a little invisible there for a minute."

Now Colleen pointed with one finger on Cassie's chest. "Not possible. How could anyone as pretty as you be invisible?" Colleen then slyly turned towards Jack and practically cooed. "Wouldn't you agree, Jack?"

Jack looked a little like a deer caught in the headlights. His mind was racing. Cassie was so pretty, but how was he supposed to respond to that question?

Immediately, a blush came to Cassie's cheeks. Cassie was so embarrassed by her friend's comment. She eyed Colleen with that "*you just had to, didn't you?*"—look.

Cassie quickly recovered. "Colleen, we better let Jack get to work now that his crew is here." As much as Jack found himself enjoying the morning conversation with Cassie, he saw an out and he jumped at the chance to take it.

Jack's eyes didn't meet Cassie's or Colleen's. "You're right; I better go meet with my crew and get the morning started."

Then remembering his manners, Jack held his cup up towards Cassie and mouthed "thank you" as he quickly headed off to the other side of the building.

Colleen watched him as he walked away. "What a fine specimen of a man!"

Cassie couldn't disagree with her, but if Colleen even remotely thought that Cassie was interested in Jack, she would set off on a path that would make Cupid hang his head in shame.

Besides, she told herself, she wasn't interested in Jack. He is a nice guy, handsome and his smile was great, but then there was that tingle in Cassie's tummy when she spotted him at the door this morning and again when her hand slightly touched his arm, but that's to be expected, right? It had been a long time since she'd been around a man who she found kind of sexy. *Sexy?* Where did that come from? Face it Cassie, she told herself, you're just feeling a little lonely and turning a few smiles and a couple of tingles into a big, fat deal in your head. Fantasize on, but the reality is that he's here for one reason and one reason only, and it's for the job only.

Colleen looked at Cassie and Cassie realized that she had been watching Jack walk away as she was lost in thought. She popped Colleen slightly on the arm and gave her a look.

"Don't say a word."

Colleen raised her hand up to her lips in that "who me" pose and batted her eye lashes.

Cassie could never stay mad at her. "Colleen, really! Did you have to ask him if I was pretty? There's nothing like putting the poor man in such an awkward position. How's he supposed to answer that question?"

Cassie's embarrassment continued. "Did you see how quickly he was out of here?"

Colleen poured herself a cup of coffee. She was completely nonchalant. "Pashaw! Jack's not a stupid man, nor is he blind. I'll bet you my last buck that he already thinks you're attractive." She nodded her head and raised one eyebrow. "It's a given, my friend."

Cassie wouldn't let herself believe it. "No, I don't think so. He's been nothing but a complete professional."

"Mmm. Perhaps that explains why the two of you were smiling at each other so sweetly while I was waiting at the door this morning."

Cassie slapped at the air. "We were just discussing wood."

Now Colleen laughed, "Wood, huh? So you were discussing hard, strong objects. I see." Colleen smiled like the Cheshire Cat. Cassie lightly slapped Colleen's hands. "Colleen, you have a dirty mind!"

Colleen smiled coyly in agreement. "I know."

In that moment, there was a flurry of activity. The rest of the morning staff had walked in the door and Jack's crew had already started to partition off one section. Soon he would be completely hidden from view and the sounds of saws and hammering would fill the shop as the morning progressed. Cassie could see that a delivery truck was pulling up and that a couple of cars had pulled into the parking lot.

Cassie looked to her friend. "Take your time and finish your coffee, but it's time for me to officially open up." Colleen waved her off. "I just wanted to stop by on the first day of construction and wish you well."

Cassie paused before heading to the door. "I appreciate that, my friend, I really do. Thanks."

Colleen remembered the other reason she had stopped by. "Do you want to come by for dinner Friday night?"

Cassie leaned over and kissed Colleen's cheek. "I would love that. What shall I bring?"

"How about a nice bottle of chardonnay?"

"That I can do. I can't wait to spend an evening with you and Kevin."

Cassie started to walk away, but then walked backwards the three steps back to Colleen. "You're not going to try some sneaky 'blind date' thing and invite Jack are you?"

"No, darling, of course not." Honestly, the thought had crossed her mind. In fact, she mentioned it to Kevin just this morning as they drank their morning tea, but he warned her to lay low, at least for now.

Cassie looked one more time towards the rising partition and Jack looked towards her. They caught eyes quickly, but then they simultaneously looked away and both attended to the business of the day.

Colleen continued to sip her coffee but she noticed the quick eye contact between Jack and Cassie. She had a strong feeling that those two were a match made in heaven. Neither one may not want to admit it just yet and why should they, but she knew for a fact that both of them had been hurt by others. They might not be too eager to open their hearts; however, she could feel something in her bones and that romantic Irish blood of hers cursed through her veins and told her that with a little luck, there just might be magic in the air between Cassie and Jack.

Chapter Seven

The construction project had been going on for a full week and the noise was quite loud that day, yet Cassie tried to concentrate while one of her long-time, elderly customers complained that she had been overcharged for a sweater that she had purchased. After looking at the tag on the sweater and the receipt, Cassie could see that she hadn't been overcharged at all, in fact, the cost was only six dollars, but Cassie quickly realized that it was simply a case of buyer's remorse rather than a clerking error, so she offered to take back the sweater and refund Mrs. Moore's money. Usually in this business, it was an "all sales are final" kind of store, but Mrs. Moore was quite elderly and she had been in the store a number of times before. Cassie correctly suspected that Mrs. Moore lived on a very tight budget.

Cassie also remembered that Mrs. Moore had spent a lot of time at the glass and china section and seemed to have a fondness for it. "Wait here, Mrs. Moore. I have an idea." Cassie headed towards the temporary location for the kitchen items. She picked up a matching china tea cup and saucer set. It was delicate and fragile and something that would probably catch Mrs. Moore's eye.

Cassie approached Mrs. Moore with the cup and saucer in her hand. She could see the disappointment leave Mrs. Moore's eyes regarding her need to return her earlier purchase as she began to swoon over the pretty object in Cassie's hand.

Cassie reached towards Mrs. Moore with the two delicate pieces. "Mrs. Moore. I'm sorry for the problem with the sweater this morning." Even though she knew the error wasn't on the store's end.

"I know it's difficult to have to deal with any kind of mix-up, so I would like you to have this cup and saucer as a thank you for being a loyal customer to 'Cassie's Closet.'"

Mrs. Moore's eyes lit up. Her swollen, arthritic hands shook slightly as she took the fine china from Cassie. Mrs. Moore's smile widened and Cassie realized for the first time, that she was without her dentures and her wide grin was charming in a way that only a wrinkled, toothless little old lady could be.

"I've been a customer here for a long time. Way back when the O'Connell's owned it. But I don't remember anybody ever giving me nothin' from here before."

Cassie smiled at her. "Well, I'd say it's about time then. I hope you'll accept this small token of our appreciation as one of our most loyal customers."

"You betcha!" Mrs. Moore exclaimed excitedly as she gingerly touched the fine china. Cassie took the cup and saucer from her hands. "Let me wrap this up nice and careful so that it doesn't break on your way home"

"Thanks, Miss Cassie, sometimes on the bus, it's a real bumpy ride and I'd hate to break that pretty lil' set."

When Cassie handed the package back to her, she said to her, "When all this construction is done, I'm going to throw a big party to celebrate the remodeling of the store and I'd like you to come by and celebrate with us. After all," Cassie paused and she rubbed Mrs. Moore shoulders, "you're one of the store's best customers."

Mrs. Moore's eyes lit up. "Are you going to have some of those fancy shrimps on a kabob?"

"I'm sure we will." Cassie smiled and helped Mrs. Moore to stand and guided her to the door. "Bye now, I'll see you next time."

Cassie took the sweater and headed back towards her office. She would set the sweater aside. With the cool days of autumn approaching before long, Mrs. Moore would need a sweater. Cassie was pretty sure that if she told Mrs. Moore the next time she came in that she had forgotten it during her last shopping trip, that Mrs. Moore wouldn't remember otherwise.

Just as Cassie sat down at her desk, there was a knock at her office door and there stood Jack. This was a pleasant surprise. He had not been in yet today. His crew had been here all morning, but he was nowhere to be seen.

When Cassie arrived at her now usual, slightly early pre-opening time, for the first time this week, Jack hadn't arrived early too. She'd told herself that it was silly to feel somewhat disappointed, but for the earlier part of the week Jack had also arrived early. It was probably just a coincidence that he'd arrived early too, but somewhere deep inside of Cassie, she was hoping that it wasn't.

It was most likely a misguided illusion, but it seemed to Cassie that they had fallen into a routine, albeit a brief routine, of her pouring both of them a cup of coffee. Sometimes, only a sip or two was taken as they talked briefly about the project before a crew member arrived. Cassie reminded herself that it wasn't like they were sitting down together and relaxing over a cup of coffee and a muffin. Nonetheless, it occurred to her that she missed it this morning.

Jack poked his head in. "I just wanted to touch base with you since I wasn't here this morning. I assume my crew has been doing fine."

"They've been great and there haven't been any problems." Cassie nodded towards the area where his crew was working. "I think they just stopped for a break, but your crew member, Dani, told me what they would be doing this morning."

"Good, good. I asked her to let you know what was going on."

Jack had told himself that there was no need to explain to Cassie why he wasn't here this morning. After all, he wasn't obligated to be here, so long as his crew was on the job, but strangely, he felt obligated, no, he wanted to explain to her about his absence this morning.

"I wasn't here this morning as I had some finishing work to do at one of our other projects. Another member of my crew was supposed to do it, but his daughter fell off her bicycle yesterday and broke her arm. He felt like he should stay home with her today, since she was still in some pain."

"Ouch, I hope she'll be okay." Cassie felt foolishly relieved that she now knew where Jack was this morning. When he didn't show up early, she had flashes of him making love to a woman, probably his wife, and starting the day out with hearty sex. As she did earlier this morning, she quickly tried to erase that image from her head.

Jack started to turn away to leave the office, but then turned back towards Cassie. "I overheard what you said to your customer. That was really nice of you." Jack had been impressed. It was a simple and sweet gesture, but one he was unaccustomed to. He couldn't remember Stacey ever doing anything that he would consider sweet or kind.

Cassie could feel the color come to her cheeks, because Jack had both noticed and then complimented her on her interaction with Mrs. Moore.

She shrugged her shoulders. "She's a sweet old lady and now she has a pretty little thing to look at and brag to her friends about."

"Not every store owner would have done that, though, and it was impressive." Now Cassie could really feel the heat of the blush on her cheeks.

"Thanks." Then Cassie felt the foolish need to inquire; she had to know if he would be back in the morning. "Were you able to finish everything at the other job site?"

"Yep, everything that needed to be done, at least for today." Little did Cassie know that he had worked like a Tasmanian devil to get it done so that he would be able to be back to work on her project. "At least until Jimmy is able to return to the site tomorrow morning."

Finding no other reason to be standing in Cassie's doorway, Jack waived a two finger salute towards her. "Okay, I'll see you in the morning, Cassie."

"I'll see you then." Cassie felt a jolt of anticipation.

* * * *

Jack walked behind the partition of the construction zone. Of his crew that hadn't left the site for lunch, a few members were sitting on wooden saw horses towards the back of the building and were eating their lunches.

Dani looked at him, smirked and shook her head from side to side. Dani was the only female member of his crew. She'd been with him for six or seven years now. She was one of the most determined and skilled carpenters he'd ever met. She'd had a rough go of it at first while at work, but it was nothing she wasn't expecting. After all, traditionally this field had been more of a male-oriented occupation. Unfortunately, initially, a few of the other men were taunting and downright sexist towards Dani. She took it quietly. Jack offered to intercede on her behalf but Dani would have nothing to do with him stepping in. She swore she'd handle it when the time was right. And she did.

One Friday night after work, they all headed to Trebbiano's Restaurant to throw back a few cold ones. It was a celebration at the end of a job in which the vineyard owner had been a demanding, bellowing task master. As the night wore on, one of the newer crew members, Buddy, had a few too many beers and started to become foolishly drunk and edged his way over towards Dani.

"Mmmmm," he said as his slurred his words, "you can sure grip a hammer nice and tight, sweetheart." Buddy suggestively smiled a drunken, dopey smile at Dani and raised his eyebrows.

Dani was going to just let it go, until Buddy continued. "You wanna show me what else you can grip real tight?"

Dani stood and turned to face Buddy full-on. She put one hand on Buddy's back and seductively pulled him tight towards her. With her other hand, so eased her way down to his crouch. Buddy's eyes rolled back in anticipation of what he thought was to going happen next.

When Dani reached his balls, she squeezed them, *hard*.

"Is this what you're talking about?" She squeezed harder and the look on Buddy's face went from anticipation to pain.

Buddy was losing his ability to stand, but Dani kept him propped up. He struggled with his words as his breath was taken away.

"No, oh, stop." Dani's firm grip remained on his testicles. The color was starting to drain from his face.

Dani put her lips close to his ear. "In the future, if you're ever inclined to talk to me with anything but respect," she squeezed just a little tighter, "think again."

She then released his testicles and Buddy grabbed his crouch as he fell to the ground, temporarily paralyzed with the pain.

With that stand for her own honor, Dani immediately won, not only the respect of the rest of the crew, but she earned a little fear from them too. From then on, she was no different than anyone else on the crew. The men treated her just like they would any other co-worker.

Secretly Dani was thrilled. When she was at work, she just wanted to work, do her job, and be given the same consideration as the other guys. However, on the other hand, there was *female* Dani, who was all woman and not immune to having needs and desires, and would have loved to have those desires returned, but not by her co-workers.

However, there was one exception. A few years ago, she found herself developing a little crush on Jack. Obviously, at the time, she knew he was married and she would have never done anything to damage that marriage. It was easy to keep her crush a secret and assumed that it would fizzle out over time. However, it was difficult to keep her feelings in check when she heard lots of talk around town that Jack's wife, Stacey Shaw, liked the men - a lot! It seemed to be a secret to no one, except Jack.

Dani had been working with Jack on a job out of town on the weekend that Stacey left him. Days later, with Jack nowhere in sight at any job, his brother, Jeremy, finally told them that Jack had a personal situation to deal with and that he needed some time away from work. Not one person on the crew contemplated that it was a health scare or anything else that kept Jack away; everyone already knew. *It was Stacey.*

Jack eventually returned to work, at least physically, within a few weeks. It was clear that the body was present but his spirit was broken and gone. Jack was a changed man. He was pissed off at the world, angry, unusually reckless and careless at work. Dani overheard Jeremy calling him out for endangering one of the crew members and pleading with him to take more time off, but Jack would hear nothing of it. He told Jeremy that sitting in that empty house was the very worst thing for him. Thereafter, he wasn't reckless, but his spirit seemed lower and dropped on an almost daily basis.

Everyone on the crew cared deeply about Jack. He's a good man, a good friend and a good boss. But there was nothing they could say to help him. It was hellish to care in silence. Everyone on the crew tried to show him they cared, but they knew it couldn't be obvious to Jack, so they did little things like throwing a wrapped sandwich to him or finishing up a task when he seemed to lose steam.

One night, several weeks after Stacey left, Dani ran into Jack sitting at the bar at Trebbiano's. He was already more than half-drunk. Dani sat next to him and ordered another shot for him and a beer for herself. Jack looked her way, nodded and said nothing to her until two shots later.

Finally, in a drunken haze, with eyes red and slurred words, Jack turned towards Dani and quietly said. "She's gone."

Jack took in a deep breath and then let it out. "She said Charlie wasn't mine." Jack finally said the words that had been hammering in his head for weeks now. The tears came to his eyes and rolled down his cheeks.

"She took my boy away; my sweet boy and I don't know where he is."

Not Jack's child! No, it wasn't possible. Was it? Dani didn't know what to say. From what she knew of Jack, he was a great dad and lived and breathed Charlie. Any stranger who met Jack and spent more than five minutes with him, learned at least one thing about him, and that was he was the proud Dad to little Charlie. She never knew anyone who loved being a Dad more than Jack. It was so obvious that Jack and Charlie adored each other. She sat in stunned silence doing the only thing she could do at the time – rubbing Jack's back.

Dani knew she needed to get Jack home. After getting a little help from one of the regulars at Trebbiano's, she had him in her car. Ten minutes later, they were at Jack's house. As they walked in, Dani was stunned. The house had been *completely* emptied. There were a few coffee cups on the kitchen counter, crumpled fast food bags and a coffee pot. That was the contents of the kitchen. There was an old VCR on the living room floor that wasn't even connected. Besides that, there wasn't even a television in the room.

Dani looked at the empty house in stunned silence. She had anticipated being able to aim Jack towards a couch, cover him with a blanket and leave, but there wasn't a couch or chair in sight.

With Jack half slung over her, she struggled down the hallway and could see a bedroom door ajar. She kicked it the rest of the way open. Still in shock by the emptiness of the house, she again felt stunned when she looked inside the bedroom and there wasn't even a bed in the room. Jack had a sleeping bag laid out on the floor. Next to it was a lamp and a clock radio. They were the lone furnishings.

Dani was now even more furious with Stacey! The bitch had literally removed everything! It wasn't enough that she took the one person in the world that Jack lived for, but she'd completely robbed Jack of the simplest comforts.

After than night, Dani became somewhat of a confidante to Jack. Jack wasn't one to talk about his emotions or feelings, but sometimes, when the pain was so intense, and he had to relieve the building pressure, he needed to talk, and Dani would listen and comfort him the best way she could. None of that comfort was in a physical way, unless you counted hugs and Dani rubbing his back. It was also around that time that Dani realized that her friendship with Jack was far more important to her and that any crush she may have had on him was gone and replaced with feelings of friendship only.

Jack told her that, besides the closest members of his family, no one else was aware of Stacey's claim that Charlie wasn't his son. Dani was sure Jack would have never told her about Stacey's claim, except for the fact he was so drunk, but she vowed, both to him and to herself, that he would never regret sharing that information with her. It remained in her confidence to this day.

Jack realized in time that Dani was safe. She never judged him. He knew he could trust her. Maybe it was because she had seen him at his lowest. Maybe it was because she never said stupid things that he couldn't deal with then like, "It will get better, hang in there." *How in the hell was it supposed to get better?*

Now, during the lunch break at 'Cassie's Closet," Jack looked at Dani eating her lunch and noticed her head moving slowly from side to side and she was looking in his direction.

"What?"

Dani nodded toward Cassie's office, although it was hidden from view by the partition. "I've just never noticed you needing to talk to a customer so often."

Jack was immediately defensive. "What? I don't talk to her all that often." Jack twisted the top off a bottle of water and took a long drink.

"Every time I check in with her, it's related to this project." Jack's arms swept the construction area, as if that movement was all the proof he needed that his statement was true.

Dani chuckled. "Mmmm, hmmm. Sure it is. Besides, I've never known you to be such an early bird on a job."

Jack started to interrupt, but Dani continued. "Seriously, until this job, when is the last time you beat me to any job site?"

Jack finished the water, crumpled the empty plastic bottle and tossed it towards Dani.

"Bite me, Dani."

Dani just laughed at his comment. "Thanks, but I'll pass." She threw him an apple from her lunch bag and Jack took a big bite out of it before walking away.

As much as Jack wanted to deny it, Dani could see that there was something about Cassie that Jack was very drawn too. Since Stacey left, it wasn't that Jack had never been with a woman, but it was always for one purpose only -- simply getting his physical needs met. Since Jack's divorce, she'd never known him to show up early for work on a regular basis. Not that he was a slacker, actually anything but a slacker, but he often stopped by the office first or went from project to project checking on the status. Maybe she was wrong, but Dani could almost sense a new bounce to his step now. Dani was betting that bounce was because Jack was attracted to Cassie. Her instincts were usually pretty good, especially when it came to Jack.

Dani wasn't surprised that Jack denied a possible attraction. He had no desire to be part of a couple again, or at least that's what he'd told her a hundred times. He'd been burned so badly by Stacey and he was mighty cautious now. Still, Dani could sense something and she knew Jack better than most.

Dani just prayed that if Jack felt something towards Cassie that she was a decent woman. Dani had been with Jack every step of the way during his divorce. The divorce and loss of Charlie had twisted him inside out. It took him a fair amount of time to get over the divorce, although she didn't think he'd ever get over losing Charlie.

Dani truly believed that Jack deserved to have a good, loving, loyal woman in his life. She said a silent prayer. If it was Cassie that Jack wanted, please God, let her be a really good woman and nothing, absolutely nothing, like Stacey.

Chapter Eight

Several mornings later, Cassie walked into the local coffee shop. The rich, bold smell of coffee filled the air, along with the sweet, mouth-watering aroma of cinnamon, nutmeg and baking pastries. Cassie's empty stomach grumbled and let her know it was time for breakfast.

She woke up this morning thinking that Jack's crew had been so considerate to her customers and employees as they did their very best to keep their work area free of debris and the noise down, that she should stop here this morning and pick up some muffins and assorted pastries for the crew. Not to mention, some treats for her frazzled, but faithful employees who were dealing with the consequences of construction.

Cassie perused the heavenly-scented pastries and silently counted calories in her head along with the amount of time she would have to walk tonight if she ate one itty-bitty, little muffin or one itty-bitty, little donut. *She reprimanded herself, oh what the hell, of course, I'm going to have one of them, so just decide which one looks the yummiest and go for it!*

As Cassie stood in line, lost in thought about the pastries, the coffee shop door opened once again and Jack walked in. He noticed that the line was long with several customers. When he was getting ready for work, he told himself that he'd have his usual coffee when he got to 'Cassie's Closet,' but he was awake earlier than usual this morning and he didn't think Cassie would be at work yet, so he decided to stop by the coffee shop.

Besides, he reminded himself, Cassie had offered him coffee every day since the project began. He should return the favor. He should bring her coffee for a change. *Right?* That was only fair. He was pretty sure she would like one of the mocha coffees or a vanilla flavored coffee or one of the fancy kinds that were so popular these days. His brows furrowed at the thought. Don't most women like specialty kind of coffees? Jack realized that it had been a long time since he considered what a woman would like to drink, other than tossing down a cold one at the bar. That was a different kind of woman though and certainly not one that he would spend time thinking about what kind of coffee she might like. Cassie on the other hand, was very much someone who he'd gladly buy coffee for and wonder what kind she would enjoy the most.

In fact, it was Cassie's face that he envisioned when his eyes sleepily opened this morning. He had been dreaming of her. He didn't recall all of it, but enough to remember that Cassie was naked, straddled sitting on top of him. Her long, dark hair hung down across her breasts and belly, with a single nipple peaking at him through the dark maze of chestnut-colored hair. Jack woke up with a massive erection and images of Cassie's naked torso haunted him even though he took a shower that was so cold, it was almost unbearable.

Trying to shake the morning dream from his mind, Jack considered the possibilities on the menu. He looked towards the menu hanging above the cashier and was caught off guard. *Was that Cassie?* He couldn't see her face and only her backside was facing him, but he smugly and proudly told himself that he'd recognize that cute behind anywhere. He had to admit to himself that he had caught himself several times trying to watch her, discreetly, of course, as she walked away. Not only did he recognize her fabulous backside, but he knew it was Cassie by the long, straight, chestnut colored hair flowing down her back. The hair streaming down her torso in his vivid dream this morning. A new tightness began to pull at his crotch and he quickly told himself to stop thinking about that dream and now!

Although he didn't need any further verification that it was Cassie, he suddenly caught a glimpse of her reflection in the glass display case. He thought to himself that she really is so beautiful. He could watch her all day and never get bored.

On impulse, Jack ignored the other waiting customers and walked towards Cassie. He gently touched her on the elbow and she turned around to face him.

Cassie jumped. It was Jack! Here at the coffee shop. With a sense of irony, Cassie realized that she had just been wondering what kind of pastry Jack might like for breakfast.

"Hi, Jack." Cassie practically stuttered the words at the sight of him. "What are you doing here?"

Before Jack could think of a reasonable sounding excuse, he found himself telling her the truth. "I thought I would pick up a coffee for *you* this morning, since you've made me a cup of coffee every day for weeks now."

Cassie was genuinely touched. It seemed like it had been an eternity since anyone had considered something so simple, yet so sweet, for her.

"That is really thoughtful of you. It's not necessary at all," she grinned and her smile grew, "but still, very thoughtful."

"I guess great minds think alike." At Jack's puzzled looked, she explained. "I stopped by here this morning to pick up goodies for breakfast for you and your crew."

Now it was Jack's turn to smile. "You don't have to do that Cassie."

"Oh, but I want too. What would they like to eat?"

Suspecting that there would no changing her mind, Jack smiled and spanned his arms across the display case. "They're vultures and will eat anything!"

The cashier signaled Cassie that it was her turn. She placed her order and added a vanilla latte for herself and asked Jack what he'd like to drink. He ordered a strong, dark robust coffee, which didn't surprise Cassie at all. Nor did it surprise him that she ordered a vanilla latte. Jack pulled out his wallet, but Cassie bumped his arm out of the way.

"No, my treat for you and the crew, remember?"

"Remember that I was going to treat you to a coffee?" Jack handed over his credit card to the cashier, with a satisfied grin on his face. Some battles were fun to win. Cassie quickly scanned her credit card and with the "approval" light flashing, Cassie smiled broadly as the cashier handed Jack his card back. Jack took it in stride and thought to himself that it would give him another opportunity to buy her coffee later.

When the coffees arrived at the counter, they were in glass mugs and not in to-go mugs. Jack and Cassie both looked at the glass mugs like they were aliens. Finally, Jack looked towards Cassie and reached for the cups.

"Unless you have to be at the shop right away, why don't we just drink these now instead of getting burned and sticky trying to pour them into the to-go mugs."

"That makes sense." Cassie looked at the remaining tables and eyed a bistro-style table with two chairs near the window and away from the noisy customer line.

Jack sat the coffees down across from each other and held the back of the chair for Cassie. That small gesture didn't go unnoticed by her. Cassie took a sip of her coffee. "Mmmm." She then shook one of the bags that the pastries were in and the noise took Jack's mind off of Cassie's lips as she licked the vanilla flavored crème off of them. Amusement was in her eyes. "Hungry?" *Oh, if it was hunger he was starting to feel in the pit of his stomach, then yes, he was famished.*

"Starving." Normally, he was more of a cereal kind of guy and definitely a bacon and eggs kind of guy on the weekends, but this morning, having a sweet breakfast seemed like the perfect way to start his day.

He looked towards the bag. "How about the chocolate-walnut muffin?"

"Wise choice and one of my personal favorites. Here you go." Cassie handed him the muffin on a napkin and took out an almond croissant for herself.

They both took a bite of their pastry. Cassie knew that she should ask him about the project, but she really didn't care about it at the moment. Instead, she found herself wondering, once again, if Jack was married or had a girlfriend. She told herself that it didn't really matter as she wasn't looking to be in a relationship, but there was something about Jack that made her inquisitive about him and left her with a desire to know more.

The realization of this was a little surprising to her, because she hadn't looked at a man like that for quite a while. Her faith in solid men had left her some time ago. Peter had rejected her, in so many ways for years, even before the divorce, that it was still an emotional injury that stung sometimes.

Without thinking, Cassie stopped blowing on her latte. "Is everyone in your family an early riser, Jack?" Feeling suddenly school girlish, Cassie quickly took another bite of croissant and looked towards her latte innocently.

"God, yes, my parents are early risers and so cheerful in the morning too." Jack quickly realized that she probably wasn't asking about his parents and now he felt a little foolish. He was nervous being around her and didn't want to sound like a dimwit, yet, that's exactly what happened. God, now he felt so stupid.

Fortunately, he recovered quickly. "I, on the other hand, am nothing like my parents. I roll out of bed, shower and find my way to the nearest place where I can pour caffeine into my veins."

Hmmm. No mention of a wife, or girlfriend, or children to get ready for school. Then again, Cassie considered, he might just be one of those guys that doesn't talk about his significant other much?

Cassie inquired further. "So you're not one to wake up and read the paper or fix breakfast for your family?" *There, she'd asked. It didn't sound like she was fishing. Right? Just a normal, everyday question that you'd ask any new person you were getting to know. Certainly!*

Jack looked up from his coffee cup and into Cassie's eyes. With soft, yet serious eyes, he responded.

"When I was married, I liked hanging around the house in the mornings and I never left for work early. I enjoyed making breakfast, listening to the news," *and watching Sesame Street with Charlie, he thought to himself* "and having coffee at home." Jack took another drink of his coffee. "Now, there's no reason to stay home in the mornings."

Cassie watched Jack as he spoke and was trying to read his emotions. There was something that she couldn't quite put her finger on. At that moment, he seemed to have a certain sadness about him, but there was something else. She remembered from her own divorce that there were a vast array of emotions – loneliness, bitterness, rage, loss, despair, but Jack's sadness didn't seem to reflect on his marriage, but something else. Maybe she was reading too much into it. She reminded herself that she really didn't know him all that well. Most of her friends that had gone through a divorce were women, so perhaps their perspective was different. Maybe with a man, in their eyes, divorce just felt and looked different.

Suddenly, she realized that he had never mentioned the word "divorce." Maybe he was a widower! That would explain the sense of loss about a loved one that she could almost feel from Jack. She didn't want to pry and had no idea how to ask that type of question, nor would she.

Cassie spoke again. "I can understand that now that my son is away at college." Cassie lifted her cup to her lips. "After I divorced, the mornings were still so busy trying to get both myself and Brett ready for school and work, that I never left the house until the very last second." She took another sip of her latte.

"Now, with Brett off at college, the mornings seem eerily quiet. I guess I'm not use to it yet, although I should be." She paused, as she remembered. "During summer, Brett was like a hibernating bear until noon each day."

Jack laughed at the image of a grumpy man-bear being awakened by his mother at noon. Cassie laughed too. "Brett sounded like a bear – a wounded bear, when I had the audacity to wake him up."

Jack shook his head from side to side and feigned support for Brett. "Of course he did, all teenagers are surely entitled to sleep every day until noon."

Jack then found his own mind wondering about staying in bed until noon with Cassie, but it had nothing to do with sleeping, and more to do with his dream this morning.

Since the project at Cassie's Closet had started, Jack wondered if Cassie was married or not. He told himself, that he was just curious and that it didn't mean anything. He didn't see a ring on her finger, but that wasn't always the case. He knew Stacey had left her ring off most of the time, using the excuse that her finger was larger after the pregnancy, even saying the size wasn't "quite right" when Jack had it sized. Looking back, it seemed like the excuses were endless, but at the time, he wasn't willing to allow his heart to go where his head was heading.

Jack was no fool. Still, he didn't want to face it then, he couldn't face it then. He wasn't unaware of the talk around town, the looks from neighbors and even his own mother telling him what she'd heard about Stacey while shopping at the local grocery store.

God, it was so hard to consider all the ramifications back then. Charlie was so little and Jack was so conflicted about what to do and the best way to do it. Jack knew deep in his gut that if he threatened Stacey with a divorce that she would threaten to try for full custody of Charlie. Stacey always made some threat to Jack about Charlie when she didn't get her way. Little did he know then that that scenario would have been preferable to never seeing Charlie again!

Jack knew Stacey had nothing to base her claim on for full custody, yet the overriding fear of putting little Charlie in Stacey's care without him around to buffer or shield Charlie from her emotional immaturity, kept Jack from thinking further about leaving her, at least until Charlie was school-age. His protectiveness toward Charlie was paramount in his mind. He could let everything else go and numb himself emotionally to the pain and embarrassment that Stacey was causing him.

Jack shook the memories from his mind and in a hurry to think about something else, he unexpectedly and hurriedly asked Cassie if she'd ever remarried.

"No" Cassie looked into her cooling latte. "I guess no divorce is fun, but my divorce left me reeling. I didn't expect it to happen and I wasn't prepared for it to happen in some ways." Cassie looked into Jack's eyes and sensed his alertness about what she just said.

Cassie paused and then collected her thoughts before she continued. "I knew that things weren't perfect between Peter and me, but I was afraid to face life without him. I met him when I was a junior in high school. I felt lost and frightened when I thought about having a life that was so different than what I had known all my adult life."

Cassie continued. "Brett was my primary concern. I wondered how a divorce would affect him. How could I change the family dynamics and do that to Brett when he was simply an innocent bystander in my shaky marriage?"

Jack thought to himself how much he could relate to Cassie. Hadn't he dealt with all the same fears? It sounded like they both had a mountain of considerations then. He thought he was considering the needs of Charlie, first and foremost. So, yes, Cassie's divorce was something that he could absolutely relate to.

"My ex-husband, Peter, ultimately made the decision that he didn't want to be married to me anymore, and he left after a very brief, matter-of-fact announcement."

Cassie looked at Jack directly in the eyes. "Even though it felt devastating to me at the time, ultimately, I'm glad that we're divorced. We're very different people and we weren't meant to be married for life."

Cassie looked into her almost empty coffee cup and thought a moment before raising her eyes to meet Jack's again. "It sounds so simple, but I honestly think we were just meant to have Brett together, but we weren't meant for each other."

In that moment, Jack had the deepest desire to touch her, hold her and stroke his fingers down the length of her back and up and down her arms. He didn't know all the facts and only what Cassie just told him, but in looking across the table at the tender, gentle soul that Cassie seemed to be, he decided then and there that Peter was an enormous ass and quite possibly the stupidest man on the planet!

On top of that, Jack could completely understand the pain of a matter-of-fact announcement by the person you were married to. He remembered his own discovery that his marriage had ended.

It was a little over two years ago. After a long, hot, physically draining out-of-town, project for work, he pulled up at the house and was somewhat surprised to see that the house was dark. Then again, Jack remembered thinking, no doubt that Stacey would be up to her usual tricks. He incorrectly assumed that she had probably dropped Charlie off with his Mom and was spending time with "her girlfriends" – her code for going out on the town.

Dammit! It pissed him off when she did that and pissed him off even more when she didn't tell him in advance. He could have stopped by his Mom's house and picked up Charlie on the way home. He was hot, tired and sweaty and all he wanted was a shower and to spend a little time with Charlie before it was time to read him a bedtime story. Besides it was late and Charlie needed to get his rest.

When Jack walked in the front door, he tried to turn on the living room light, but nothing happened. Jack recalled thinking that the bulb must have burnt out. Jack walked to the kitchen and turned on the overheard light. Suddenly, his spider senses were tingling and they quickly danced down his spine. Something was terribly wrong. He slowly turned towards the living room and with the light on from the kitchen, he could see that there was nothing there except for a VCR lying on the floor next to the cable cords. Every stick of furniture was gone. Every picture was removed. Literally, everything was gone!

Alarm bells screamed inside Jack and to this day, he doesn't know if they were verbal screams or the inner sirens made out of his pure fear. Naively, he ran to Charlie's room. Under his breath, he prayed to God, to let Charlie be there and be okay. Charlie's room was just as empty as the living room. Even though he knew he would find the same thing, he still ran into his own bedroom, only to find it completely empty.

Jack raced to the telephone hanging from the kitchen wall. His only thought was to call his brother, Jon, at the police department. It was then, on the kitchen counter, that he saw two pieces of paper. The first, a letter from Stacey, saying that her "true love" was back in her life and that she and Charlie would be happy and to not look for them. She said it was for the best. *For who, Jack screamed?* Stacey's letter also included an apology, not for leaving, but for not telling Jack before Charlie was born that Charlie wasn't his biological son. She went on to briefly explain that she had ordered a DNA test and had taken a sample of his saliva while he was sleeping.

The document next to Stacey's letter was the lab results from a DNA test, which showed the test results. Jack's eyes blurred with tears, but he managed to make out words to the effect that the likelihood of paternity between Jack and Charlie to be less than one percent. A pain seared through his gut that felt like a hot sword was cutting him in half. At that moment, he was certain he was dying.

Jack stumbled backwards and his back hit the kitchen wall. He slid down the wall and to his knees. His knees were drawn up to his chest and he sobbed terrible, heaving sobs that left him too weak to stand. *Charlie, not my son!* It wasn't possible, was it?

He had dated Stacey only briefly before they married, but he never doubted Charlie's paternity for one second. When they found out that she was pregnant after only a month of marriage, he was thrilled! It never occurred to him to question that Charlie might not be his and Stacey never said anything to the contrary, even during one of their many arguments.

After Stacey left with Charlie, Jack sat paralyzed on the kitchen floor, he felt the waves of nausea consume him. What the hell just happened? What was he going to do without his son? Was Charlie his son? Another man's son? Of course he was his son! Although, every fiber in his being screamed that Charlie was his son, he also knew that Stacey hadn't been faithful to him during marriage so why would she have been faithful to him *before* marriage?

That night, as the minutes turned into hours, Jack's position on the kitchen floor remained the same. He felt so lost already. He missed Charlie deeply and only hours had passed. It sounded like such a cliché, but he really felt a happiness that he had never known before when he was with Charlie. Being with him filled Jack with such joy that it was almost indescribable. Quite simply, he loved every second that they were together.

Jack remained on the floor, with tears still sliding down his face until the next morning when his brother, Jeremy, walked in looking for him. As Jeremy looked at the empty house and the broken man crouched on the floor, he didn't have to ask what happened. He knew, or at least knew some version of what happened. *Goddamn you Stacey!*

Lost in the memories that he tried so hard not to think about any more, Jack didn't realize that Cassie had been watching him. Eager to remove the horrible memories from his mind, he blurted out the first thing that popped into his head.

"I think your ex-husband is a damn fool. No man in his right mind would reject a woman as beautiful as you." Jack stopped himself from saying more. He quickly looked towards the activity outside the coffee shop window.

At Jack's unexpected outburst, a slow grin turned into a big smile across Cassie's face. Jack's defense of her and as his compliment settled into her head, she was feeling genuinely flattered and somewhat surprised, Cassie also said the first thing that popped into her head. "That was honestly the nicest compliment I've had in a very long time." Not knowing what else to say at that moment and both of them feeling awkward, they both started to stand.

Still a little surprised at Jack's compliment, Cassie was the first to speak. "Thanks for having breakfast with me, but I should let you get to work now."

She smiled up at Jack. "I heard you are working for a very difficult customer and if you're late," she whistled, "who knows what will happen to you." Jack touched her back to guide her away from other customers and towards the door.

He chuckled, "So, you've heard about my new boss too. You're right, she's quite the shrew and I better get to work and fast." They both laughed as the door closed behind them.

As Cassie walked towards her car, she continued to feel the warmth of the unexpected compliment and, more surprisingly, the warmth that remained on her back where Jack had touched her gently to guide her out the door. She couldn't recall ever feeling the slightest touch lingering on her body for so long. It was as if his hand was still there.

Starting the day off by having coffee and breakfast with Jack had been very interesting. She still didn't know why his marriage had ended, but one thing was now very clear to her. Jack was not married. That was one lingering question that had been racing around in her head since she met him. Not that it should matter, but somehow Cassie felt internally better and at peace knowing that a wife wasn't in the picture.

The morning had certainly taken an interesting and unexpected twist. Cassie thought to herself. She was supposed to see Colleen and Abby later in the day. No doubt, they would turn an innocent and unexpected breakfast into a romantic "meant to be moment."

At the thought of Abby and Colleen's likely misguided notion of a romance ran through Cassie's head, the radio played a song about finding eternal love. Cassie unwittingly sang along as she drove to work.

Chapter Nine

Colleen, Cassie, Abby and several other members of the "Dig It, Dudley" production team sat around the large, messy conference room table at the Pueblo Valley Playhouse. There were scripts in front of each member of the team, half empty coffee cups or cans of soda, vibrating cell phones and chatting people. It was unorganized chaos at its finest.

When the noise level reached decibels that would make a dog lay down and cover it's ears, Colleen, banged the first thing she could find on the table, which happened to be a large book. Everyone at the table quieted and looked her way.

"People, people, now that I have your attention," Colleen looked from one set of eyes to the next, "we really need to stay focused on the agenda." At her own words, Colleen picked up an agenda in her hand and waived it in the air. "Opening night will be here before you know it and we are *way* behind."

A frazzled Colleen looked towards Kevin and immediately a tender tone entered her voice. "Kevin, darling, please start by telling us how the cast is doing, about the upcoming rehearsal schedule and whatever else we need to know."

Kevin winked at his wife and then looked to his notes. "As you all know, the cast is larger for this production than most of our productions, so it presents some challenges." Kevin paused and scanned his notes once again, "because this production is a musical comedy set in the 1970's, we have approximately fifteen secondary performers that are primarily part of the disco scenes and the choreography is really starting to take shape."

Kevin looked towards Cassie. "I will need to work with you on additional accessories for the costumes, but I'll get to that in a minute."

Kevin asked one of the team to close the conference room door completely shut before he continued.

"The main character roles have all been cast and we've started a pretty intense rehearsal schedule, but there is one problem." Kevin looked towards Colleen and she knew what was coming. She rolled her eyes in anticipation. This wasn't the first time that they had dealt with this situation. Kevin explained to the rest of the committee, although some of the more seasoned members suspected what was coming.

"We have once again cast Liza Beardsley in the lead female role." A collective sigh fell across the room.

"As we all know, Liza is an extremely talented performer and she brings in not only an established audience, but a high volume of people, mostly through her own social circle but also because of her talent."

Kevin took a breath and continued. "As most of you know, she is extremely demanding. Liza is concerned that she'll get lost within the larger cast and 'not shine.'"

Kevin had worked with demanding actors for years, but Liza's demands and need for attention was right up there at the top. Liza was very much the typical diva. "She has been quite vocal that the audience, many of whom are her friends, will not get the show they bargained for if she isn't front and center most of the time."

At the staff's chuckles and queries of "huh," Kevin clarified. "Her words, not mine. Needless to say, Liza is demanding two additional musical solos, including a sexy 'dirty dance' with one or two of the men, not to mention that she wants several very ornate costumes."

Colleen shook her head in frustration. There was a bad apple in every crate and Liza Beardsley was their token bad apple. Both fortunately and unfortunately, it was true that Liza was extremely talented. When the curtain rises, she transforms into the character she's playing and she has a beautiful, lyrical voice that completely envelopes you.

Not only that, but since she married, Tom Beardsley, an older and prominent winemaker a few years ago, Liza's own social circle grew significantly. Many of the theatre's newest season ticket holders were due to Liza's influence, or more likely perhaps, because of her husband's influence. Colleen was more than a little frustrated. She didn't like being over the barrel for anyone, but she was also a business woman and she knew when it was time to keep her lips zipped.

Then a memory of the old Liza, before her marriage to Tom Beardsley, provided Colleen with enough amusement to induce an internal chuckle. She remembered that Miss High Society Liza, used to be one of the town "flirts," and Colleen was being more than generous in that description. Liza was known to sleep around with just about any available man, particularly if he was older, or if Liza thought his wallet was a little thicker than the average Joe's.

Suddenly the amusement was gone as Colleen recalled that Liza and Jack Shaw's ex-wife use to travel together in pairs. She remembered that they were thick as thieves. What was Jack's ex-wife's name? *Hmmmm,* she hadn't thought about that for a few years, so she'd have to try to remember what she'd heard.

Colleen's attention returned to the sound of Kevin's voice. "Cassie, you'll need to meet with Liza to get an idea of the costumes and accessories that she has in mind." Cassie nodded in agreement as she made notes on her tablet.

Kevin continued. "Cassie, Liza will want costumes that are super sexy and you'll need to bring it to my attention and let me deal with her if she gives you any grief." Kevin had worked with Cassie many times in the past, so he knew that she would be able to tackle Liza's demands. "Keep in mind, that it's okay for some sex appeal, after all, this production is set in the 70's which was in the full swing of the sexual revolution."

Everyone snickered. "But still, this is a family show and, like the circus, it's for children of all ages."

Cassie recalled working with Liza in other productions in the past. Liza was opinionated and treated everyone as a subordinate. Her behavior got worse after she married a rich husband, but Cassie wouldn't let her get to her. Besides there was an incredibly large cast for this production and she would have her hands full trying to meet all their needs, so she'd give Liza an adequate amount of attention, but others in the cast needed her attention too.

Cassie's ears perked back to attention when she heard Colleen stating that Jack Shaw would be doing some construction work for the stage set. That was surprising news! Cassie had been volunteering at Pueblo Valley Playhouse for close to ten years now and she never remembered Jack volunteering there. Other than the work he was contracted to do, she'd never heard about him helping out before. She wondered how that came to be. She made a mental note to ask Colleen about that.

After the meeting was over, the rest of the staff and volunteers trickled out of the conference room. Cassie stayed behind, as did Abby. There were a few things that she needed to address with Colleen about the costumes, but honestly, she admitted to herself, she was still a little giddy from her impromptu breakfast with Jack that morning. She felt like a schoolgirl as she waited for Colleen to finish her conversation with another volunteer.

Finally Colleen was done and the three of them scooted their chairs closer together. Abby tucked one leg under the other and scooted herself into a relaxed position. She enjoyed volunteering at the playhouse, but obviously she couldn't always make the meetings due to the delivery schedule of her patients, but today she was able to make it and now she would have a few minutes to touch base with a couple of girlfriends.

"Tell me what's going on with you two." Abby looked from woman to woman. "I haven't seen either one of you for a day or two."

For once, Colleen paused before speaking and Cassie jumped at the chance to get the first word in.

"Well, something kind of surprising happened to me this morning." She looked from friend to friend and they could both see the twinkle in her eye.

Abby uncurled her legs and sat forward towards Cassie with keen interest in her eyes.

"What?"

Cassie had a sly grin on her face and she relaxed back into her chair, crossed her legs at the ankles and looked towards her friends until they both said "what" again in unison.

"Well, it so happens that I had breakfast with Jack this morning." She looked from woman to woman. Colleen smiled from ear to ear and Abby cried out for more details.

"Wow! How did that happen? Was it prearranged?" Abby looked from Colleen to Cassie. "If so, why didn't I know about it?"

Colleen interrupted Abby, "Please tell me it was breakfast in bed after the two of you realized you're hot for each other and you couldn't wait to ravish one another for one minute more."

Cassie laughed, "God, I wish, but no, it wasn't like that." Suddenly realizing that she had said "God, I wish" she quickly continued. "It was kind of sweet how it happened."

Cassie leaned in closer and looked to make sure the conference room door was closed. "I woke up this morning thinking that I should buy some pastries for Jack's crew because they've been really terrific about keeping the noise down as much as possible, keeping the dust down, and so on, so I decided to stop by the coffee shop."

Abby and Colleen both listened with rapt attention. "As it turns out, Jack woke up this morning and he decided that he was going to stop and pick *me* up a specialty coffee because I've been giving him a cup of coffee every morning."

Abby jumped in. "Oh that was sweet of him. Most guys wouldn't think to do that."

"It really was very thoughtful and it touched me that he was thinking about a way to thank me."

Now it was Colleen's turn to jump in. "I told you all along he's a great guy, but I bet he was thinking about more than thanking you." Her knowing smile grew as she thought about it.

Colleen continued. "I bet he gets coffee from lots of his customers. Come to think of it, when he worked here, I gave him more than a cup or two of java and I don't recall him ever buying me a specialty coffee." Colleen paused. "I think he's sweet on you."

Cassie wasn't so sure. "Oh I don't know about that. It's not like he asked me out for a breakfast date or anything. It was just one of those things." Cassie considered her thoughts before she continued. "Even having breakfast together was an accident. I just assumed that our coffees would be in to go cups, but then they accidentally put them in glass cups, so we decided to drink it there and eat a pastry while we drank our coffees."

Abby looked at Colleen, caught eyes and then looked at Cassie. "I think Colleen has a point. Jack is sweet on you." Cassie tried to interrupt without success. "No, I don't…"

Abby continued. "First of all, he was thinking about you this morning." Abby looked at Colleen to confirm.

With Colleen's eyes agreeing, Abby continued. "Seriously what do most guys think about first thing in the morning?"

"Sex!" Colleen and Abby answered in unison.

Abby now had a theory and she shared her thoughts on what must have happened "Since Jack was thinking about sex, he started thinking about you because he wants you."

After a half second of pause, Abby continued. "But since you weren't there with him, he was thinking about a way to do something nice for you, aka, which leads to sex later on. See, ta da! That's how guys think."

Cassie nodded her head from side to side in disagreement, although she smiled at Abby's thought process. Internally, she was torn. On the one hand, she so wanted to believe her friends and could admit what they were saying was a slight possibility, but on the other hand, apprehension gripped her. It was just so hard to let her mind believe that it might be true that Jack thought about her in that way.

Abby leaned over and put her hands on top of Cassie's hands. "Listen, I know you think we're being silly and I'm sure this feels like high school to you, but I think Jack might be starting to look at you like someone he could be interested in."

Abby was much more experienced with men that Cassie. "It's just my experience that when men have you on their minds, they think about little things like that."

Colleen leaned over and put her hands on top of Abby's hands, whose hands were on top of Cassie's hands. "That's been my experience too. Abby and I might be wrong, but I don't want you to miss an opportunity to at least consider the possibility that he could be interested in you. Then let yourself decide whether or not you could be interested in him too."

Well, Cassie commented to herself silently, she already knew the answer to the second part of Colleen's statement. *She was very interested in Jack Shaw.*

Cassie squeezed both of their hands and then sat up straighter in the chair. "I love you both, you know." They knew. "I guess I just haven't been able to let myself believe that someone could be interested in me."

With a knowing looking to both of her friends, she said, "You both know it took me forever to get over Peter's rejection of me."

Abby couldn't control her tongue when it came to Peter. "Peter is such a moron."

Cassie kind of chuckled. "It's funny that you say that, because at breakfast this morning, I told Jack a little bit about my divorce and when it was all said and done, he said something to the effect that Peter was a damn fool for rejecting someone as beautiful as me."

Colleen slapped her leg. "Woo hoo, you just confirmed everything that we've been telling you."

Cassie grinned. "I have to say, that when he said that I was 'beautiful,' it didn't go unnoticed; my tummy did a little flip flop."

Colleen inquired. "So has your tummy ever done a little flip flop when you've been around Jack in the past?"

Cassie thought carefully before answering. She could no longer avoid admitting it to her two closest friends. "Honestly, since the moment Jack walked in the door to give me an estimate, I haven't been able to stop thinking about him."

"Yes!" Both Abby and Colleen clapped their hands together in a good ol' high five. Their glee was obvious.

Now Cassie laughed out loud. She had finally admitted her attraction to Jack to her friends. She didn't know what it was called -- a crush, an interest, a feeling, a whatever, but it was about Jack and it had been a very, very long time since she couldn't get a man out of her head.

Cassie's eyes then narrowed and she looked at Colleen. "Colleen, don't you dare say a word to him."

"I wouldn't think of it!"

"Oh yes, you would. I just remembered you or Kevin saying that Jack was going to do some work on the set, so don't you even think about it!"

Colleen chuckled. "Who me, of course, I wouldn't do that to you."

She shook her finger at Colleen. "You better not." She didn't think Colleen would really say anything to Jack, but then remembered Colleen asking Jack if she was pretty.

Then the curiosity got to her. "By the way, how is it that Jack will be working on the set stage for you?"

"Oh that! It was perfectly innocent. I ran into him at your store the other day. He was sitting out in his truck, finishing up a phone call, so I walked over to say hello. We talked for a while and I asked his opinion on how to do a large moving wall that will serve multiple purposes in this production. Jack ended up volunteering to help us out, at least with the preliminary design and basic construction."

Cassie was still suspicious and thought that Colleen was leaving something out. After all, they had used moveable walls in the past, but she elected not to question her further.

For now, it felt good to simply be with her two best friends and consider the possibility that a very attractive man, might, just possibly might, be interested in her.

Chapter Ten

A few days later, Cassie was at work. It was late in the afternoon and she'd been unusually busy. She was starting to get tired, yet she perused the racks of women's clothing looking for some items that might be appropriate for Liza Beardsley to wear in "Dig It, Dudley." Liza was supposed to stop by Cassie's Closet at some point before closing. Cassie was dreading it. Liza wasn't her favorite person and her demanding ways were just exhausting; more so after a particularly long and busy day. However, she reminded herself, this was just a preliminary search and there was a volunteer seamstress that would be dealing with Liza most of the time.

Sometimes there were obvious pieces that Cassie could quickly pull for a production; other times it was her keen eye for color, pattern and fabric. She didn't have a lot of bell bottoms and wide bells in the store, in large part, because there had been a recent come-back in 70's fashions and teenage girls couldn't get enough of them. Cassie pulled a few pieces that might work for Liza, or some of the other cast members, and then a few pieces that had vivid, bold patterns that could work for the wild, polyester prints of the 70's.

As she pulled the clothing, Cassie could smell Liza's presence before she actually saw that she was near her. Liza's perfume was powerful and strong. For all the money she apparently now had, her perfume smelled like cheap baby powder. It hit Cassie's throat and a tickle started to grow in her throat. Cassie coughed and Liza jumped back.

"God, Cassie, you don't have a cold do you?" Liza's ash blonde bob bounced softly as she moved back in disgust. Distain was etched in her crystal clear, blue eyes.

Cassie sighed. The appointment was off to an encouraging start. "No, Liza, it's just something in the air."

Liza waved her hand in front of her face and wrinkled her perky nose. 'I'm sure there is. This place smells musty."

Cassie tried to keep her simmering rage at bay. One thing that she had taken from the O'Connell's, and continued throughout her operation of Cassie's Closet, was that they washed and dried every piece of clothing that came through the door. It was expensive, time consuming and Cassie's Closet was the only thrift store that did it, but she felt it was important to give her customers the sense that they were purchasing an item that had been laundered instead of wondering if the clothing had been laying on someone's garage floor, or worse.

Liza's arrogance continued. "I can't possibly catch a cold now, Cassie, with the play fast approaching." Cassie nodded in agreement, but fumed inside. She took it personally when someone was so callous and insensitive about her business.

Liza was smug. "Although I'm sure I could pull off a sexy, throaty sounding character, but I have several numbers, including my solo, and I need to be at the top of my game. After all, *everyone* in the audience expects perfection from me." Liza seemed to think that she was the only reason people attended any production that she was in.

Cassie ignored Liza's overblown arrogance and tended to the business at hand. "I don't have a lot of articles of clothing here that will work for you, but I've pulled a few pieces that you might consider."

Liza looked at the pieces, but tried to avoid touching them. Cassie draped a few men's shirts over her own arm. "Take a look at these, Liza. They would need to be altered, of course, but the fabric and design are perfect for your character."

Cassie stroked the fabric of the shirt. "Wouldn't this be great with a fringed vest over the top, a pair of brightly colored bell bottoms and platform shoes?" Liza didn't have Cassie's creativity or clear vision. It wasn't until Cassie described the outfit to her, that she was able to see it.

Yet, she would never admit that. "That's exactly what I was thinking!" Cassie doubted that. Cassie silently reminded herself that Liza would be leaving soon and that Cassie could leave, get some dinner and relax the rest of the evening.

Without warning, Cassie heard Liza call out "Jack Shaw, is that you?" in a sexy, purr-like voice. Cassie whipped her head around in the direction of Jack. Jack stood several yards away, frozen in place. His tool belt hung low at his hips, his feet were spread apart and his eyes were darker and blacker than Cassie ever remembered seeing them. There was an absolute rage and fury reflected on his face. Cassie looked from Liza to Jack and back to Liza's face again. Where Jack's face showed astonishment and fury, Liza's face eerily showed shameless satisfaction, but for what, Cassie didn't know.

Without a word, Jack literally turned around the other way and walked towards the enclosed partition where construction was ongoing. Cassie could see that Jack was incredibly angry. So much so, that the pit of her stomach turned at the silent interaction that had just occurred. Her first thought was to run after him, but she was confused and didn't know what to do.

Clearly, Liza was someone he knew. Yet there was no doubt about that glare; which was pure bitterness across his face. The questions jumped around in Cassie's head. It just didn't make sense. Could Liza be an old lover of Jack's? The thought made her feel physically ill. Would Jack ever be with someone like Liza? In that moment, it was the only explanation that Cassie could come up with that made any kind of sense. She would have never pictured Jack with someone like Liza, but then again, opposites attract. Still, the thought of them together was dumfounding and it left her feeling stunned.

For the reaction that Jack had, Liza seemed to have the exact opposite reaction. She shrugged her shoulders and looked back towards Cassie. "Apparently, Jack is busy now." Cassie hadn't found her voice yet and tried to focus on the clothing racks.

Liza thumbed through the clothing with little or no notice of Cassie's reaction. "I can see that you are under construction. I should have assumed that Jack's company would be handling your project."

After a slight hesitation, Liza continued. "Jack is the very best after all." Cassie's stomach lurched once again at the implication.

Twenty minutes later, Liza finally left the store. She had selected some pieces and instructed Cassie to send them to the seamstress. Apparently, she assumed that Cassie was her personal assistant. Cassie didn't argue. She was suddenly bone-tired and the odd exchange between Jack and Liza had left her feeling confused and emotionally drained. Cassie was eager to lock-up. The last customer had left and the building was silent except for some small noise from the construction side of the building. It sounded like a crew member or two was cleaning up for the night.

Cassie finished locking up and turned off the lights. She then walked through the partitioned plastic and found Jack unplugging cords and putting saws back up on the tables. The rest of his crew had left. Little did she know, but Jack was doing everything he could to control his emotions, even twenty minutes after spotting Liza.

The very thought that Cassie might be friends with Liza made Jack sick to his stomach. It was obvious that they knew each other and not just as a customer. Besides, Jack knew that Liza would never shop at a thrift store, no matter how nice it was. It just didn't make sense. Liza's heart was black as the night and Cassie's heart was... No it couldn't be possible that they are friends. Could it?

Jack heard Cassie approaching but he didn't look her way. His eyes were downcast. He didn't want Cassie to witness the raw rage he still felt. Cassie could still see some of Jack's emotions on his lowered face and in his body movements.

Even feeling her uncertainty about what she witnessed with Jack and Liza's interaction she still had the strongest urge to touch Jack. It was unexplainable to her, but she just wanted to comfort him. Upon closer inspection, it appeared to Cassie that the shock and turmoil she had witnessed on Jack's face earlier, was now replaced with quiet sorrow maybe?

In a soft voice, Cassie said, "Jack, I've locked up for the night? Are you ready to leave?"

Looking up, Jack turned in Cassie's direction. Although he knew it was none of his business, he had to know. With a controlled voice, he simply asked,

"Is Liza Beardsley a friend of yours?"

Even after asking her, he knew he had no right to ask her that, but he had to know.

"No," Cassie answered softly.

Jack's eyes slowly rose to meet Cassie's eyes. "What was she doing here then?" Jack sounded both relieved and as exhausted as Cassie felt.

"You know that I volunteer at Colleen and Kevin's playhouse. Because I own this store, I often have the task of gathering clothing and accessories for each production."

Cassie could see more relief leave Jack's body. "I'm sorry Cassie; I don't have any right to ask you who your friends are. I just have this..." Jack shook his head and paused, "...this history with Liza, that's complicated."

Jack tenderly looked at Cassie. "I didn't think the two of you would be friends. I guess I was just surprised to see her here and talking to you."

At the mention of a "complicated history" with Liza, Cassie felt ridiculously jealous. Full-on, no doubt about it, jealous! She hadn't felt that way, since, when? When she thought Peter left her for another woman? She had no right or reason to feel this way about Jack, yet clearly she did.

Not wanting to think about her childish jealously anymore, she told Jack, "No, I wouldn't be friends with Liza. I can barely tolerate her to work with her during the plays. Fortunately, it's usually just a brief meeting or two with Liza."

A slight grin formed at the edge of Jack's lips. "I give you credit Cassie, because I can't stand her." Jack couldn't stand her? Interesting! There was a new twist to this "strange connection" that Jack had with Liza. Suddenly Cassie wasn't feeling jealous and exhausted anymore. Amazing how a few words could change her mood from envy to relief.

Jack took three steps closer to Cassie. He too, was tired and hungry. On impulse, he asked. "It's been a long day and I'm starving. Is there any chance you'd like to join me for dinner at Trebbiano's?"

Cassie looked at Jack and saw all the earlier rage and confusion gone. Once again, the twinkle and light was back on in his black eyes. Cassie's stomach growled then, loud enough for both of them to hear. She laughed. "I guess that's your answer!"

Jack laughed too as the last of the tension left his body. Once again, he gently touched the small of Cassie's back and guided her out the back door of Cassie's Closet.

Chapter Eleven

The lights at Trebbiano's were soft and low, but it wasn't too dark. The atmosphere was relaxing and enjoyable. Jack sat across from Cassie. By now, she had a glass of wine in front of her that was almost empty and Jack's beer was sitting in front of him, with more than half of it gone. The basket of bread was almost gone after Jack and Cassie had eaten a couple of pieces. Their dinner orders were in. Cassie sat back and relaxed herself into the comfort of the high-backed chair, sitting across from her, Jack did the same.

The tension and long day had left Cassie's body. She looked around at the rich, mahogany wood of the bar, the rustic wall colors and the colorful, Italian pottery that lined the shelves on the wall.

"I haven't been to Trebbiano's in quite a while. I don't remember it being this nice." Cassie raised her hand and pointed toward the bar area.

Jack, also more relaxed and feeling better with a little beer and bread in his stomach, felt a little cocky about the hand he had in the renovations.

"It was recently remodeled; it hasn't always been this nice." Cassie nodded in agreement.

Jack continued. "I went to school with the owner, Doug. He wanted to upgrade the place, almost like a thank you to his customers. He has good food, a strong following of the locals and visitors, and great wine. He wanted his customers to relax and feel good in here." As he said that, Jack raised his glass in a symbolic toast. Cassie raised her glass.

"Cheers to good food and wine." Their glasses clinked together.

Suddenly Cassie realized that Jack must have had a part in the remodel. "Jack, were you and your crew a part of the remodel?"

"Actually, we were. We finished up just days before I started on your project."

"Oh Jack, it's beautiful in here now. I like it and it's not too pretentious or intimidating."

Jack felt proud and maybe a little bit smug. He was usually very satisfied with the work that he did, but somehow knowing that Cassie responded to it favorably, made him feel particularly proud.

"I'm glad to hear you say that. If you feel that way, I accomplished what I was supposed to do. Doug wanted this place to reflect an establishment where you could come in and grab a drink after work, eat at the bar, or relax a little longer and eat at the tables."

Cassie looked at the deep, rich wood of the bar and then at the simple, yet sweet table where they sat. Besides the bread basket, olive oil and their glasses, it had a small candle that flickered softly. That's all that was needed; casual elegance.

Jack started to tell Cassie more about the remodel when suddenly a strong hand slapped his back. Jack turned quickly to see his younger brother, Jon. Jack started to stand to greet his brother, but Jon quickly ignored Jack and leaned over towards Cassie.

"Hello, beautiful. I am Jon and your name is?"

Cassie grinned at the compliment but was also somewhat confused, as she didn't know who this man was.

Jack stood, patted Jon on the back and simultaneously, but good-naturedly pulled Jon several inches back from Cassie.

Looking at Cassie, Jack playfully explained. "This ugly bastard is my brother, Jon."

Jon bumped his shoulder into the still standing Jack, but looked at Cassie. Relieved to now know what was going on and who this handsome man was, Cassie stuck out her hand to shake Jon's hand. "Hi, Jon, I'm Cassie. It's nice to meet you."

Jon looked from Jack and then back to Cassie. "Cassie, as you can see, I'm the looker in the family. Why don't you leave Jack here and join me for dinner?"

Cassie giggled at the surprise attention, although she recognized instantly that it was all in good fun. There wasn't a trace of anger or annoyance on Jack's face; instead enjoyment flickered in his eyes.

This time Jack tried to elbow Jon slightly, but Jon escaped the jab quickly enough to grab a chair from another table and slide it next to Cassie.

Jack returned to his seat and signaled Nicki at the bar to bring another round, including a drink for Jon.

"So, Cassie, what's a beautiful woman like you doing here with what's-his-face and why haven't I seen you before?"

Fully relaxed and charmed, Cassie giggled, enjoying the lighthearted playfulness of Jack's brother.

"I was just telling Jack that I haven't been in here for a while. It looks really nice after the remodel."

The waitress brought over the drinks and asked Jon if he would like to order something for dinner. "No, he doesn't want anything." Jack answered for his brother.

"Did you help Jack with the remodel here?" Cassie remembered that she had dealt with Jack's brother, Jeremy, initially in the contract negotiations and recalled that it was a family business.

"No, I leave all the sawdust and dirty work to Jack here. I, on the other hand, am a police officer for the Sheriff's Department. It's my job to serve and protect and serve is what I do best." Jon cocked his eyebrows at Cassie and it made her laugh.

Jack rolled his eyes in mock horror at Jon's description of his job. "I think you have a 911 call, lil' brother. Go protect someone."

Jon ignored his brother and turned once again towards to Cassie. "You still haven't told me what you are doing here with my older, uglier brother."

With a full glass of wine in her now and after watching the playful exchanges and eye rolls between the brothers, Cassie was completely relaxed and enjoying Jack and Jon immensely.

"Jack is doing some work at my store, Cassie's Closet." She pointed to the window and in the general direction of the store.

Jon nodded. "I've actually been to your store. It's a great store. I bought some camping gear there a few years ago." Jon paused, took a drink of his beer and resumed his conversation. "Our mother actually loves your store too."

Cassie was so pleased to hear that Jon liked her store, but she was particularly pleased that Jack's Mom enjoyed her store.

"Now if you'll excuse me for a moment, gentlemen." Cassie left for the restroom.

As soon as Cassie was out of ear shot, Jon asked his brother. "Wow, she's a looker, big brother. So what's the scoop? Are the two of you dating?"

Jack looked towards the bathroom. "No, we're not." He let out a breath. "I don't know, maybe," Jack took in another breath, "no, it's just a casual dinner after work."

Jon smacked his elbow into Jack's. "All I know is that I haven't seen with you a woman at a dinner table in a very long time. Most of the time, you are up at the bar and the women are, well, waiting up at the bar too."

Jack knew what he meant. He hadn't taken a woman out to an actual dinner since before he was married. It wasn't until he met Cassie that he discovered that he actually wanted to spend time with her and get to know her.

"Wait until I tell Mom about Cassie. Now at Sunday's dinner, she'll ask you all about Cassie, instead of asking me when I'm going to get serious about someone. Yee ha!"

With a smile, Jack smacked Jon on the arm. "Go, lil brother, go and make eyes with Nicki."

Cassie returned from the restroom. This time, Jon stood and pulled her chair out for her, but he remained standing. "Cassie, it was a pleasure to meet you, but I'm going to let you and the ugly one here enjoy dinner together."

"You don't have to leave." Cassie was sincere and didn't want Jon to feel like he couldn't stay and spend time with his brother.

"I'll take a rain check, but next time let's leave Jack at home." Jon leaned down and took Cassie's hand and kissed it lightly. Jon turned to Jack and Jack stood. They did the quick guy hug that men do and Jack returned to his seat.

Jack looked towards Cassie. "I hope Jon didn't offend you."

"No, he's great. I enjoyed meeting him. He's a character."

"That he is! He's the baby of the family and loves to have all the attention. He's a major flirt. Are you sure he didn't offend you?" Jack didn't sense that Cassie was annoyed with Jon, but he wanted to make sure.

"No, not at all!"

The waitress came with piping hot plates of food and sat it down before them. Suddenly the bread that had been holding off Cassie's hunger was gone. Her eyes delighted at sight of the steaming, hot plate of pasta.

Throughout dinner, Jack told Cassie stories about his family, particularly his brothers and when they were growing up. He had her laughing with pleasure at the antics of three boys, all of them about eighteen months apart in age and Jack's stressed out mother chasing their rambunctious butts out into the yard, when she'd had enough of their fighting and doing damage to her house. At Jack's story-telling, Cassie could easily see a frazzled, frustrated Mom trying to control three young boys. Having one child had been a challenge for her once in a while when Brett was little. She couldn't imagine having two other mini versions of him around when Brett was so little, yet she wouldn't trade being a Mom for anything. She sensed that Jack's mother would agree with her completely.

Finally, with a full belly and completely satiated by an incredible dinner, Cassie leaned back in her chair. Jack did the same. He had a great time regaling Cassie with stories about his childhood. It made it all the better to hear her laughter and the periodic sympathy moans for his "poor Mom" and all she'd been through with them.

The unexpected dinner had been completely enjoyable. It was almost worth it to run into Liza. At the thought of Liza, Jack realized that he probably owed Cassie some explanation for his reaction to seeing her. Now, after spending an evening with her, he was relaxed and could talk to her about it, without feeling the bile rise in his throat. Yet, he was conflicted. He didn't really want to think about Liza, but, in another surprising revelation, he realized that Cassie was someone he could talk to. It had been a very long time since he wanted to share something, especially something so personal, with a woman.

Accepting that, Jack cleared his throat and leaned forward towards Cassie. He locked eyes with Cassie.

"I'm sorry if it seemed like I barked at you today after Liza left the store." Jack could see compassion, kindness and understanding flick across her hazel eyes and knew for sure that he wanted to be upfront with her.

"You didn't bark at me, but I could see that you were upset."

Cassie swallowed at the thought of what was to come next. "I take it that you and Liza know each other?" Cassie's inquisitive gaze prodded Jack to respond.

Jack sighed and took a drink of his beer. "Unfortunately, I do." Knowing that he shouldn't or couldn't leave it at that, he continued.

"Liza was good friends with my ex-wife, Stacey. The two of them were always in cahoots with each other and pretty constant companions. Where one of them was, the other wasn't too far behind."

That question was finally answered Cassie thought. Cassie remained silent, allowing Jack to talk.

"This was before Liza married Tom Beardsley." Jack took another drink of beer and told himself that it was his final drink for the night.

"When I married Stacey, I thought we wanted the same things out of life. To settle down, raise a family and build a life together. That feeling of settling down, didn't last long with Stacey. She wasn't ready for that lifestyle. I knew it at the time, but I couldn't really face it."

Jack amended his statement. "I didn't want to face it."

Cassie nodded in understanding. Flashes of her own marriage skimmed across her mind. She also thought that she and Peter would settle down and share their lives together. When she realized that Peter had been unhappy and dissatisfied with their marriage, it had been a devastating blow.

Cassie listened as Jack started to talk again. "I can't tell you how many nights I came home and Stacey was gone. Sometimes there was a note; most times there wasn't. Invariably, I discovered that she was out with Liza." Jack was lost in his thoughts for a moment, yet the sorrow was gone. Somehow it made a difference to share it with Cassie.

"Stacey always claimed that it was just a 'girls' night out' and that she and Liza went to the mall or to the movies. I wanted to believe it and I did," Jack paused, "for a while." Jack took another drink of his beer, ignoring his earlier promise that he wouldn't drink any more for the evening.

"Word was getting back to me, through my friends, my crew and even my mother, that Stacey and Liza were out drinking, dancing and spending time with different men."

Cassie sucked in a breath and did a silent whistle. Ouch! For all her beliefs that Peter had left her for another woman, no one ever told her that directly, especially her mother! Cassie reached over and quickly stroked Jack's forearm. "God, Jack, I'm so sorry." She was genuinely sorry and couldn't understand how Stacey, how any woman for that matter, could do that to Jack.

Jack shrugged his shoulders. "It's all in the past now. I know it's for the best that Stacey and I aren't together, but seeing Liza today stopped me in my tracks. I hadn't seen her since…" Jack looked at his beer, pulled his shoulders back and decided against another sip.

"I hadn't seen her since Stacey left." Jack looked up into Cassie's eyes. He didn't see pity; he saw concern.

"I discovered Stacey left me when I returned home from an out-of-town job. I walked into a dark house only to find that everything, and I mean *everything*, was gone."

Cassie clasped her hand to her chest and realized that her mouth was agape. She quickly shut it. "Jack, I don't even know what to say." Cassie was genuinely stunned. What a horrible nightmare Jack walked into, yet Cassie didn't know the half of it.

"As you can imagine, I went out of my mind. I called everyone Stacey knew and no one knew anything. Obviously, the one person who would know for sure where Stacey was, would be Liza. I called her several times, but she never returned my calls."

Cassie was still dumbfounded. To make a commitment to marry someone and then leave, yes, of course it happens, but to leave like that? To disappear into thin air and take everything. Cassie didn't understand the need for that. It was such a horrible way to handle the end of a relationship.

"Finally, I drove over to Liza's apartment. Liza answered the door, but refused to tell me where Stacey was. In fact, she denied even knowing where she was or that she had left. That was the biggest line of bull, but I had no doubt that she knew where Stacey was. She just refused to tell me."

Cassie always knew that she disliked Liza whenever she had to deal with her at the theater, but to now know the role that Liza played in

Jack's marriage, and its demise, was incorrigible. She said as much to Jack.

Jack nodded. "I agree with you Cassie. Even when I returned to Liza's apartment several weeks later, I was much calmer and explained that there were legal papers and issues that we had to deal with. I didn't even ask her where Stacey was because I knew she wouldn't tell me."

Jack had a flashback to that day. "Liza was getting ready to marry Tom Beardsley and in the process of moving. She was eager to have me out of the way. She said that she would ask Stacey to call me." Jack looked up at Cassie and she was listening closely.

Jack continued. "When she said that, it was obviously confirmed that she knew where Stacey was, but I didn't push her further. At that point, I thought she was the only open door that I might have to get to in touch with Stacey."

Cassie inquired. "Did you ever hear from Stacey?"

Jack shook his head. "No. Not a word. It was like she vanished into thin air. After hiring a private investigator and still not finding her, my lawyer had to finalize our divorce by taking all these extra steps that were necessary."

Cassie was struck by what Jack had experienced. "Jack, I can't imagine experiencing something so hurtful."

In response, Jack thought to himself that maybe someday he would tell her about Charlie, but for today, he just couldn't bring himself to do it. Talking about Stacey was enough for one night. But when and if he told her, then she would understand what horrible really was to him. For today, it was a relief that he felt comfortable enough that he was able to tell Cassie about the circumstances of his divorce.

Cassie took the last sip of her wine and looked Jack straight in the eye. "I remember when I told you about my ex-husband and you said something to the affect that he was an incredible ass."

Jack nodded in agreement. "I remember saying that *and* he is an incredible ass."

Cassie smiled and again leaned forward to touch Jack's forearm. This time she left it there. "I will say the very same thing about Stacey. She's an incredible ass and so is her best buddy, Liza."

This time it was Jack who laughed. "I couldn't have said it better myself."

At that point, the waitress stepped up to the table to return Jack's credit card. Jack stood and held out his arm for Cassie. "Can I walk you out?"

"Absolutely!"

The night was still warm and the stars were out. Downtown was lit up with white lights strung throughout the trees that lined Main Street. It was so pretty and Cassie enjoyed being outside and looking at the effect of the lit trees. Cassie looked from the trees and then to Jack.

They stopped walking and Jack's face was inches from hers. Jack discovered that he couldn't stop himself and he didn't want to try to stop himself. He needed to kiss Cassie. It's what he had wanted to do from almost the moment he met her. Tonight, he shared with her something that he had shared with very few people. Her compassion and kindness left him feeling cared for.

Jack raised his hands and held Cassie's face tenderly and she felt his lips gently touch her own. Her heart leaped as his lips touched hers, ever so gently. Then, he pulled away, but only slightly, just long enough to look into her eyes, before leaning down to kiss her again. This time, the kiss was a soft, yet lingering kiss.

When Jack pulled away, Cassie felt her heart beating wildly in her chest. Her lips tingled slightly and she could still feel Jack's kiss on her lips. When she opened her eyes, the white lights in the trees gleamed like a thousand stars.

Jack smiled at her tenderly before removing his hands from the softness of her face. He waved a taxi down and Cassie pointed to her parked car. "We'll get your car tomorrow, but you've had lots of wine."

Cassie nodded in agreement. Jack helped eased her into the back seat and handed the taxi driver money.

"I had a wonderful night with you Cassie," Jack briefly touched his lips to hers again. "Thank you."

Cassie relaxed back into the taxi's back seat. She thought to herself that it was a good thing that she wasn't driving. How could she possibly concentrate after Jack's kiss? No, wait, not just one kiss, she reminded herself, but several! Cassie reached up to touch her lips with her finger. The delicious feel of Jack's lips still lingered on her lips.

Jack started walking down the street. Jon's house was close by. He'd crash on his couch tonight. He needed to walk. God, it had taken all the control that he had to not pull Cassie fully into his arms and cover her with deep, lingering kisses, but he knew the moment he did that, there would be no stopping himself. He ached for her even now. Jack shook his head to clear the cobwebs.

What in the hell had he done? Now all he wanted to do was kiss her again, hold her close and never let her go.

Chapter Twelve

The next morning, Cassie pulled into a parking spot in front of one of the outlet stores at the mall. It was Saturday morning and the sky was a beautiful blue, without a cloud in the sky. On a whim, she called Abby to see if she was available to meet her. She told Abby that she had talked to Brett and he mentioned tearing his jeans while playing a rousing game of football with his friends. That part of her phone call was true and she did want to send Brett a few new pair of pants and maybe a couple of t-shirts, but mostly she needed to talk to Abby and get her feedback on what happened with Jack the previous night after dinner at Trebbiano's.

Since she woke up this morning, she went over the evening and the kiss, no kisses, she reminded herself a dozen times. Cassie had alternated between convincing herself that it was grand passion and a romance was looming, and then, boom, she would turn around and convince herself that Jack simply had too much to drink and gave in to a kiss after sharing such a painful story about his divorce.

When she went to pick up her car that morning, thanks to a ride from her next door neighbor, she noticed that Jack's truck was still parked where he had left it. She wondered if he took a taxi home, or if he lived close enough to walk home. Before driving a way, she looked to the spot where Jack had kissed her the night before and she was filled with a warm, tingling sensation all over again. She reminded herself that it wasn't a dream and that it had really happened.

Now in the rearview mirror, she noticed Abby walking towards her from the adjacent parking lot. Cassie got out of her car and met her halfway.

"Hi there." Cassie gave her a quick, but firm hug. "I'm so glad that you could meet me today."

"Me too! It's been way too long since we've been shopping together."

They chatted as they walked into the Levi's store and began perusing the racks. Abby held up a pair of jeans and checked them out. "What style of jeans does our rambunctious guy want?"

Cassie picked up a pair herself to check them out. "The kind that's on sale." They both laughed.

Abby inquired of Cassie. "Is Brett enjoying school? I got a text from him a few days ago, but it was a human biology question. Yesterday, another text, but this time it was a joke."

Cassie grinned. That sounded like her boy; serious student, or at least semi-serious student, one minute, jokester the next minute.

"It seems like he's doing great now. I think he's finally over the adjustment hurdle and he's starting to settle in now."

"Is there anything new with you Abby, at least that I haven't heard about since we talked yesterday morning?"

Abby threw an old school KISS t-shirt over her arm. She would send a gift to Brett with his Mom's care package.

"No. Not much. I slept for about eleven hours yesterday after we hung up. The Johnson birth was most of the day and night before," she emphasized the *day and night* "and it was a tough one, but I feel well rested now and ready to spend some time with you!"

Cassie was trying so hard to focus on jeans and catching up with Abby, but it was unbelievably difficult to not shout out that Jack had kissed her.

Abby looked up towards Cassie. She suddenly realized that Cassie was smiling at her. One of those sly, cat-that-swallowed-the-canary kind of smiles. Abby walked towards her and stood close to Cassie. Abby knew her friend well.

"Why are you grinning like that all of a sudden?"

Cassie leaned over closer to Abby and lowered her voice. "Jack kissed me last night!"

Abby's mouth dropped open in surprise, but she lowered her voice to a near whisper, which was almost impossible considering her excitement. "What! Oh my God, Cassie!"

Abby jumped up and stood on her tippy-toes, with both hands clasped on Cassie's upper arms. "Okay, okay, let's grab this stuff, pay for it and then go get coffee. You have to tell me *everything*!"

Within five minutes, they had both purchased their items and where walking out the door and towards Starbucks. Abby was dying for the details, but she knew that a story like this had to be told when they were sitting down, had a drink and Cassie could tell her every little detail. Still it didn't stop either one of them from looking at each other occasionally and giggling like school girls.

Finally, they were sitting at an outside table in front of Starbuck's. Not only was it warm and beautiful outside, but it was much more private than inside where it was crowded and kind of loud.

Cassie was still in the process of scooting her chair closer to Abby and to the table, when Abby banged her hands on the table. "Details, details, I need details, my friend."

Cassie took a drink of her coffee and looked Abby in the eyes. As much as she would like to drive Abby crazy and make her wait even another five seconds, she just couldn't do it. She was already about to burst!

"Last night right before I was ready to close up Cassie's Closet, there was this strange incident with Liza Beardsley."

"Ugg, Liza Beardsley, God, what did she do now?"

Cassie told Abby everything that happened, starting with Jack's odd reaction to Liza and then his later inquiry about Cassie's relationship to her. Abby listened intently. She didn't understand yet, but Cassie promised her that once she heard the entire story, that she would understand completely.

Cassie continued on about the impromptu dinner invitation to Trebbiano's afterwards, about Jon's fun, but harmless flirting, and Jack opening up to her about his divorce and Liza's involvement with Stacey and their good time ways. Abby shook her head in distaste.

"We've always known what a self-centered, arrogant, little witch Liza is." Cassie nodded in agreement. She never cared for Liza at all, but she simply dealt with her quickly whenever it was related to a play. Any displeasure she had in dealing with her was quickly replaced by her allegiance to Colleen and Kevin and the success of their theater.

Cassie didn't want to think about Liza anymore and continued on with her story. "So after dinner, we were completely relaxed. We'd both had two or three glasses of wine or beer, we had full bellies and we were just enjoying being there together."

Cassie looked away dreamily, "the flames were flickering on the candle on the table and it just felt so right to be there together."

Abby sighed. She could envision it all in her head but nodded towards Cassie for her to go on. She knew the kiss was coming soon and she couldn't wait to hear all about it. It had been far too long since she'd been on a date, so it was fun to live vicariously through her friend.

"Besides being relaxed and comfortable after dinner, Jack seemed relieved to tell me about his past." Cassie took another sip. "I can't really explain it. I think it's just something that I sense more than anything, but I get the strong impression that Jack isn't one to share a lot about himself, especially something that's so private and painful."

Abby didn't really know Jack, just the different things that Cassie shared with her recently, but she had heard about their morning conversations over coffee at the shop and their casual breakfast together, so she was starting to feel like she knew Jack a little now too.

"I agree with you, Cassie. Men don't often share their inner feelings with other people. They tend to hold it in and deal with it in their own way."

Cassie bobbed her head in agreement. Then she locked eyes with Abby and did a little drum roll on the table. She couldn't keep it in one second longer. Abby maintained direct eye contact with Cassie in anticipation of what was coming next.

"So after dinner, I thought Jack was walking me out to the car. It was parked only a few spots away, but we were kind of strolling slowly. You know how the trees are all lit up each night on that street," Abby nodded, "and I was looking at them, and thinking how pretty they looked, when all of a sudden we stopped walking. When I looked up at Jack, he leaned down and before I knew it, his lips were on mine!"

Abby clapped her hands in delight!

Cassie looked at Abby dreamily. "It was one of those soft, tender kisses that just make you melt."

Abby gushed. "Oh, I love kisses like that!"

"I do too! When Jack pulled away from me, literally stars were dancing in my eyes. I don't know if it was the stars, or the trees, or the kisses, but there were stars!"

They both laughed again. It just felt so good to feel happy; Cassie for herself and Abby's happiness for her.

"When Jack pulled back from the kiss, we locked eyes and held it for a split second and then he leaned down and kissed me again!" Suddenly Cassie's excitement overflowed and she could barely sit still in her chair.

"That kiss was deeper and I swear to you Abby, I could feel Jack's lips on mine for such a long time afterwards. I kept touching my fingers to my lips." Even as she told her story, she unknowingly touched her fingers lightly to her bottom lip.

"Oh yay, Cassie! Those kisses sound amazing! Hell, the whole night sounds incredible."

Cassie nodded in absolute confirmation. "It was amazing! After that kiss, Jack flagged down a taxi for me and gave him the money to take me home. Before he helped me into the taxi, he thanked me for a wonderful evening and kissed me again!"

Cassie stared off again, remembering that last, soft kiss and once again felt the tiny tremors along her skin.

"Cassie! I'm so excited for you!" Abby genuinely was. There was nothing more she wanted than for her best friend to find that special kind of happiness.

"So tell me everything. How do you feel? You are obviously attracted to him. Right?" Abby paused, "even if you won't admit it to yourself, Colleen and I have been able to see it for weeks now. Do you want to see him again?" Abby was loaded with questions.

"I would like to see Jack again." Putting all her jitters aside, she thought carefully. "I really would." She paused again briefly. "I care for Jack, maybe even more than I am willing to admit and even though it scares me." She had to be honest with Abby. She could be nothing less with her.

"Why? You have a handsome man who obviously wants to spend time with you. Why are you making yourself crazy about this?" Abby knew her friend all too well and already suspected Cassie's answer.

Cassie was frustrated with herself because in every other area of her life, she felt self-assured and competent, but since meeting Jack, she discovered that the old wounds caused by Peter made her question herself or Jack's interest in her.

"Because one minute I think that Jack enjoys spending time with me and that maybe, just maybe, he's starting to care about me, and then, wham, the next minute I have myself convinced that Jack was just overcome with the emotions of talking about a terrible divorce, or that he had too much to drink, and that he kissed me just because he let his guard down." She sighed. "I don't know. What do you think?"

Cassie's eyes explored Abby's, "please tell me what you really think?" It had taken her a long time before she could ever let herself care about another man, and she needed the reassurance that she wasn't completely off base about Jack's possible interest in her.

Abby took Cassie's hands into her own and looked her deeply in the eyes. She was serious, "Cassie, let's go over this together." Cassie agreed.

"You said that Jack comes in to Cassie's Closet early almost every morning for what is now a coffee ritual," their eyes clicked together and Cassie nodded for her to go on, "and you have said that the conversations aren't really about work so much anymore and that you're starting to talk about a lot of different things now."

Cassie couldn't deny that and silently urged Abby on.

Abby continued, "The two of you also shared that nice little breakfast together."

Cassie started to interrupt her and Abby quieted her thoughts away. "No, don't even go there. I know what you're going to say and trust me, if Jack didn't want to spend time with you at breakfast that day, he would have asked for a to-go container."

Cassie let out a sigh. "Okay, okay. I'll give you that one."

"Thank you, because I am right." Abby now squeezed Cassie's hands into her own hands even tighter.

"Cassie, we both know how easy it is to convince ourselves of one thing, when the reality is that it's something else, but I honestly think we both know the truth this time. Just trust your instincts. I honestly think it's telling you whatever the truth is."

Abby looked deep into Cassie's eyes and she could see that what she said had clicked for her. She just needed that reassurance. It had been so long since Cassie had been in a new relationship, more than twenty years really, so it was difficult for Cassie to allow herself to believe it might be the start of something wonderful. Maybe now she could.

Abby wanted to lighten the mood and bring her friend back to feeling all the joy of a new relationship and to forget about all her misguided insecurities.

"So did I hear you correctly when you said that you were undeniably attracted to Jack and that you don't ever remember feeling this attracted to anyone before?"

Cassie just laughed. Ah, but her friend was a sly one. "Funny, I don't remember saying those words *exactly*." Abby just peered at her with raised eyebrows and waited impatiently. Cassie raised her own eyebrows. "I don't remember saying it quite like that, but I have to say, I've certainly thought it!"

Abby was thrilled and let out a loud whoop.

Now that all the seriousness was gone, Abby shook Cassie's hands free of her own. "There's only one thing left to do. Since Jack said that he had a wonderful time with you at dinner, I'm thinking there's a pretty good chance that he's going to ask you out again." A smile spread across Cassie's face at the thought of being with Jack again.

Abby stood up and signaled Cassie up. "The heck with more clothes for Brett, let's go shopping girlfriend! We need to find you something sexy to wear!" Cassie laughed. Thank God for girlfriends. Abby just turned around all of her insecurities and made her believe that there would be a next time with Jack.

Chapter Thirteen

Jack groggily stretched his arms and legs and in the process, he realized he was almost to the edge of the couch. He quickly rolled himself back onto it before he fell off the edge and onto the floor.

He heard Jon's chuckle, along with "Good morning, Sleeping Beauty."

Jack slowly turned to face him. Jon was sitting across the living room in his recliner, wearing a t-shirt and black shorts. His shoes and socks had been kicked off and were on the floor, off to the side of the chair.

"You're bright and cheery this morning, little brother."

"That's what a good run will do for you." Jon smacked his rock solid abs with one hand and held a cereal bowl with the other. "The ladies like it when I'm nice and fit."

Jack sat up on the couch and peered more closely at Jon's bowl. "Yep, buddy, I bet that run does you a lot of good when you eat Frosted Flakes afterwards."

Jon shrugged off the comment and nodded towards the kitchen. "The box is on the counter if you want some."

Jack stood up and slipped his jeans on and padded to the bathroom in his bare feet. When he returned, he could smell coffee and he headed towards the kitchen.

When he returned, Jon was still sitting in the recliner but he had set his bowl on the end table. He was texting someone. Jack assumed it must be Jon's flavor of the month.

Jack folded the blanket and laid it on the end of the couch. He sat at the other end. "Thanks for letting me crash here last night. I wasn't drunk, but it wouldn't have been smart to drive home either."

"No problem. I'm glad you came here. Unfortunately, I see way too many assholes on the road that don't make the same decision and it costs innocent people's lives."

Jack nodded in agreement and sipped his coffee. It was robust, rich and tasted heavenly. He needed to wake up. It had been a long night. He had tossed and turned for several hours before falling asleep. He just couldn't shut his mind off. Images of Cassie's beautiful face, dark hair and full lips flashed through his mind. The memory of the taste of her lips lingered. Those images resulted in strong stirrings that couldn't easily be quieted.

Jack tried to force himself to think about anything else, even trying to count the proverbial sheep in his head, but as the sheep were jumping over the bed, he'd think about Cassie being in bed with him and all hope of sleep was lost.

Finally, sometime shortly before dawn, his body finally found the peace that he needed and he drifted off to sleep.

Knowing his brother and that he needed a few minutes to wake up and drink coffee first, Jon remained silent and continued to text. He was surprised when he ran into Jack with Cassie last night. Although he had teased Jack about it, he was sincere when he said that of the few times he saw Jack with a woman, it was usually a woman at the bar, which left Jon with little doubt as to the nature of their 'relationship.' Now there was little doubt that last night was more than a simple mutual hook-up for Jack and Cassie. He honestly couldn't recall ever seeing Jack eating, laughing and talking with a woman at a nice restaurant – not even his lying, cheating bitch of an ex-sister-in-law.

The anger in Jon started to rise at the mere thought of Stacey. Not only had she destroyed Jack by taking Charlie, she had hurt every single member of his family. Jack wasn't the only one who had lost Charlie. He and Jeremy had lost a nephew. His parents had lost a grandchild. Hell, his parents still had pictures of Charlie hanging up on the wall in the hallway of their home. They just couldn't bring themselves to take them down.

When Stacey left, he did everything that he could to find Stacey and Charlie. He used every resource available at the Sheriff's Department to try and track her down. He personally, along with several of his buddies on the force, most of them on their own time, scouted places and surrounding areas where they thought she might be hiding. At the time, they thought Stacey was probably playing an incredibly immature and painful trick on Jack to punish him for telling her to stay home more and be a responsible mother. Either that, or whatever man she presumably left with, tired of her ways quickly and that she would return to Jack with her tail between her legs.

The whole situation was completely infuriating to him. *He was a fucking cop! If he couldn't help his own brother, or his nephew, who the hell could?* He still checked the bulletins regularly regarding women that fit Stacey's physical description or that of Charlie. It scared the hell out of him that Stacey could be her usual irresponsible self and leave Charlie home alone. It had always been Jack, with a little help from their Mom that had taken almost sole responsibility of Charlie before Stacey left. So Jon checked everything that came through the wires regarding a male child about Charlie's age now. He was filled with relief each time a severely injured child or dead child wasn't Charlie, but then instantly filled with sadness that it was someone else's child.

One thing that he knew for sure, was that he would never stop looking for Charlie. Charlie deserved to be back with his Dad and the rest of his family. He didn't even care if Charlie wasn't biologically related to them by blood. The entire family wanted Charlie and loved him. There was no question that Jack, his parents and Jeremy all felt the same way. Charlie needed to be safe, well cared for and with the people who genuinely loved him.

Jon looked back towards Jack. He could see the faraway look in Jack's eyes as he sipped his coffee. Jon was aware that Jack was probably struggling with whatever feelings he might have for Cassie. It was obvious to Jon, by the way that Jack looked at Cassie, that something was there. Yet, Jack had been horribly burned by Stacey. What Stacey did to Jack wasn't a typical break-up. It was nothing less than cruel.

Jon, Jeremy and their parents all secretly agreed that it would take an incredibly special woman to get into Jack's heart again. Up until last night, Jon wasn't completely convinced that it could ever happen for Jack again.

"Cassie seems like a nice lady. So what's up with her? Are you guys dating?"

Jack considered carefully before responding. "She *is* a nice lady; a very nice lady. Like I told you last night, I don't know if you could say we're dating. It wasn't like I asked her out on a date," he paused, "but, I like being with her, *a lot*."

Jon did a silent "*yes*" in his head. The one other thing that he wanted for his brother, besides having Charlie back, was to settle down with a really special woman. Jack was the type to settle down. Jon wasn't so sure he himself was the type, but Jack definitely was. Jack's marriage, if you could call it a marriage, had been crappy since practically day one. Jack had sworn a hundred times that he would never get married again. He'd just been hurt too deeply.

"If you like her, why don't you ask her on a real date?"

In avoidance, and to give him a minute to answer that very question, Jack stood up and went to pour himself some more coffee. When he returned from the kitchen, Jon's eyebrows were raised. Jon teasingly bounced his eyebrows up and down.

"So, big brother, are you going to ask Cassie out?" A mischievous smile spread across Jon's face. "If you're not going to ask her out, I will." Although Jack knew his brother was teasing him, he reached for one of his dirty socks on the floor and threw it at him. Jon raised his arms to block the sock and laughed.

"If you aren't going to answer me whether or not you're going to ask Cassie out," Jon grabbed his phone and shook it at Jack, "then you'll have to answer to Mom because I texted her this morning to tell her about running into the two of you." Jon started laughing hysterically. "She's only texted me back about a hundred times wanting 'details, details, details.'"

Jack set his coffee down and good-naturedly started picking up anything he could find off the floor to fling at Jon. His socks, DVD cases and game jackets were tossed at Jon as Jack teasingly snarled, "Gee, thanks, little brother, dinner at Mom and Dad's house tomorrow is going to be so much fun." As Jon blocked whatever was being hurdled at him, both men continued to laugh.

Later that morning, when Jon dropped Jack off at his truck, he threw the final jab at Jack. "See you tomorrow, sucker. I'm looking forward to Mom's inquisition being turned on you."

"Bite me, little brother." Jack grinned and took his keys out of his pocket. "Thanks again for letting me crash last night."

"Anytime." Jon sped away.

Jack got into his truck and noticed that Cassie's car was no longer there. He briefly looked at the place on the sidewalk where he had kissed her last night. His stomach muscles tightened, both in remembering the kiss that had left him tossing and turning all night and the thought of asking Cassie out on an official date. He just wasn't sure he could bring himself to do that. *Could he really let himself trust another woman?*

Chapter Fourteen

After brunch at Jack's parents' house, Jack sat on the porch swing in his parents' backyard. It was going to be a late Fall this year, as the leaves on the maples trees were just starting to turn burgundy. A few had turned yellow and gold and had fallen to the ground. Jack looked across the fenced yard and could see his Mother's vegetable garden in the corner of the yard. It wasn't too large, but it sustained his parents each season. Jack had received the benefit of extra vegetables quite often and even this morning, brunch had consisted of a Denver-type omelet, with fresh tomatoes, onions and mushrooms with a side of homemade hash browns.

Jack had been more quiet than usual through brunch. He could feel his Mom's eyes trying to read his mind when he didn't give in to her questions of "what's new with you Jack?" Jon and Jeremy had done their fair share of "yeah, what's new Jack" when he failed to answer the question that his Mom was really asking. He knew she wasn't satisfied with his response when he talked about work, or told her that he was thinking about going camping again before it got too cold.

After brunch, it was Jeremy's turn to do the breakfast dishes and Jon went to the computer to show his parents how to do something on the computer. Jack took the opportunity to escape to the backyard and collect his thoughts. He wasn't trying to avoid his Mom's inquiries. He knew that she wasn't just curious, but that she asked out of love. He just wasn't sure he had the answers yet that she was looking for.

Since he'd had dinner with Cassie, he had struggled to make sense of his thoughts and feelings. Cassie was beautiful, sexy, funny, sincere and completely desirable and he knew she was a different kind of woman than Stacey. He knew that it was so unfair for him to compare her to Stacey, but it was hard not to. Stacey had betrayed him so deeply, that he was having a difficult time believing that he could trust his own judgment about someone's character again. He had never had to question a woman's character before now. Since Stacey left, there wasn't a single woman that made him consider, even for a single second, that he might want to date her or spend time with her. Then he met Cassie.

Jack could hear the pull of the sliding glass door as his Mom walked through and into the backyard. She sat down next time him on the porch swing and the two of them sat in silence for a couple of minutes. The birds chirped and fluttered from tree to tree. Jack and his Mom swung slowly in the swing and Jack's Mom looked straight ahead. Finally, she turned to face Jack. She smoothed back a stray lock of his hair and then put her hands back down in her lap.

"Sweetheart, I'm not going to pretend that I haven't heard that you were having dinner with Cassie Reed the other night?"

Jack turned towards her, somehow surprised that his Mom knew her full name. "Do you know Cassie?" Barbara Shaw had lived in this town her entire life, so it didn't surprise him that she knew so many people, but he found it intriguing that she might know Cassie.

"No, I don't know her, not really, but I've been into her shop several times." After a brief pause, she continued. "After Stacey left, I shopped at Cassie's Closet from time to time and that's where I purchased most of the furniture and small appliances for your house."

Jack nodded. He should have known. After Stacey left, he would come home from work and notice that there was a new bookshelf, a toaster oven or even a recliner. He had forgotten until just this moment, that he'd find a note from his Mom on the kitchen counter, saying that if he didn't like the piece, that the owner of Cassie's Closet said she would accept it back within ten days.

The furnishings his Mom chose for the house were always fine. Jack was too numb at the time to even think about furnishing his house, but he knew that his Mom was desperate to help him in any way that she could. She was doing anything she could to provide some level of comfort to her broken son.

"I don't know Cassie personally, but every time that I've dealt with her at the shop, she's been very nice."

Jack remained silent, but nodded in agreement.

Barbara Shaw had been married to her husband for forty years and had raised three rambunctious boys. She knew her husband and sons like the back of her hand. There was no way that she could press Jack, or any of the men in her life, to talk when they weren't ready to talk, but it didn't mean that she had to remain silent.

Turning away from Jack and looking up towards the cloudless sky, Barbara spoke softly, yet with intention.

"Son, I know you pretty well and I can see that you are troubled by the possibility of considering someone new in your life."

Barbara could feel Jack's eyes turn towards her, but she continued to look at the sky. She knew that if she looked at Jack directly in his eyes, that the tears would flow and that's not what either one of them needed at this moment.

Barbara continued. "We both know that I want to know every thought, every detail and whatever it is you're thinking or feeling, but I also know that you're not ready to talk about it."

"I appreciate that, Mom." Jack briefly leaned over and touched his head to his Mom's head. When he lifted his head and sat back up, she continued.

"I just want you to remember that not every woman is like Stacey." Her voice choked with emotion, but then she recovered. "Sweetheart, I don't want you to spend the rest of your life alone because of what that evil woman did to you."

Jack could feel his own emotions swell. His Mom knew him so well. He didn't have to say anything for her to be aware of his internal conflict.

"I don't know too much about Cassie, but I do know that your brother said that you seemed like you were enjoying yourself at Trebbiano's." Barbara knew that Jon could be a man-boy by teasing his brothers sometimes, but one thing was certain, probably because of his work as a police officer, but Jon was incredibly observant and astute and if he said that Jack was grinning from ear to ear, then Barbara trusted her youngest son's observation.

For the first time, Jack broke his silence with a chuckle. "Jon has always been a little tattle tell."

It was Barbara's turn to giggle. "This is true. I'm glad he told me though. It made me happy to hear it. It's been too long since I've seen my oldest son happy."

Barbara took in a deep breath. She felt the next words had to be said. For a while now, Barbara had toyed with saying something to Jack or deciding if she should remain silent. She had chosen to remain silent, but that no longer felt right. She certainly didn't want to cause Jack more pain, but the timing to share her concerns seemed right at this moment.

"Jack, I don't think it would hurt for you to finally face your responsibility in your troubled marriage."

Jack turned to her quickly with stunned surprise. He started to speak, but his mother cut in.

"I'm not saying that you were responsible for what ultimately happened in the end, no, no, not at all." Barbara shook her head from side to side and took a deep breath before considering her words carefully.

"Stacey wasn't the right woman for you, even in the beginning. There were red flags all over the place, but you closed your eyes to who she really was."

Jack agreed with her assessment. It was true, he knew that now. After Stacey left, how many hours had he laid awake remembering sign after sign that he chose to ignore.

Barbara continued. "Son, I know that you chose to ignore the signs because Stacey was pregnant and then after Charlie was born, you had to consider Charlie first." Barbara inhaled deeply. "You were struggling to keep your family intact and that's admirable."

Barbara looked into her son's eyes. "You're a good Dad and you were trying to do what was best for your son." Barbara's voice filled with emotion and she looked back towards the sky. "I just don't want you to make the same mistake again. I want you to be with a woman that loves you unconditionally and that honors your relationship every day with the truth, and that all her actions are based on love and made in consideration of your relationship together."

Now she could turn towards Jack and with her hand on his cheek, she turned him to face her. When they were eye to eye, she spoke again. "I want you to think about everything that I just said carefully, but I also don't want you to let this chance pass you by. If you're interested in spending time with Cassie, just do it, and don't walk away because you are afraid of being hurt again."

Barbara could see that Jon was about to open the sliding glass door, but she gave him the "in a minute" look and he turned away from the door.

"Stacey already took everything away from you. If you let her take this chance for happiness away from you, then she's won again and I just can't bear the thought of that." Her eyes were damp, but the tears didn't flow. "Please don't let her take anything else from you, Jack."

Jack leaned over and gave his mother a huge hug. He knew, hell, he'd always known, just how much his Mom loved him, but on days like this, he was reminded just how wonderful she really was.

They both stood and he put his arms around her. "Thanks, Mom. Trust me, I don't want Stacey to take anything else from me either."

He felt like he'd been dying a slow death since Charlie was taken. Now, he felt alive again and it felt good to laugh and feel like he was part of the human race once again. It didn't go unnoticed to him that all those feelings started when he met Cassie and he discovered that he couldn't get her out of his head.

More aware and realizing that he needed to think about everything his Mom said, Jack told his Mom. "How about this, I promise you that I will give everything you said very, very serious consideration."

Jack kissed her temple and they both walked back in the house. Barbara hugged him back tightly and silently prayed that her oldest son wouldn't run away from a chance at happiness. *Jon had told her that Jack had been beaming when he was with Cassie.* With her fingers crossed behind her back, she decided to let that bit of information go unmentioned for now.

Chapter Fifteen

It was bright and early Monday morning and Cassie was about to open up shop. Jack hadn't arrived for their usual morning coffee routine and that struck her as a little odd, since it had turned into a daily event, or so it seemed to Cassie.

Since they had shared their kiss on Friday night, Cassie had thought about it, and Jack, all weekend. She and Abby had talked about it while they were shopping. Cassie was in such turmoil. Is this a new relationship? Do I kiss him when I see him next time? Will he kiss me? Do we pretend like it never happened? It all felt so confusing to her.

It felt like high school all over again and she was just as unprepared for dating now as she had been then. It's quite possible that she might even feel more awkward now because her feelings for Jack were very real and very adult like. He wasn't a high school crush. He was a man. Cassie sighed in frustration. It was so difficult to know what to do or how to act. She dated Peter through the latter part of her high school years and then they married practically right out of school. She had never learned the fine art of dating, flirting or how to pick up on signals from the opposite sex.

After their divorce, she didn't date for the longest time. Besides being a busy, single Mom, she wasn't anywhere ready to date again and Brett certainly wasn't ready to accept a new person in her life at that point. He had struggled so much because of Peter's relationship with another woman; if Cassie had brought someone new into the picture, she's not sure how Brett would have handled it.

Besides the emotions were just too raw so soon after their divorce and Cassie was trying to figure out how to be a single Mom and deal with a young son and a new business. Cassie had known for a long time that her marriage wasn't the type of marriage that she had always envisioned as a young girl. She had innocently believed in finding your one true love and living happily ever after. Even when she was a little girl, her favorite line from the fairy tales, was always "…and they lived happily ever after."

Peter had been home so rarely and Cassie knew that he was unhappy being married, or at least married to her. She tried so hard to please him and thought it would pass as he got older and they developed more history together as a couple and a family. Unfortunately, Peter's feelings of being tied down as a young man never changed and his resentment grew day by day. Still, Cassie put blinders on until Peter started seeing someone else. It took her a long time to accept that there had probably always been other women in Peter's life.

Long after the divorce, dating still wasn't a regular part of her life and when she did date, it all felt very uncomfortable and forced. The men she had dated before weren't interesting, or they were full of bitterness about their exes, so much so, that the evenings dragged on and Cassie couldn't wait for the evening to end.

Now Jack had kissed her and it felt right -- so right! The dinner, the date, or whatever the heck it was, didn't feel forced or uncomfortable. It was relaxing, fun and interesting. Jack was a great conversationalist and she enjoyed his company. Then there was the kiss and there was no question in her mind that it felt good and very right. There was little doubt in her mind that she wanted another kiss from Jack. All weekend long, she had envisioned those kisses. The firm pressure of their lips touching, the feel of his hands as he cupped her face, the smell of his body and the warmth of his breath near her face.

Only time would tell, if that kiss with Jack was an isolated event, then so be it. Then Cassie sighed a little, even if it was the most amazing kiss she'd ever had!

Better With Time

* * * * *

The day at Cassie's Closet had been grueling and her back ached. Cassie stood up and stretched from the crouched position she had been in for hours now. Every couple of weeks, she and another employee went through the various donations and items from the estate sales and sorted through them. They were looking for name brand items on clothing, purses and shoes and checking jewelry to see if the gems were potentially real or fake. The jewelry that was possibly more valuable was set aside for the gemologist to review during her next stop at Cassie's Closet. With the jewelry, it was amazing how many pieces went through the shop that looked like costume jewelry, yet turned out to be quite valuable. The same thing happened with artwork.

Oftentimes, Cassie would purchase items from an entire house after the owner had passed away or moved into long-term nursing care. Most often an adult child would arrive from another state, or they lived here, but they had their own busy lives to lead, so they didn't have time to clean out a house and deal with removing years' worth of furnishings, clothing, artwork, glassware and tools. After the family members took out the mementos and pieces they wanted, Cassie's Closet would send a crew over with a large truck and take everything away from the house and bring it back to the shop. Cassie's Closet was the only thrift store currently doing this and the need for her services was in high demand.

Cassie usually met with the family and viewed the contents of the home. Of course, there were some homes that had terrible conditions, whether from animal feces, poor maintenance or hoarding issues and Cassie wasn't willing to accept the items in those homes. However, fortunately, most of the time, the homes held years' worth of treasures, both old and new and it allowed Cassie to keep her store inventory interesting and ever-changing.

Throughout the day, Cassie had glanced back towards the construction area. Of course, she couldn't see anything as the plastic partition was still up, but she found herself wondering if Jack was working back there, although she suspected he wasn't. She couldn't recall a day when he'd been working and he hadn't come over to her and said hello, or brought her up to date on the days' timeline.

Needing to stretch after crouching over the sorting table for so many hours, Cassie told herself that it was okay to walk in the back and take a look at what had been accomplished today. Even though she didn't think Jack was there, she was still a little curious.

Walking through the plastic, Cassie quickly scanned the area and didn't see Jack. Dani noticed Cassie and walked towards her.

"Hi, Dani. Boy, it looks great back here."

Dani swept her arms around and towards the kitchen area. "We will be finished with the kitchen today." Although it was covered in sawdust, the kitchen area looked amazing. The granite was absolutely beautiful and the dark, open-doored cabinets complimented the granite perfectly. Cassie's vision of how the kitchen would look was coming to life. Now, all of the small appliances could be on top of the counters and the dishes, glasses and other glassware could be displayed and easily be seen from the open cabinets. Cassie couldn't help but to smile.

"Dani, this is just beautiful."

Dani was proud of their work too and she beamed with pride. "I think so too. I wish my kitchen at home was this nice."

Cassie laughed. "I agree," if only her kitchen at home looked so updated.

Dani continued. "We're going to keep this area covered for now, but Jack told me this morning that we're going to start on the dressing rooms and the infant area tomorrow."

Cassie was surprised at the mention of Jack being here this morning. "Was Jack here this morning? I didn't see him."

Dani shook her head. "No, he called me earlier this morning. Actually, I don't know where he is. I thought he would be here today."

Maybe he regrets the kiss the other night? Cassie shook her head, trying to cast away any self-doubt about the other night.

Cassie was angry at herself. She tried to remind herself of her own promise to not turn the kiss into something that it wasn't. Remember, it might just be an innocent, but meaningless kiss, or an action without thought by Jack after a few drinks? Maybe it was something she made bigger in her head than he did.

Forging ahead, Cassie had a brief conversation with Dani about the dressing room work and told her that she would ask her employees to clear the area the crew would start to work on tomorrow. Then she excused herself.

There was an hour left before closing and Cassie needed to make some calls and adjust the schedule. Hopefully, some of her part-time employees would be able to come in to work in the morning, at least for a few hours, and get the areas ready for the newest construction project. Additionally, she needed to temporarily put two trucks worth of stuff into storage, to make room both for construction and to hold some kitchen items that she didn't have room to display until the new kitchen was unveiled.

After several phone calls and schedule changes, Cassie hung up the phone, sat back in her chair and sighed. What a day!

It was then that Cassie heard a soft knock on her office door and Jack peered in. He had been standing outside the door for several minutes. He could hear that she was on the phone, but more than that, he just wanted to hear her voice. He had been away all day, no, he had *stayed* away all day, but suddenly, before he knew it, he was in his truck and hitting the gas pedal. Without really understanding why, he just knew that he needed to get here before closing. It felt wrong to stay away even a minute longer, yet he couldn't explain why to himself. He didn't try to, but followed his gut instincts instead.

Cassie looked up, the surprise showing on her face. "Hi, Jack." She sat a little straighter and smiled up at him. "I didn't expect to see you now," she looked at her watch, "at closing time."

Jack grinned sheepishly. If she only knew how often his thoughts had wondered to her and to this store all day. He told himself that he wasn't going to come in today. He was determined to stay away. When he woke up this morning, he felt like he needed time to think and Dani and the rest of his crew were more than capable of running the ship.

Impulsively, he had thrown a fishing pole into the back of his truck and headed out to his favorite fishing hole. The stream was quiet, except for the rustle of the leaves in the trees. With a hot coffee in the thermos beside him and the daily newspaper, he propped his pole against a rock and settled himself in a foldable captain's chair. It was just where he needed to be and maybe he could quiet his brain in the silence of the trees and babbling serenity of the stream.

Throughout the day, he thought about his conversation with his Mom. She was right to point out that he needed to take responsibility for his own failures in his marriage, if you could call it a marriage. He had been facing his mistakes, for several months now, but it seemed important to really consider the choices he'd made and why. He wasn't proud of the fact that he chose to ignore all the signs that Stacey was cheating, that she didn't want to be a Mom to Charlie, or that she didn't want to be in a relationship with Jack. Sadly, Stacey pretended just enough to calm his concerns and he allowed himself to believe her. That was a shame that he would probably always carry, but also he learned a powerful lesson about not trusting his own instincts out of fear of change, so he had promised himself then, that from now on, his gut always knew best and he would listen to himself more closely.

Now his gut was telling him something else; something new and unexpected. After his divorce and the loss of Charlie, it never occurred to him that he might meet a woman that made him laugh or that he'd find himself thinking about her throughout the day.

With a light wind blowing and the warmth of the sun on his back, along with the feel of the slight bobbing of his fishing rod in his hands, Jack finally understood that he knew one thing for certain and that was that he wanted to spend more time with Cassie. He didn't want to compare her to his past; he just wanted to be near her, and often. That was a big step for him and it would have to be enough for now.

Jack realized that Cassie was still looking at his face and searching his eyes for an answer. "I needed to be away from the store today. I had some things to take care of."

A rush of relief filled Cassie. Although she did not want to admit it, all day long, she had an underlying concern that Jack had stayed away because he didn't want to be near her after their kiss. That worry faded away instantly.

"I noticed that your car was still in the parking lot, so I wanted to stop in and let you know that I'll be here tomorrow."

Cassie was suddenly filled with anticipation for the next day. "Oh, good, okay. Dani told me what was happening tomorrow and I think I'm…" Jack interrupted her. He had to say it now before his courage left him.

"Cassie," Jack cleared his throat and made eye contact with her, "there's this vineyard in St. Helena that shows movies on a big screen on Saturday nights out on the vineyard floor. I heard it's pretty nice to bring a picnic basket and watch a movie under the stars."

Jack took a deep breath, which he hoped Cassie couldn't see. With his eyes still on her, he asked, "would you like to go with me this weekend?"

Cassie's heart jumped into her throat. *Oh my God, Jack just asked me out on an actual date!* Remembering that she hadn't answered him yet and that his eyes were still searching her eyes, she smiled. "That sounds wonderful. I would like that a lot." Now letting the breath out that he had been holding in, it was Jack's turn to smile at Cassie. "Okay, a date it is."

Jack's smile broadened as he turned and left. Cassie leaned back in her chair in stunned silence. Wow! That was unexpected. Oh boy, this was going to be a long week waiting for Saturday night to arrive.

Cassie walked around the building locking doors and turning off lights. She got into her car and remembered Jack's final words to her "Okay, a date it is!" *A date!*

Chapter Sixteen

It had been a long week and Saturday had finally arrived. Before that, Jack arrived at Cassie's Closet early every day and they had fallen back into their routine of having a quick cup of coffee. Sometimes they talked about the work being done that day, or what they had watched on television the night before, or the latest news about the upcoming musical at Pueblo Valley Playhouse, just anything really. It was always an easy and relaxed conversation. Cassie thought that once she caught Jack looking at her and she got the feeling he wanted to kiss her, but he didn't. She certainly wanted to feel his kiss again. Sometimes she swore she could feel the electricity between them and wondered if Jack could too, or if it was all part of her over active imagination.

Now Cassie stood in her bedroom and looked at her reflection in the full length mirror. She took another look at her appearance for about the tenth time that evening. It was going to be a warm early autumn night, so the tan colored denim capris and copper colored tank top were perfect. Her tank top had the slightest hint of shimmer and it complimented the soft tan on her shoulders, chest and face. She would bring her brown cardigan with her in case it cooled off later. She looked at her feet and questioned her sandals, also for the tenth time. She wondered if she should put on another strappy, more elegant pair, but decided to keep the more casual sandals on instead. After all, they would be walking on grass most of the evening.

A final look at her make-up and a quick application of more lip gloss and Cassie's stomach did a little flip flop. There wasn't anything else to do except wait for Jack to arrive. Yesterday she asked him if there was anything she could bring and he said no, he had it all covered.

The doorbell rang and her stomach did another flip flop. *Jack's here!* Letting out her breath before opening the door, Cassie opened it to find Jack standing there with a big smile and a gorgeous bouquet of sunflowers, orange lilies and yellow chrysanthemums.

"Oh, Jack, they are so beautiful! Thank you" Jack handed her the bouquet and she breathed in the sweet, perfumed musk of the lilies.

"Come in." Cassie waved Jack in as she walked over to the coffee table and set the vase of flowers down. After another admiring glance at the flowers, she turned back around towards Jack.

Jack picked up Cassie's hand and raised her arm high as if he was going to twirl her like a ballerina. "Cassie, you look stunning." Cassie could feel the heat rise in her face. She was so thrilled that Jack admired the way she looked tonight.

"You look pretty darn handsome too."

"Why, thank you." Jack took her hand. "Shall be go?"

Cassie reached for her cardigan and purse and they headed out the door.

* * * * *

When they walked out onto the vineyard, Cassie broke into a huge smile. There was a large grassy area where couples and families had spread out blankets and sat on low beach chairs or pillows on the blankets. Most people had picnic baskets of food and wine. Several people had small, flat tables set up and they were either eating off of it or playing cards before the movie started.

In front of the grassy area was a large screen that was about eight feet by ten feet; certainly smaller than a movie theater, but Cassie thought it was absolutely perfect. On each side of the valley floor were the hills of St. Helena. It was stunningly beautiful and green, and you could see the perfectly symmetrical row after row of grapes growing on the vines, reaching towards the peak of the hills.

Jack carried a picnic basket and blankets and Cassie carried the bottle of wine that they had purchased at one of the wineries on the drive there.

They selected a spot on the grass and spread out one of the blankets. Both Jack and Cassie sat down, stretched out their legs, took their shoes off and laid them to the side of the blanket. Cassie was still in a little bit of awe over how beautiful the winery was.

"How is it that I've lived here most of my life and I've never heard of this wineries' movie night?"

Jack laughed. "I just heard about it recently myself. One of my crew members brought his family here a few weekends ago."

The cork popped from the bottle that Jack was opening and Cassie held a glass in each hand for both of them. Jack filled their wine glasses.

Jack continued. "They usually show an old school movie, like a Hitchcock movie, or the Sound of Music." Jack looked at the screen. "Tonight they are showing 'Some Like It Hot' with Marilyn Monroe, Jack Lemmon and Tony Curtis.'"

Cassie clapped her hands in excitement. "I haven't watched that movie in years, but I remember it being so much fun."

Jack was happy that Cassie was excited about the movie choice, and he was too, but in all honesty, for him, they could be showing the worst movie ever made and it wouldn't matter to him. He was sitting next to an incredibly beautiful woman, a woman he might add, that he forced, literally forced himself not to kiss all this week. As hard as that was, he knew they had a date tonight and he was trying to keep it professional while they were at Cassie's Closet, but restraining himself proved to be an incredibly difficult thing to do.

It was dusk now and there were low-lights on at the corners of the grass area. People were still enjoying themselves before the movie started. Jack started pulling containers out of the picnic basket, a basket which he borrowed from his Mom. To her credit, his Mom didn't say too much, except "will you be seeing Cassie then?" When Jack told her yes, she patted him on the back. He was sure it took all her will power to keep from saying anything else, but he was glad that she didn't. He just had to take it one step at a time for now.

Cassie helped Jack open the containers. There were containers of pesto pasta, chilled fruit, sliced grilled chicken breasts and cranberry spinach salad. Cassie licked her lips. "Jack, you sure know how to pack a picnic basket."

After staring at the deli counter for a good twenty minutes, Jack was happy that Cassie was pleased with his choices for dinner. They put their plates on their laps and started to eat. Jack smiled as Cassie said "ummm" to the first bites of everything she tried. Teasingly, he told Cassie, "if you play your cards right, I might be convinced to share with you the fudge brownies that I have hidden in the basket."

Cassie just laughed. "First good wine and food, pretty soon the stars will be out and then you have chocolate too! I might just try and play those cards."

Jack smiled at Cassie. "I thought bringing chocolate was an excellent play on my part."

After they ate and the dishes were rinsed off under the fountain and put back in the picnic basket, Jack refilled their wine glasses. He'd waited long enough and the movie was about to start. Jack pulled Cassie close to him. He could feel her arm touching his and feel the length of her leg along his own leg. Just that slight touch sent electricity through his body. Still, he grabbed the other blanket and wrapped it around their shoulders as he didn't want Cassie to be chilled. Cassie smiled up at him. Jack admired her dimple for about the hundredth time since he'd met her. There was just something about it that made his heart melt. Jack returned her smile. As he shifted the blanket over them and settled down closely next to her, from under the blanket, Cassie took his hand and their fingers entwined.

The stars were out now and shining softly down on them. The movie screen flickered and an old Bugs Bunny cartoon started playing before the movie began. Cassie repositioned herself slightly and slid closer to Jack so that her head could lean on his shoulder.

Jack took it all in. The twinkling stars in the sky, the scent of honeysuckle from Cassie's hair, the sensation of her hand in his own hand, and the feeling of being happy in this moment with Cassie.

Jack's lips brushed the top of Cassie's head. Cassie squeezed his hand a little tighter and they both turned their attention to Elmer Fudd trying to outfox Bug's Bunny.

Chapter Seventeen

After the movie, Jack pulled up in front of Cassie's house and quickly ran to the other side of the truck to open her door. It had been a great night at the movie on the vineyard. They had laughed several times during the movie and Cassie teased him on the drive home about how he would look dressed up as a woman. Jack went with the flow and they teased more about the type of dress that he should wear to really stand out as a woman. They both chuckled at the thought of him walking in high heels.

As they approached the house, Cassie wondered to herself about how to handle the rest of the evening. Should she invite him in for coffee? A drink? Stop at the door? Just thank him? She just felt really unsure of normal dating routines. It had been such a terrific evening and she didn't want to worry about what to do next. One thing was for sure, it had been a very long time since she enjoyed herself this much and she wasn't sure she was ready for it to end yet.

At the front door, Jack took her keys and unlocked the door before handing the keys back to her. He turned to her and took both of her hands into hands.

"I had an amazing night with you, Cassie."

"I did too," she said sincerely. "It was wonderful."

Jack released her hands and instead put his hands and arms around and onto her back. He pulled her body closer to his and leaned down to kiss her. His kiss started out soft and gentle. He pulled away slightly, looked into her eyes and then pulled her into another kiss. This time it was firmer with more passion. Cassie's lips reached up to meet his and she felt the sweet pressure of his lips against hers. Their mouths parted and there was the soft touch of their tongues against each other.

Jack felt a low growl in his belly. Cassie stood even closer to him now. She could feel the length of him along her body. Jack had lowered his hands to the top of her hips and pulled her towards him. Her arms were encircled around his neck and shoulders and she wasn't ready to let go of him yet.

He didn't know how he did it, but somehow he forced his lips away from hers. He was dizzy from desire. He had waited almost an entire week to kiss her. Cassie, too, was breathless from the jolt of sensations that traveled through her body. She had never felt anything like that from a kiss. Her arms remained around his neck and shoulders, but she tilted her head back. She could see the same desire in his eyes that she felt running through her veins.

Without thinking about whether she should, or shouldn't, and just feeling the passion and need within both of them, Cassie asked softly, "Would you like to come in?"

Jack pulled her a little tighter. "God, yes!"

They were both inside the door instantly. There was a soft glow from a light in another room. The living room was fragrant from the lilies and roses and the sweet fragrance of them sent another sensation through Cassie. After standing in the living room for several more minutes, and with each kiss increasing the desire within them, Cassie took Jack's hand and headed up the stairs. Cassie thought to herself, to hell with dating protocol or to falling into bed on the first date (or was it the second?) or whatever! She was a grown woman who was deeply attracted to an incredibly sexy man. Jack sent shivers through her body whenever he looked at her. When he kissed her passionately, all hope was lost of stopping then!

When they got into Cassie's bedroom, she quickly lit the candle that was on her dresser with a silent thank you to Abby for reminding her to pick up a scented candle, in the event that something romantic should happen after their date. Then she turned all her attention back towards Jack.

Jack pulled her to him again and covered her lips in wet, luscious kisses. His arms were fully around her and he pulled her towards him as tightly as he could without hurting her.

God, all night he had been dying to kiss her, to touch her, to make love to her. It had been absolute torture to not hold her as closely as he wanted to. The smell of her hair and her body; the feel of her hand in his, the touch of her leg along his, all of it had almost driven him into madness. Now, he was here, in Cassie's bedroom. As much as he wanted to rip every shred of clothing from her body, he couldn't rush, not yet, not with her. God, he prayed, please give me some kind of control.

Jack slowly laid her down on the bed and he let the length of his body match her own. They clung to each other tightly. Their kisses were becoming more and more passionate. Their tongues were quickly searching out each other, entwined as much as their legs were. Now, he needed to feel her skin without clothing, stroke her body with his hand and then with his tongue, taste her.

He sat up and guided her up and lifted her tank top off over her shoulders. As sexy as her soft crème-colored, lacy bra was, he had to have it off and now! Jack reached behind her and unsnapped Cassie's bra. As he did so, Cassie kissed his neck and throat. This time a growl escaped from low in his belly and through his throat. Cassie eased the rest of the groan out with her tongue by slowly moving it up along Jack's throat. With her hands working just as quickly, she pulled Jack's shirt up over his shoulders. A loud thud from his shoes dropping on the side of the bed could be heard. Cassie's own shoes followed on the opposite side of the bed.

As the bra released, Jack thought he would go out of his mind. Cassie was the most beautiful woman he'd ever seen! She eased back down and Jack quickly pulled her capris and panties over her legs. Jack looked at Cassie's naked, golden skin, the long chestnut-colored hair cascading over her shoulders and across her breasts and he had little doubt that he had died and gone to heaven.

Now it was Cassie's turn to lean up and unbutton Jack's pants. When she pulled the zipper down, she could feel that his bulging erection was screaming to be freed from his clothing. Cassie hooked her thumbs through the top of his jeans and lowered his pants to his knees. Cassie cupped his erection in her hand and stroked the length of him, slowly and seductively. With her touch, Jack could barely hold himself on his knees. Sighing at the delicious feel of her touch on him, Jack removed her hand, readjusted his body and pulled his jeans the rest the way off.

Their naked bodies were now side by side. Each of them held the other tight. With their kisses deepening and the fire burning, Jack pulled himself away from the glorious taste of her sweet mouth. He softly kissed each eyelid, the tip of her nose, her chin and then his tongue found her throat. This time it was Cassie who groaned as Jack's tongue ever so slowly found its way down her throat and to her breasts. Jack's delicate, teasing flicks across her nipples made Cassie purr with delight and tingles danced across her skin. As his teasing flicks became more intense, Cassie could feel the gentle stroke of his hand move from her stomach, to her hip, to the top of her leg, to her groin and then stop. Cassie was full of anticipation and started to arch herself up, when Jack suddenly moved his hand away to stroke her other nipple. Oh, what a delightful tease he was!

Cassie was torn with delight at the sensation on her other breast, but her body cried out for Jack to return to where the fire was now burning from the all too quick touch of his hand.

Sensing her need, Jack somehow pulled away from her breast and looked up at her beautiful face. Cassie was still running her hands through Jack's hair, but her eyes were closed and she was moaning softly. Jack could see that her nipples were still hard and moist from his mouth. He ached to get back to them, but lowered his head again to the center of her chest. With gentle, butterfly kisses, he kissed her a dozen times on her chest and each of her glorious breasts. Then he took his tongue and started the slow, thrilling process of making its way down Cassie's stomach.

As the first flick of his tongue hit Cassie's fire, she cried out. Jack could feel her legs tighten and then release. Still keeping his tongue darting quickly against her softness, he opened his eyes and looked up at her. Her head was tilted back and her nipples were hard as a rock and her breathing was fast. Now her hands were searching for Jack. Jack knew the moment was almost here. He gave several more flicks of the tongue and Cassie cried out. He could feel the moment building and he didn't stop until she stopped bucking and her legs started to relax on his shoulders.

Feeling a desire, unlike one he had never felt before, Jack lifted himself up and towards Cassie. Cassie partially sat up until she was able to reach out to him and she pulled him fully on top of her. Cassie didn't want one more second to pass without feeling Jack on top of her. Cassie could now feel his massive erection next to her and she was burning alive for the want of him.

With a throaty, sexy voice, Cassie whispered, "Oh God, Jack, I need you *now*!"

Hearing her plea, Jack was no longer able to hold back. He needed her at that moment just as much as she needed him. Jack thrust himself inside her and Cassie cried out in pleasure. She raised her legs around his hips and back, which allowed her to move freely with him, movement to movement, thrust to thrust.

In unison, the passion in both of them began to build and grow. Cassie felt the climax growing through her body. Suddenly the raging explosion burst through her body like a shock wave. Almost shocked at the depth of sensations, Cassie began to shiver.

Now overcome with the need to make Jack feel what she had just experienced, Cassie again moved her hips to meet Jack's thrusts beat for beat. Jack's pace quickened, his stomach muscles tightened and he felt the surge of passion in his own fiery release.

Jack collapsed onto Cassie, both of them breathing heavily. His head was close to her breast and he was softly stroking her thigh with his hand. Cassie had one hand running her fingers through his hair, the other hand lay limp at her side.

As their breathing returned to normal, Jack still sprawled across Cassie, panted, "I would get off you, but I'm unable to move. I might be like this forever."

Cassie laughed. "That's okay. I want you right here. I'm not sure I can move either. I think we'll be stuck like this for a long time."

Jack grinned. "One could only hope."

Later, Jack found the energy to scoot up closer to Cassie's face. He propped himself up on one elbow. He looked into her eyes and the flecks of gold from her hazel eyes shone brightly. God, she was beautiful. She smiled at him and stroked his cheek.

"You are an amazing woman, Cassie."

"I can say the same thing about you Jack. That was…" She paused and looked up at the ceiling, trying to find the words. Then she turned back to look at Jack. Her heart skipped a beat and she said simply, "incredible, just incredible."

Jack thought so too. He had imagined all kinds of moments like this with Cassie, but even in his wildest fantasies, he didn't think that making love to her would make him feel the way that it did.

They lay there together, silent, but stroking the other's arms, thighs, throats and back. They looked at each other and shared sweet kisses. There was no need to say a thing in that moment. It was more than enough for them to each feel close to the other.

Finally, realizing that Cassie's skin had cooled a little bit, Jack sat up and Cassie looked at him, curious about what he was about to do. Jack pulled the sheet out from the bottom of the bed and pulled it up over her. Cassie wasn't just some hook-up that he rolled in the sheets with and then left after a few hours without another thought or even a goodbye. Cassie was much more than that. Jack then pulled the sheet in tighter around himself too and pulled Cassie close to him.

"Cassie, I want to spend the night with you, okay?" Cassie wiggled herself against Jack even tighter than before and looked into his sparkling dark eyes. With a quick and satisfied smile, she told him, "Yeah, that's okay by me."

Chapter Eighteen

Liza Beardsley tapped her foot impatiently as the phone on the other end rang for the fifth time. After so many rings, she expected the voice mail to come on. Finally, a sleepy sounding female answered.

"Hello."

"Stacey, its Liza."

On the other end Stacey forced herself awake. "Oh, Liza, thanks for finally calling me back." She emphasized the 'finally.'

Liza could hear the irritation in Stacey's voice. "Well, I almost didn't. What the hell are you doing calling me at the house?"

Stacey started to answer, but Liza interrupted her. "If Tom finds out that you've been calling the house, he'll have me skinned alive! I've told you a hundred times to always call me on my cell phone."

"I'm sorry," Stacey started sniveling, "but it's so important that I talk to you and I thought that Tom might not be home."

Liza was still angry. "Don't ever assume that. He's getting even older and he's home more and more all the time now." She sighed loudly. "Unfortunately."

It was difficult enough for Liza to pretend to be a dutiful wife after Tom's work hours, but with the added hours that he'd been home lately, it had been downright exhausting.

Liza continued. "Well, it worked out this time. Fortunately, the housekeeper told me that you called me while Tom was in the shower." Liza tried to run her point home to Stacey about the importance of her calling the house.

"On top of that, I had to promise her an extra day off with pay next week, just so that she won't say anything to Tom about you calling."

Stacey was unimpressed with the overture Liza had to make to the staff. She knew Liza well, too well. In fact, they had known each other since they were six years-old and in the first grade. It was a regular occurrence that Liza could feel troubled by even the slightest event. Still, she shouldn't have called the house. She knew that was a big no-no.

"Okay, okay, Liza, geesh, I said I was sorry, but I really need to talk to you."

Liza sat in her car and her eyes darted from side to side. She and Stacey had always been there for each other. Neither one of them had much in the way of family, so she felt like they were more like sisters, but like most sisters, Stacey still pissed her off sometimes.

Liza thought for a minute. "Okay, okay, but I really can't talk to you today, except for a minute. I had to sneak out to call you." From her car, her eyes darted from side to side. Seeing no one she knew, she continued. "Tom wants me to go to church with him. I told him that I had to run to the market and pick up a cake for one of the needy families, so he's expecting me back any time."

Stacey laughed a big old belly laugh. "My, my, you in a church! I just can't imagine." But she knew that Liza would get angry if she didn't get to the point soon, Stacey stopped herself and continued.

"Liza, I was calling because I am going to be in San Francisco next weekend."

Liza was genuinely surprised. "You are! Why?"

Stacey sighed. "Richard wants to talk to a specialist. He's desperate to have another child. I convinced him that the best doctor was in San Francisco."

"Will Richard be with you?"

"Luckily, he won't be joining me until Sunday night." Liza could hear Stacey draw in a long drag from a cigarette.

"I convinced him that I haven't been away forever, which you know is true, so I'll be flying in Friday afternoon. Then I have Friday and Saturday to be free as a bird."

Liza's mind was racing. She knew exactly why Stacey had called now and she was starting to get excited. It had just been forever since she'd seen her best friend. Besides, the thought of a weekend away from Tom's boring ass thrilled her.

The excitement was building in Stacey. "So, do you think you could meet me there?"

Liza thought quickly. "Yeah, I think so. I'll have to come up with some reason to go into the city without Tom."

"Couldn't you tell him you have to meet someone in the city about the play you're doing?"

Liza shook her head no. "I don't think he'd buy that, but listen, I'll come up with something. I just have to think about it, but don't you worry about that," Liza paused, "you know me and I'll figure something out."

Now fully awake and excited at the thought of seeing her best friend, Stacey mouthed a silent 'yes.'

"It's been too long. I have a lot to talk to you about. I miss you Liza."

"I miss you too and we'll have a nice long talk this weekend. It's long overdue." Stacey agreed. "We talk on the phone all the time, but I haven't seen you since," she took a drag from her cigarette, "well, you know, and it's just been too long."

Liza couldn't agree more. Even though her life had changed night and day since she married Tom Beardsley and it was so nice to not have to worry about money any more, there were still lots of nights that she missed the good times when she and Stacey used to play together, at least that's what they called it.

With the two of them together, there was nothing more fun than flirting with men, especially older, lonely men who usually didn't receive too much attention from the ladies. Stacey and Liza had turned it into an art form, with both of them believing from a young age that it was their only ticket to better their lives.

Of course, older men were their freedom tickets, but younger, sexy men were flat out exhilarating and both of them had many a good night enjoying the company of those gorgeous, energetic hunks too.

Thinking about the prowl once again, Liza felt shivers tingle down to her groin. Yes, it had been far too long.

Suddenly she realized that they might not be able to go out on the prowl together if Stacey wasn't alone. "Stacey, will Charlie be with you?"

"Pleeeassseeee, not a chance in hell. That's what the housekeeping staff is for."

Liza breathed a sigh of relief. Reading each other's minds and knowing each other so well, they were both looking forward to a few new conquests.

"I'll call you later in the week and find out where you're staying and we'll make plans from there. But, don't call the house again."

"Geesh, enough already. I won't call."

Stacey took in a breath and held it until Liza answered. "Liza, there's no chance that Jack would be in San Francisco would there?"

Liza shook her head no. "No, he's always just hanging around town. I see his truck everywhere. I don't think he ever leaves the county."

Stacey was relieved, but curious. "Is he still moping around because he misses me?"

Liza laughed. "Oh boy, he did have it bad for you, huh, you sexy thing."

With Stacey's ego newly inflated, she smiled and looked at her reflection in the dresser mirror. Damn straight, I'm a sexy thing. Jack could never resist me.

Stacey knew that she was pushing her luck now by staying on the phone much longer. They'd have a lot more time to talk this weekend and she didn't want Liza to be on the outs with Tom.

"Now, go be a good wife and buy a frickin' cake for church."

Liza tapped "end call" without a further response to Stacey. There was nothing else to say to her at this moment. She would hear every little detail this weekend. What a fabulous weekend this was going to be! Now, what to tell Tom that he'll believe. How was she going to get her weekend in San Francisco without him? Hmmm, her mind was racing with possible excuses as she sped to the grocery store.

Chapter Nineteen

With the soft glow of the morning sun filling Cassie's bedroom with light, Cassie woke up and could feel Jack's arm spread out across her waist. She could hear his soft breathing, so she gently tried to lift his arm without waking him. She had one leg on the floor, when suddenly Jack pulled her close to him.

"Where are you going?" Jack nuzzled his nose in her hair. Cassie giggled and swatted his arm loose to free it.

"I'll be right back."

After returning from the bathroom, Cassie hurried and jumped back in bed. She was eager to be back in Jack's arms. What a night! Cassie realized that she felt downright sexy for the first time in... When? When had she genuinely felt sexy? She didn't think she ever had.

Happy again to have her back in bed, Jack pulled her close towards him.

"Watching you walk back here from the bathroom was just as enjoyable as watching you walk to the bathroom." Jack snickered as Cassie giggled and playfully slapped at his hands.

She teased him. "Hey, you're supposed to be a gentleman and not look." Jack pulled her a little tighter by cupping her buttocks with his hands. Now they were face to face again.

"In that case, I'm not a gentleman, because I don't want to ever stop looking at that entrance or that exit." Cassie giggled. "That's not fair. It's all bright and sunny and I'm a mess."

Jack kissed her full on the mouth. When he pulled back, he told her sincerely, "You're beautiful, day or night."

Cassie kissed him back, appreciative of his sincerity. "How about I go fix us some coffee and maybe some eggs?"

Suddenly, Jack had a devilish look in his eyes and Cassie was pretty sure she could read his mind. Intending to go in the kitchen, she sat up, straddled Jack and sprawled her legs over his stomach. As she was about the slide off to one side, Jack stopped her.

"Oh no, you don't, Jack." Cassie's smile grew. "I know what you're thinking and we did that most of the night!" Cassie laughed out loud. "We need food and coffee."

Jack grabbed her hips with his hands and then eased his hands up her back, until he had pulled her chest flat against his.

"You're not doing a very good job of convincing me that I should have eggs and coffee instead of you." Jack stroked his hands up and down her back and down her buttocks. Cassie moaned close to Jack's ear. "Well, maybe we can wait on that breakfast."

Jack quickly rolled her over and he was on top of her. He started nuzzling her neck. "Hmm, I know what I want for breakfast."

Cassie just leaned her neck back so that he could feast on her. Cassie couldn't help but think that this was the best Sunday breakfast ever!

* * * * *

An hour or so later, Cassie and Jack were sitting at the breakfast nook, drinking coffee and they were finishing up eating their eggs and toast. They were both ravenous and ate quickly. They both sipped on their coffee. Jack looked in the living room and noticed the pictures hanging on the wall. He picked up his coffee cup.

Jack nodded towards the living room. "I take it that those are all photos of Brett."

Cassie put down her coffee and took Jack by the hand. She led him into the living room.

As they got closer to what was obviously Brett's graduation picture from high school, Jack could see that Cassie was beaming with pride as she approached the photo.

"Yes, this is Brett." Jack had seen some of Cassie's pictures in her office, but not these more recent photos.

Jack took the framed photo into his own hands and looked at it carefully. He could see that Brett resembled his Mom a great deal. "He's a really handsome boy. He looks like you."

Cassie spread her arms out towards other pictures lining the wall. "Thanks. I think he's pretty darn handsome too, but I'm prejudiced."

Jack had a twinge in his stomach, remembering Charlie and his brown wavy hair and the half-dozen freckles that were sprinkled across his nose. Jack always thought those freckles were so cute, but he suspected that Charlie would grow up and not like them. He wondered what he looked like now, or if those freckles had blended into his skin, or if his hair was still wavy and brown.

He watched Cassie as she continued to point out pictures of Brett playing baseball in school, his prom pictures and different family members. He heard her, yet his mind wandered. He knew he had to tell Cassie about Charlie, he just didn't know how to tell her. What would she think of him? How could he possibly explain something to her that he didn't understand himself? Cassie didn't know Stacey and how she was such a flirt around town, or that she devoted about one percent of her time to Charlie. Would Cassie believe that or would she assume that Jack was some kind of monster for Stacey to take Charlie away from him? He sighed at the thought of his predicament, yet somewhere deep inside, he already knew the answer to that question; Cassie would believe him.

Then and there, he promised himself that he would tell Cassie all about Charlie when the time was right. But today wasn't the day. They had just shared a magical night together that was only about the two of them. There was time for the story of Charlie later, but for today, they both needed to think or feel nothing except what they had just experienced together.

Two hours later and after a steamy shower together, Jack left. At the door, he kissed her softly. When their lips parted, he held her chin gently with his fingers.

"Cassie, last night was not only incredible," he stopped what he was saying and held her eyes to his, "but it meant something to me." Cassie could feel a flutter in her chest.

"It did for me too, Jack."

Jack kissed her again. "I don't want you to think that this was a one-time thing."

Cassie smiled and was touched that Jack made a point to tell her that. Jack ended it by saying what really didn't need to be said at that moment, but he felt it was important.

"I'm crazy about you." And he was.

This time it was Cassie who kissed him. "I think I just might be crazy about you too, Jack Shaw." Saying that, she knew full well that she was more than just crazy about Jack; she just might be falling in love with him.

Chapter Twenty

Abby slid into the booth next to Cassie and hugged her when she got close. A second later, Colleen slid in and sat opposite Cassie. She was looking around Trebbiano's.

"Cassie, you're right. This place looks so nice now." Abby agreed.

Cassie took another look around herself. "Thanks for meeting me tonight on such short notice."

Colleen waived for the waitress. "I'm so glad you called. Kevin had me running errands all day. Whatever happened to Sunday being a day of rest?"

The waitress came and took their drink and appetizer order. Colleen looked at Abby and then stared at Cassie.

"You're a cruel woman, Cassie!"

Cassie grinned. "What! Why am I cruel?" Although she already knew the answer to Colleen's teasing accusation.

Abby jumped in. "You're cruel because we've both been waiting by the phone all day to see how your date with Jack went."

Colleen nodded her head affirmatively.

With feigned exasperation in her voice, Abby continued. "No phone call, no text, nothing, until we get your call about meeting here tonight." She teasingly continued, "which we were happy to do, but it just meant more waiting."

Cassie laughed. "I was going to call you both, but it would take too long to tell you both on the phone. So I thought it would be more fun to get together in person."

Cassie saw the waitress approaching with their drinks and waited until she sat them all on the table and walked away before telling them about the date.

Cassie put her hand to her heart and smiled. She couldn't wait one more second to tell her best friends. "It was an amazing date!"

Colleen and Abby clapped their hands together in a joint high-five. "Yes! We want to hear all about it."

Colleen held up her hand to briefly stop Cassie. "Don't leave out a detail either. We've been waiting ten years for you to go on an incredible date."

"Okay, okay. Well, I told you that we were going to a movie at one of the vineyards and it was so romantic." She took a sip of her wine and then continued. "The first thing we did was stop by one of the vineyards and pick out a bottle of wine for the picnic."

Both Colleen and Abby sighed. "You know how beautiful the vineyards are and it was such a relaxing, nice way to start the date."

Cassie knew she had their complete attention and she left out no detail about the vineyard, the movie, the picnic basket and that Jack had been so attentive to her by keeping her warm and close to him all night.

Colleen leaned over and gently squeezed Cassie's forearm. "I told you that he liked you! I could see it in his eyes from the first day he started on the job."

Cassie smiled. "I don't know about that, but I'm pretty sure he likes me now."

Abby rested her chin on her hands and sighed again. "That sounds very romantic and I'm so happy for you. When you first told me about the date, I thought it sounded like a romantic setting, but I wasn't sure if you would be able to talk much."

Cassie nodded her head in agreement. "I was kind of worried about that too. With a regular movie, once you're in the theater, it's kind of quiet and there's no talking, but last night, we enjoyed each other's company at the winery while we were picking out a bottle of wine for dinner."

Cassie looked from friend to friend and she still had all their attention. "Then we had the picnic dinner together and we sat on the blanket and talked and ate for a long time before the movie started."

Cassie then told them all about their teasing on the way home and that Jack walked her to the front door.

Abby needed more information from her friend. "You left out a very important detail. Was there a kiss goodnight?"

Cassie tapped her fingers lightly on the table and looked down at them briefly and then back up at her friends. Both their expressions were frozen in place as they waited for Cassie to answer.

"There was a kiss at the door."

Ever the romantic, Colleen jumped in. "What kind of kiss? Like a peck or a...."

Cassie filled in the blanks for them. "Or like an incredibly, soft, sexy kiss that said he had a really good time."

All three of them lifted up their glasses and made a toast to soft, sexy kisses.

Colleen and Abby started chattering on about how romantic the date was. They quickly concluded on how could it not be romantic when you're sitting under the stars? Cassie sat smiling at both of them, but didn't say a word. Within a moment, they looked at Cassie and realized that her smile was growing wider and wider.

It was Abby that restarted the interrogation. "Cassie, did anything happen after the kiss?"

Cassie giggled. "A lady never tells."

Colleen jumped in. "A lady never tells in mixed company. We're not mixed company. Out with it now!"

Cassie never dreamed of keeping it from them, but it was sure fun to watch them squirm a little bit.

"There was another kiss." She paused, and then added with a smile. "And another kiss." Cassie arched her eyebrows and her hazel eyes just glowed. "I guess you could say there were several more kisses, with the last one being when Jack left my house early this afternoon."

Colleen bounced up like a kangaroo and almost dislodged the table from its base. Abby steadied the wine glasses. Both Abby and Colleen were trying to ask a dozen questions at the same time.

Finally after her laughing spell at their shock, Cassie held both hands to her chest. "It was… no, he was incredible."

Colleen pointed to Cassie. "Why didn't I see it when I got here? I guess I was distracted looking at the renovations, but look at you. You are glowing. Isn't she glowing?"

Abby nodded her head. "It's that 'I just had sex that rocked my world,' kind of glow."

"Well, that's a pretty damn good description, because every time it happened, I thought I was in heaven."

Abby was the one to arch her eyebrows this time. "Every time it happened?"

"Oops, you caught that one, huh? Let's just say that it was more than once and, yeah, it rocked my world."

Colleen let out a hoot and all three of them gave in to the giggles.

There was a part of her that wanted to share every detail, but she didn't need to. Her friends definitely got the picture and they were so excited for her. As much as they had laughed and teased her tonight, she knew that they were genuinely happy for her. She didn't know what was going to happen with Jack down the road, but at this moment, it felt so very right.

For weeks now, Jack had been in her head every day, heck, almost every minute. Now he'd been in her bed. More importantly, he was finding his way into her heart, but she didn't want to think too seriously about that yet or get her hopes up that something more might develop between them. For now, it just felt downright good and simply right to be with Jack.

As they ate their appetizers, Cassie shared with them that Jack said he was crazy about her and they all oohed over his sweet statements.

Colleen sipped her wine and stared at Cassie while she was laughing and talking to Abby. Colleen couldn't say that she knew Jack Shaw very well, but she knew him well enough. She'd heard about and witnessed a man that had been tortured when his cheating ex-wife left town without a word. He'd been a zombie for a long time after that. Cassie couldn't possibly know it yet, but Jack must feel strongly about her already. She correctly assumed that Jack wasn't the type of man that would jump into a relationship after what happened with his ex-wife, that is, unless Cassie was somebody who was very important to him.

Colleen was liking the sound of this more and more by the second.

Chapter Twenty-One

Liza slowly slid her naked body up Tom's body until she reached his neck, where she planted several kisses. Tom stroked her back and moaned in satisfaction. In his younger days, he would have been able to flip Liza back over onto her back and take her again. Sometimes he longed for those days, especially with a much younger, sexy wife.

Liza kept kissing his neck and throat, but whispered loudly enough for Tom to hear. "Did you like it, Baby?"

"You know I always like what you do to me, darlin'."

Liza nuzzled his earlobe. "Good, baby. You know I just love taking care of my man."

Tom's eyes were closed and he was completely relaxed. Tom squeezed her buttocks gently. "You do a damn good job of it too, darlin'."

Yes, she did. She only wished she could say the same about Tom. He certainly took care of her financial needs, but she too, wished that he could take her again and again. She desperately missed the raw, physically exhausting sexual experiences that she'd had with other, past lovers.

Liza had grown up poor, neglected and without any real opportunities to get ahead. Her father left her mother before Liza was three years-old and Liza didn't have any memories of him. Her mother was an alcoholic and was barely aware of Liza's existence. She died of cirrhosis of the liver when Liza was just fifteen years-old. After her mom died, she lived in her mother's car and parked it on the side of Stacey's parent's house at night.

Not that there was any added security at Stacey's parent's house, but it was simply all that Liza knew. Stacey's dad was a sixth grade drop-out and he went from job to job. He was bitter at his own circumstances in life and he lost job after job because of his bad temper and know-it-all attitude. He also had plenty of run ins with the law. It started out for minor stuff like shoplifting a carton of cigarettes under his jacket or filling up his gas tank without paying afterwards and speeding off. Over time, the crimes grew from breaking and entering to his final arrest when he was caught selling speed at the local college campus. When he was busted that time, they put him away for twenty years. The last Liza heard was that his bad attitude continued in prison and he wasn't likely to get out early for good behavior.

Even before her husband's jail sentence, Stacey's mom had long since known she couldn't count on that 'good-for-nothing husband' of hers and she was quite vocal about that to Stacey and Liza. Stacey's mom learned to take care of herself in the only way she knew how. Gentlemen callers were what kept food in her belly and the lights turned on at the house. It was Stacey's mom who told Stacey and Liza that they had but one ticket out of doom and that was to use their bodies and their brains to get what they wanted in life.

With no other kind of knowledge or faith in themselves and believing Stacey's mom was right, Liza and Stacey concocted a plan for their future. That plan consisted of seeking out older, rich men who were looking for trophy wives. Although there had been many men in her life, Liza never lost sight of her true goal and she never wavered from her plan until she had a ring on her finger from Tom Beardsley. Their quickie wedding in Mexico was almost two years ago now. Stacey waivered from their plan briefly, with Jack, but then she wrapped her wicked little finger around Richard and now she was secure too.

Although their plan had been successful, Liza couldn't help but think about what other lovers could do to her long neglected body and she began to burn inside. Meeting Stacey in San Francisco was the perfect opportunity to have a couple of harmless little sexual escapades and there would be no risk of seeing anyone from this sleepy little town, or more to the point, anyone who might know Tom. She would be very, very discreet, of course, but a girl just needed to have some fun once in a while. Seeing her best friend, her sister really, was just the icing on the cake.

Of course there were opportunities in this town and men still flirted with her on a regular basis. Liza was confident that she was both beautiful and sexy. She found it to be incredibly difficult to walk away from the men who flirted with her. It was probably the hardest thing that she ever had to do was just casually flirt back and not have any physical contact with those men and the attention she craved so deeply. Although she played out those scenarios in her head, it wasn't a risk she would take if it could get back to Tom.

On the other hand, if there was a chance that she was completely safe, Liza would take that chance. She recalled her deliciously, exciting indiscretion that happened about a year ago. His name was Marcel and he was visiting California from France. Liza had been at a restaurant in Napa, asking them to donate a dinner to the silent auction for one of Tom's charity events. Already bored and awaiting approval from the restaurant manager, she noticed Marcel sitting at the bar and the two of them made eye contact several times. He was very young, tall, dark and strikingly handsome. Liza was even more intrigued when she heard his European accent as he was asking the bartender about the location of a local winery.

Liza did another glance around the restaurant and didn't see anyone she knew. She approached Marcel, sat down next to him at the bar and introduced herself. Liza discovered that Marcel had been on a driving tour of the Napa wineries and had missed getting back to the limo at the time it was to depart. Now he was waiting for a taxi to take him to the next winery where his friends were waiting for him.

Liza told herself that she didn't want the people of France to think that Californians weren't friendly, so she offered to drive Marcel to the winery and he quickly agreed. On the drive over, Marcel referred to her often as "a beautiful American woman" and eventually slid his hand under her dress. She didn't resist. Liza couldn't and wouldn't risk finding a motel. It was the middle of the afternoon and she needed to be home soon. With her mind racing, she noticed a large barn up ahead with an access road on one of the vineyard properties. She turned and drove down the access road and pulled in behind the barn, which was completely hidden from the street. After she parked the car, she looked around and couldn't see anyone else on the land. With a nod to Marcel, they both got into the back seat of the car. He was inside her within thirty seconds.

Tom knew everyone in town and if he ever found out that she had cheated, he'd throw her out on the streets without a dime, lock the door and never look back. He'd made that perfectly clear when they got married.

Pushing Marcel out of her head, Liza remained on top of Tom and slid her hand down to his flaccid penis. She knew it wouldn't get hard yet, but she stroked it lightly. Tom was super relaxed after the sex and sleep was quickly approaching. She had to get his attention now.

"Tom, Baby, I want to ask you something."

Tom's eyes remained closed. "Mm, hum, darlin'."

"Well, you know the play is going to start pretty soon and I'll have performances several times a week." Liza looked up at him and could see that he wasn't asleep yet.

"I'm excited to do the play, but it's been pretty exhausting with all the rehearsals and then such a heavy performance schedule coming up."

Tom patted her on the back. "My poor overworked girl. You have been working too hard. How about if after the play ends, I take you on vacation and we can relax together. How does that sound?"

Liza cringed inside. Damn, of all the responses she expected him to take, she felt stupid that she hadn't anticipated this one.

She inched her way back up to Tom's neck and got close enough so that when she talked, Tom would feel the warmth of her breath against his skin.

"Baby, you know there's nothing I'd enjoy more than going on vacation with my handsome husband," she peppered his throat with kisses now, "but that's still a ways off and I'm exhausted now."

Tom's eyes were open now. "What did you have in mind?"

Liza raised herself up and kissed his mouth. "I was thinking that I would go to San Francisco this weekend. It's not too far away from home and I could stay in a nice hotel and spend some time at the spa. It would be just what I need to get a facial and a massage."

"That would be nice for you darlin' and you should have some spa treatments before the play gets going." Liza breathed a silent sigh of relief.

Tom started to reach for the phone on the nightstand. "Let me call up my secretary and she can reschedule any appointments that I might have for this weekend."

Liza's breath caught in her throat. What to do? That's the last thing she wanted to have happen. Liza urged herself to think. Then it hit her.

"Tom, Baby, as much as I would love, just love, a mini honeymoon with my sexy husband," she leaned up and kissed him and then licked his bottom lip with her tongue, "I kind of wanted to go by myself this time." Tom looked at her suspiciously.

Not wanting Tom to get suspicious, she added with a sexy smile, "I didn't want to tell you and I wanted to surprise you, but your birthday is coming up soon and I won't have time to do much shopping with the play and all and I thought this trip would be the perfect time to treat myself to a spa day *and* look for your special birthday gift."

Liza could see that he was starting to soften and she went in for the kill. "Baby, you work so hard and you're so good to me all the time. I want you to have something special for your birthday. I can't find the perfect gift for you here in this little town. I need to go to someplace like San Francisco to find my wonderful husband the best birthday present ever."

Tom searched her face and could swear that he saw the face of an angel. Liza looked sweet and loving and he couldn't find a reason in the world to tell her no, yet his gut was telling him that something wasn't quite right.

However, not wanting to disappoint his young bride, he agreed. "Okay, darlin', you go shopping in San Francisco and get plenty of spa treatments."

Liza excitedly planted several kisses on Tom. "Honey, you'll be amazed at how rejuvenated I am after going to the spa."

Tom was asleep a short time later, but Liza was so excited she could barely contain it. When she was sure that Tom was in a deep sleep, she put on her robe, took her cell phone out of her purse and went to the kitchen downstairs. On the second ring, Stacey answered. In a whispered voice Liza told her, "It's all set. I'll be in San Francisco this weekend." She could hear a loud "yippee" on Stacey's end. "Okay, I've got to go now. I'll call you tomorrow."

When she hung up, she immediately deleted the 'calls made' to Stacey's number from her cell phone, which she always did, both before and after she talked to Stacey, as Tom would never allow them to remain friends. Tom was more than aware of their reputations before he married her.

After the phone call to Stacey, Liza went into the home office and got on the computer. She would have a Rolex watch, beautifully wrapped for Tom, delivered to the hotel in San Francisco. She certainly wasn't going to waste a minute of her own precious time in San Francisco searching for her husband's birthday gift.

Little did Liza know, but Tom checked her phone log the next morning while she was in the shower. Seeing nothing suspicious for now, he elected not to change his mind about Liza's trip to San Francisco. He wouldn't stop her from going.

Chapter Twenty-Two

Cassie started the coffee pot and turned on the lights at Cassie's Closet. There was a chill in the air and Cassie turned on the heater, just high enough to take the chill off the air and not to suffocate the customers or Jack's crew once they arrived.

The thought of Jack made her feel warm and happy inside. Then again, she hadn't really stopped thinking about Jack since he'd left her house yesterday. Going out with Abby and Colleen last night and telling them all about their date; sharing it all with her best friends, was just the icing on the cake.

Now it seemed surreal that it was just a little more than a month ago that she dropped Brett off at college. After being divorced for ten years and Brett going away to college, she really believed that her life would consist of building up Cassie's Closet, spending time with her family and friends and helping out at Colleen and Kevin's playhouse, and she was okay with that. It was enough and she didn't feel unsatisfied with where her life was going.

However, she admitted to herself, that some days she still watched romantic movies and read romance novels and tears would run down her cheek when the couple finally realized that they were meant to be together. After reading the novel or watching the movie, she would let herself think about having someone special to share her life with, but until recently, it didn't seem like a possibility at this point in her life.

For a long time, she attributed that belief to her insecurities because of Peter's infidelity. Then when she reached the point that she thought about dating again and it wasn't very successful, she accepted that meeting a man wouldn't live up to the expectations she now wanted if she was to ever have a relationship. She knew that if she was ever to get involved again, she had to trust him completely. It had taken her several years to get over Peter's betrayal. She didn't want the young love she had with Peter where she was completely dependent on him and lived or died by his moods, thoughts or needs.

She wanted a relationship with mutual trust, shared interests, someone who laughed easily and wasn't afraid to share himself. A relationship where there was support to the other, no matter what happened. She wanted not only that incredible love, but to genuinely find and be someone's best friend. On top of that, she wanted to give and receive unconditional love. She had a firm belief that he would always be there for her and that he knew that she would always be there for him.

Cassie really believed in that kind of love. Now she'd had the most romantic date with Jack and was still stunned by how drawn she was to him. Even before their date, she knew she felt something towards him. She looked forward to their mornings together having coffee and talking to him; looking into his eyes and seeing that little twinkle. She could swear that there was a star in his dark eyes. She found herself thinking about him often. Then she admitted to herself that she thought about him more than often, it was virtually all the time.

As she was getting to know Jack and learned more about his life, meeting his brother and listening to his stories about growing up, she was finding that he was simply a very good man and that was insanely attractive to her. After hearing about his divorce, he could have easily let himself become a bitter man, when Stacey took everything and left, but he wasn't, or didn't seem to be.

Still, there was something, some part of his divorce that she could sense that had a huge effect on him. She didn't understand where this intuitive sense came from or why, but Cassie knew in her heart that there was more to his story. She only hoped that Jack would trust her enough to eventually tell her. Hopefully they would continue to grow closer and he could let himself confide in her.

Smelling the just perked coffee, made Cassie looked at the clock. She thought that Jack would be tapping on her door any minute. She genuinely looked forward to the cup of coffee with him in the mornings, before the staff and crew arrived and the day got busy with customers.

Today she was more eager to see Jack. She hadn't seen him or talked to him since he'd left her house yesterday after breakfast and she wondered if their mornings would be different now. Would it feel strange to either one of them because they were working together? Would it feel awkward to be around each other now? She didn't have to wonder much longer as she heard the familiar tap at the front door.

Cassie headed to the front door with a smile on her face and she could see Jack through the glass doors, along with Dani by his side. Oh no, as much as she was starting to really like Dani, she was so disappointed that she was with Jack this morning. For Dani's sake, she hoped the disappointment didn't show on her face.

Putting her disappointment aside, she chirped out a spirited, "Good morning you two."

Jack smiled at her. "Look who was already in the parking lot when I pulled up?"

Dani seemed unaware that she had interrupted a morning routine that both Jack and Cassie looked forward to, more so after their passion-filled weekend.

Dani smiled at them and sniffed at the air at the scent of coffee. "There was no traffic this morning, so I got here early and now I can get a head start."

Disappointed that it wasn't just the two of them, Cassie silently hoped that they would find a moment alone together sometime today. She started to tell herself that she needed to look into Jack's eyes and just make sure that nothing had changed for him and that the twinkling star was still there, but quickly admitted that it had nothing to do with that. She just wanted to feel his lips on hers again.

Nodding towards the coffee pot on the back wall, Cassie asked them if they'd like a cup of coffee and they both accepted.

Cassie handed Dani a steaming cup. Dani took it and blew on it softly before taking a sip. Cassie handed Jack a cup and when she handed it to him, his hand touched hers. She looked into his eyes and he winked at her. An instant smile beamed across her face. Just the slightest touch of his hand and a wink was all it took and the butterflies in Cassie's stomach fluttered.

The three of them talked about the project for several minutes. Now that the kitchen was done, the remaining projects wouldn't take as long. They had already done a lot of work on the dressing rooms and this week would be the baby and infant area. After that, the faux living room area and remaining work would be done. Cassie had a sudden thought of no more coffee with Jack in the mornings and she immediately felt a sense of loss, so she quickly pushed that unthinkable thought out of her head.

After they finished with the work talk, Dani gulped the last swig of her coffee and walked to the small sink and rinsed out her cup. As she was doing so, Jack brushed his arm lightly against Cassie's. The butterflies took flight again.

Dani thanked Cassie for the coffee and looked at Jack. "I'm going to start work. Are you coming?"

"I'll be there in a minute. I need to run some cost estimates by Cassie."

Cassie wrinkled her nose. "Oh no, not cost estimates on a Monday morning!" Dani chuckled softly and headed towards the plastic barrier.

Jack nodded towards Cassie's office and indicated he wanted to talk to her there.

They walked in to her office and Jack closed the door. Without saying a word, he took Cassie in his arms and planted a big kiss on her lips. Cassie didn't budge from Jack's firm grip and she melted into his kiss.

Afterwards, she looked up at him dreamily. "I want to talk about cost estimates every day!" Jack laughed "It's a deal." He kissed her again.

Cassie looked into Jack's eyes and the twinkle was there again. She was sure that his twinkle was reflecting back into her own eyes, as she suddenly felt alive, excited and exquisitely happy.

In that moment, it hit her and she didn't want to think about being careful with her words; she just wanted Jack to know what she was thinking. It was simple and to the point. "I missed you after you left yesterday."

This time it was Jack's stomach that jumped. God, it was so wonderful to think that someone missed him; that he was on someone's mind. It made him feel like he mattered.

He cupped Cassie's face into his hands and leaned down to kiss her again. "I haven't stopped thinking about you either, Cassie."

He hadn't either. Not when he was driving away from Cassie's house, not at his parents' house later, not in his own bed last night or on his way to Cassie's Closet this morning. No, he hadn't stop thinking about her for one second.

Cassie felt another soft, warm kiss on her lips and heard his words only an inch from her lips. She was thrilled and delighted that he had been thinking about her too. Cassie knew then and there that she wanted to be with Jack, no matter what and she was as certain of that as she had been about anything in her life.

Hearing that the front door of the building had opened and knowing one of the employees must have walked in, Cassie looked at Jack. "I thought that maybe I could interest you in a home cooked dinner some night this week."

"I think I could be persuaded." Jack kissed the tip of her nose. Then he grinned. "I would like that very much."

Now hearing footsteps approaching her office, Jack gave Cassie another quick kiss, winked at her again and reluctantly broke his hold.

When Cassie's employee, Andrew, opened her office door, he heard Jack telling Cassie, that he'd be back later to discuss another cost estimate.

Before she knew it, the day was upon her and employees and customers were filling up the place, the phones were ringing and the sound of Jack's crew were sawing and hammering away. The sound of construction had almost become soothing to Cassie, either that, or maybe it was just knowing that Jack was on the other side of the partition, but she liked the sound of the tools and the smell of the wood.

On the other side of the partition, Jack whistled as he worked. Dani looked up at him and listened to him whistle. Whatever song it was, it was a catchy little tune and Dani suddenly became aware that Jack had been full of smiles this morning. Dani burrowed her brow together in concentration. She couldn't remember the last time that she'd seen Jack happy and whistling. Then it hit her! What a dummy, she thought to herself. She slapped her forehead. Why didn't she see it this morning? It was as obvious as night and day. Jack and Cassie had been making eyes at each other and sharing smiles for weeks now and Jack was smiling like a monkey. Hot damn! If she was right, she couldn't be happier for the guy. He absolutely deserved to feel good. By Dani's way of thinking, feeling good was long overdue for him!

Later on during the lunch break, Jack and Dani were sitting on the tailgate of his truck. Jack was eating a sandwich and Dani eyeballed it, with its dripping mayo and mustard, Dani suddenly found her grilled chicken breast and grapes to be quite unappetizing. Not only was she looking at his sandwich, but she was watching Jack to see if there were any other tell-tale signs that she missed.

Jack turned to her. "What?"

Dani shrugged her shoulders and smiled. "Nothing, Jack. I just noticed that you were whistling today while you worked and it was kind of nice."

Jack looked over at her and knew that she was teasing him. She'd figured it out! He should have known that Dani would put two and two together before too long. Honestly, he didn't mind that she knew; she'd seen him through a lot.

Jack pushed her with his shoulder a little bit. "What! A man's not entitled to whistle to help pass the time?" He grinned and took another bite of his sandwich.

Dani pushed him back a little with her shoulder. "Oh you can whistle any time you want too, but I've just never known you to whistle on any job," she pointed her fork towards the front door of Cassie's Closet, "that is, until you started working for a very pretty client."

A chuckle escaped from Jack before he could stop it. What the hell, he didn't care if Dani knew and it felt good to talk to her about something besides Charlie and work issues.

Looking towards the front door of Cassie's Closet and then back to Dani, Jack nodded, "I think she's a good one."

Dani smiled. Now it was confirmed and she felt warm inside. Jack wasn't just her boss, but her friend. "I'm happy for you Jack. I really am." And she was. Jack wasn't the type to share much, but simply knowing that he'd spent time with Cassie and was feeling good about it, that was good enough for Dani.

With a final nudge on the shoulder from Dani, she chuckled. "Cost estimates, my ass." Jack laughed out loud.

Afterwards, Jack finished his sandwich and continued to look towards Cassie's Closet. Happiness with a woman had eluded him for such a long time now. After the divorce was finalized, he came to accept that he hadn't been happy and mistrusted Stacey early on, even when she was pregnant. They were just miles apart in what they both wanted and needed in a marriage. During their marriage, all of his happiness came from being with Charlie. For Jack, Charlie was the only glue that held their marriage together.

After lunch, when the crew returned to work, Jack waited in the store and watched as Cassie talked to a customer. She was aware that he was waiting for her, but she patiently waited as her customer talked to her for a few more minutes. Jack watched Cassie as she gently touched the women's shoulder and pointed in different directions for the location of items the woman must be looking for.

Jack thought Cassie looked so beautiful. He always thought that, but today as her long, dark hair swayed as she turned her head, it was so shiny and pretty and it laid softly down her back. Immediately he was reminded of that long hair spread across her naked breasts and his mind started to wander where it shouldn't wander during work hours.

Cassie approached Jack. He told her that he wanted her to check out the progress of some of the work. He took her behind another section of the plastic partition and pointed to the dressing rooms. A smile spread across Cassie's face in delight. The first two of the dressing rooms now had doors on them.

"Oh, Jack, I have actual doors now instead of curtains. They look great!"

Jack lightly took her elbow and walked her towards one of the enclosed dressing rooms. "I want you to see if there's enough room in here and if the benches are placed correctly."

Cassie walked in and looked at the dressing room and declared that it was all just perfect.

Jack had sworn to himself driving in this morning that he was going to keep his composure while he was with Cassie during business hours. He wasn't able to keep that promise this morning, nor could he keep it now. He didn't think he could make it until the end of the day to kiss Cassie. He needed her lips on his right now!

Not able to stop himself, Jack leaned Cassie up against the dressing room wall and leaned in for a hot, sexy kiss. When his mouth stopped ravishing her mouth, he pulled away slightly and whispered to her. "I couldn't take one more minute of not kissing you."

Cassie was still breathless from the kiss, but she pulled his mouth back down to hers. When their kiss ended and their lips were inches apart, a breathless Cassie whispered back, "Good because I needed you too."

Hearing her say that and looking into the hazel eyes that were full of sexiness and mischief, Jack felt a little wobbly and he knew that they had to get back to work instantly or he wouldn't be able to walk out of the dressing room without having his way with her. The crew was so near he could hear their voices.

One of Cassie's fingers drifted down Jack's neck and then to the center of his chest. With her other hand, she took his buttocks and pulled him towards her, before giving him a deep, lingering kiss. When Jack started to lean in for more pressure against her, she pushed him away. Now it was her turn to wink and smile. "See you later, Jack." Jack stayed in the dressing room for a couple more minutes to collect himself.

Damn, but if she wasn't amazing!

Chapter Twenty-Three

Liza looked out the window of her hotel room. Surprisingly for San Francisco, it wasn't foggy and overcast. Instead the sky was bright blue and cloudless, with the Bay waters reflecting its gorgeous blue color. To her left, she could see the brightly painted orange of the Golden Gate Bridge spanning its way across the Bay, and to the right, the long length of the Bay Bridge. Down below on the street level were hundreds of cars, street cars, pedestrians and bicyclists. It was the world she craved, with tons of people, places to go and activities day and night. Tonight the city would be lit up in endless lights against the blackened sky that reflected off the shimmering Bay waters. She was so thrilled to experience it all with her very best friend, Stacey. It had been two years since she'd seen her, and she was almost as excited to see her again, as she was for their outings tonight and tomorrow night.

Liza heard a knock at the door and ran to open it. There stood Stacey with a smile as big as the sun. They both jumped in place like when they were teenagers before they pulled each other into a long hug. Liza finally pulled Stacey into the room and closed the door.

Liza held Stacey's hand, but stood back to observe her friend carefully. "Look at you! You're like a beauty queen."

Stacey touched her now lightened, strawberry blonde hair and asked "Do you like it?"

Without waiting for an answer, Stacey checked out Liza. "Look at you, Liza! You look, well, what's the word I'm looking for -- just stunning. That's it!"

Liza laughed and touched Stacey hair. "I like the soft reddish color on you. It's much better than the mousy brown you used to have."

"I think so too. I think this color is sexy and it flatters my skin tone. Besides, Richard has a fondness for it."

They both stood back to observe each other. "Liza, look at your clothes. I can tell by looking at them that they are all designer labels."

Liza smiled in satisfaction and touched the fabric of her dress. "They are!" They both felt like they were back in high school and giggled in excitement at the sight of each other.

They hugged each other once again. Stacey squeezed her extra tight. "I can't believe I'm here with you finally!"

Liza looked more closely at Stacey and besides the change in the hair color, she looked basically the same. The clothes were nicer, of course, but she still had an incredible body and the high heels that she wore with her skirt made her legs look ten miles long. Liza knew that Stacey would be showing off more of her legs tonight. As if reading her mind, Stacey touched her pencil skirt and wrinkled her nose.

"Richard was in the bedroom with me the whole time I was packing, so I had to bring the most boring clothes. Before tonight, we just *have* to go get something decent to wear."

Stacey pouted, but then patted her purse. "But I have Richard's credit card." She stroked her purse with a smile.

Liza nodded in agreement. "We'll definitely go shopping. I was in the same boat as you and Tom was in the bedroom while I was packing."

Liza looked at her reflection in the mirror. "I think the old coot is going to miss me."

With a wicked laugh, Stacey agreed with her. "Of course he is. God, you should have heard Richard. He kept trying to get me to change my mind. He wanted to come with me now, instead of arriving Sunday night. What a nightmare that would have been!"

Liza understood her dilemma completely and told her about the little white lie she had to tell Tom so that he wouldn't come with her either.

Liza pointed over to the beautifully wrapped gift box sitting on the dresser. "Tom's birthday gift; delivery guaranteed today." Stacey walked over and touched the elegantly wrapped watch. "You've always been so smart Liza."

Stacey put the package down and walked back toward Liza. She took her hands into hers. "I'm so glad we're here together. I have so much to tell you. I've been so lonely being away from you and stuck at Richard's house."

Liza understood that too. Even though she had more people around her in town than in the God forsaken place where Stacey was living, she knew that none of her friends cared for her the way Stacey did. She wasn't stupid and she knew that most of the women she spent time with did it because of their own husband's relationship with Tom or his business. It had nothing to do with enjoying Liza's company. Besides that, it was obvious to Liza that they were jealous of her youth, beauty and talent.

Stacey turned around slowly in front of Liza and with a slow side to side bump of her hip. When she was facing Liza, she smiled coyly. "Do you think that if I put something sexy on this body that I won't be quite so lonely anymore?"

Liza did her own slow roll of her hips side to side. "I don't think either one of us is going to be very lonely tonight." They both giggled and held each other tight again.

Liza grabbed her purse and Stacey's hand. "How about we do some serious shopping for something a little more revealing, then we'll have dinner here and get all caught up before we paint the town red."

Stacey was so excited to be out among the people of San Francisco and away from the dry, boring desert where she lived with Richard. To be away from Richard, his bratty daughters and Charlie's constant pestering her to play with him, to draw with him, to take him to the park. He never let up for one minute. God, that kid was so annoying! Then with the added pressure of Richard wanting another child, well, it was almost more than she could bear! She needed this weekend.

Stacey raced to the door. "First stop, Victoria's Secret!"

****

Later that evening, Stacey and Liza sat in the restaurant of the hotel. They had had a great time exploring San Francisco, shopping for suitable clothes for the next couple of evenings and getting their egos boosted from all the looks sent their way. They were wearing some of their purchases now. Stacey was dressed in strapless, ruby red dress that covered just enough of her butt to be legal. Her legs were crossed and she could feel the slight weight of the very high heels that she wore. Her feet would probably be aching by the end of the night, but she didn't care. Hopefully, she had them kicked off on the side of the bed in some young, sexy man's room before the midnight hour.

Liza wore a dress in a similar style, but it had a sexy vertical single strap and it was bright sapphire and just as short as Stacey's dress. She felt sassy and sexy.

Stacey had put soft waves in her hair and wore big hoop earrings with black diamonds that shimmered against her lightened locks. Several men had already walked by and eyed the two women hungrily. It didn't go unnoticed by either woman.

Stacey's stomach flipped over in excitement. God help her, but she'd been tamed too long. She felt like there was a beast inside her dying to get out. It only made the urge stronger to be there with Liza, knowing she was anticipating the 'hunt' as much as she was.

The 'hunt' as they used to call it was something that they did best together. Usually one of them would literally lock in the prey with her eyes and the other one would approach. Before long, both of them were circling for the 'kill' that would leave their prey laying down, ravished and unable to move afterwards. They laughed at the analogy of their 'hunt' because it so easily compared to a real jungle hunt. Past experience had taught them that when they felt sexy and desired, they felt as powerful as a hungry lioness.

But before the fun began tonight, Stacey had something on her mind and she needed to talk to Liza first. There was no one in the world that she could talk to about her problems except for Liza.

"Liza, you have no idea how much I needed to get away to someplace like San Francisco." Through the restaurant windows, she could see the twinkling lights of the Bay Bridge.

"When Richard asked me to move in with him and told me his place was in Nevada, remember how excited I was?"

Liza responded. "Of course, I remember. Everything we had planned so carefully had finally worked out."

"That's true, but I guess I heard Nevada and I thought Las Vegas and how exciting it would be to live there."

Liza nodded. She knew where this was going. After all, she helped drive Stacey and Charlie to Richard's house and realized that it was much more desolate than either one of them could have imagined.

"I had no idea that Richard would live so far away from everything that's exciting and fun! Do you know the next biggest town from where we live is Ely, Nevada?"

Without waiting for an answer, Stacey continued. "Do you know what's in Ely, Nevada?" Stacey sighed deeply.

Liza shook her head no.

"Trains!" Liza looked somewhat surprised. "Yep, that's the highlight of the town of Ely."

Liza shrugged her shoulders. "Richard is loaded. Now that time has passed and you don't have to worry about Jack tracking you down, why don't you convince Richard to buy a weekend condo in Las Vegas?"

Stacey started to pout. "I tried to get him to do that, but he said he needs to be close to the mines. Besides, he doesn't want to travel every weekend, since that's his 'down time.'"

Oh, that was definitely something that Liza could relate to! On occasion Tom would offer to take them away on vacation, but to travel at the pace she was interested in, didn't interest Tom in the least.

Stacey continued with a forlorn look. "I mentioned it to you on the phone, but it's becoming a really big deal for Richard." Stacey sipped her martini and sighed. "He really wants to have another child. He said he's owned the mines for thirty years now and he wants it to be a family legacy. The mining business is growing and he wants his children to be a part of it all."

Liza just looked at Stacey like she was crazy. "That's not what you want is it?'

"No frickin' way!" Stacey lowered her voice and looked around before she shared her secret with Liza. "You know it's not what I want."

Stacey lowered her voice even more and moved her head closer towards Liza before she spoke again. "I even faked two pregnancies to keep him off my back for a little while."

Liza took in a breath. "How did you manage that?"

Stacey still kept her voice low, although no one was close enough to hear. "Last year I told Richard that I was pregnant. You should have seen him. He was so excited. He picked me up and was twirling me around." Stacey made a circular motion with her hands as she spoke.

Liza could only imagine. "I gotta say, Liza, it was great. For a couple of months, I slept in every day. I told Richard that the first trimester was exhausting, so he had the staff completely take care of Charlie, which was such a blessing because that kid just tries my nerves most days."

Liza shuddered at the thought. Thank God that Tom didn't want children. He had adult children from his first and second marriages and he told her that he didn't want to start over again. Liza was thrilled. She had never wanted children and after returning from their honeymoon, she had her tubes tied, as Tom held her hand in recovery. They were both very clear in what they wanted in their marriage, although Liza still fantasized about pursuing her own agenda, whenever possible.

Liza was curious. "What happened next?"

Stacey smirked in satisfaction. "Between us girls, all I did was remove my vaginal ring that I use for birth control," with a satisfied smile she continued, "well, let's say that the evidence of a miscarriage began, if you know what I mean."

Liza laughed. "Sneaky, sneaky, girlfriend."

Stacey agreed. "I thought so too."

Stacey touched the large hoops hanging from her ears, that were encircled with the black diamonds. "A little present from Richard when I miscarried because he thought I was so sad."

Liza chuckled. "I'm sure your heart was just broken in two."

Stacey smiled and put both hands to her heart and sarcastically said, "It was broken in half, for sure. I had to stay in bed for another month to recover from such a terrible ordeal."

Liza nodded in approval as Stacey continued her story. "Naturally, after the 'miscarriage,' Richard was very concerned and careful with me. He didn't mention me trying to get pregnant again until earlier this year." Stacey sighed and explained that she had naively believed that after the miscarriage, Richard wouldn't want to risk it again and would back off in pressuring her to have another child.

"When that didn't happen, I became 'pregnant' again. This time Richard was completely attentive and I didn't have to lift a finger for another two months." Stacey chuckled. "Unfortunately, I miscarried that one too." Stacey used her fingers to symbolize air quotes around the word 'miscarried.'

Stacey lowered her voice once again and put her head down closer to where Liza could see her eyes. "You should have seen him, Liza." Stacey said with no remorse. "He put his head on my lap and cried like a little baby."

Liza took another bite of her scallop. She had no sympathy for Richard. Why should she? Richard had a beautiful, sexy wife and he should be happy with his life, like Tom was.

Liza learned a long time ago that if you gave into a man's weakness, no matter what that weakness was, then he had all the power, and power and control was not something that Liza was ever going to give up again. She'd done enough of that when she was younger. She even gave herself to Stacey's daddy before he went to prison, because he threatened to call the youth authority on her if she didn't give in to him. He was also the source of her food, drink and shelter when her mother's car was towed away. Liza never told Stacey and probably never would. That was the only secret she kept from her best friend. It didn't matter anyway, because it had taught her a valuable lesson that would carry her through the rest of her life, which was that sex equaled power and control.

Stacey shrugged her shoulders. "It's one of the reasons that I was able to convince him that I needed a few days in San Francisco alone before he arrived." Again, she clasped her hands to her heart. "After all that I've been through, it's only fair."

Liza arched an eyebrow and nodded towards Stacey. "Well played, sister, well played."

After they both chuckled for a moment, Stacey got solemn. "Seriously, Liza, what am I going to do? Richard really wants another child and that's why we're here this weekend, to talk to some specialist on Monday about ways for me to maintain a full-term pregnancy again."

"I don't know Stacey. I have to think about it for a minute, because I'm kind of stumped right now."

Liza knew that having another child was completely out of the question. It wasn't even a possibility that Stacey would consider, no matter how much she may or may not want to please Richard. She'd already gone that route once before. Charlie was simply an unexpected pregnancy in between Stacey switching birth control.

Liza was stunned when Stacey kept him, but she was sure that had to do more with Jack than anything else. Unfortunately, Stacey had blurted out that she was pregnant before thinking it all the way through. Later, Liza had admonished her for telling Jack before taking action to rid her body of the pregnancy. Stacey agreed and knew she'd made a serious mistake.

Even though she ended up having Charlie, Stacey certainly made sure that she wasn't going to be a full-time Mom. It had always been Jack who took care of Charlie and Stacey had her freedom. She was young, sexy and eager to live life in the fast lane, without any distractions. Stacey didn't want to be settled down with kids and when she looked at Charlie, Liza knew that all she felt towards Charlie was resentment.

Suddenly, Liza had an idea that just might work to resolve this problem for both of them! She looked Stacey directly in the eyes. "I have an idea. I haven't figured out all the details in my mind yet, but what if you return to Pueblo Valley?"

Stacey's eyes flew open. "What! Are you crazy! Jack would try and throw the book at me and his crazy cop brother would lock me up and throw away the key." Stacey still felt personally offended that Jon had turned down her advances on more than one occasion, claiming that he would never do that to his brother. Whatever! Jack would never have had to know. Stupid man!

Now the wheels had really started to turn in Liza's head and she continued on. "No, Stacey, Jack wouldn't throw the book at you, especially if you asked him to take you back."

Liza paused for the desired dramatic affect and was rewarded with Stacey' full attention. "Jack was always crazy about you, but he was also so crazy about Charlie. If he had Charlie back in his life, he wouldn't put you in jail."

Stacey was starting to arrive at the same page as Liza. "Yeah, if I begged and pleaded with Jack and told him that I'd made a terrible mistake and that we wanted to be a family again…" Liza finished Stacey's thought. "Jack would take you back in a New York minute!"

Stacey was starting to like the idea more and more. If their plan worked out, she would live close to Liza again and be back in Pueblo Valley. Even though it was a small town, at least it wasn't in the middle of the desert and she could drive to the ocean, to the city, anywhere that she wanted. Best of all, Jack would be so happy to have Charlie back, that there's no way he would say no to her. The icing on the cake would be that she wouldn't have any responsibility toward the whole kid thing. Her time would be her own. Stacey recalled that of all the uncertainties in life, the one certain thing, was that Jack was crazy about that kid.

"Has Jack been seeing anyone in town that you know of?"

Liza shook her head no. "I told you that he was Mr. Mopey for the longest time after you left. I think he still is. From what I can tell, all he does is work."

Liza sipped her cocktail, before adding. "He's probably making even more money now doing all those projects to fill the void."

Stacey smiled an evil smile. "Your idea is definitely worth thinking about."

Liza nodded in agreement. The more she thought about it, the more she liked the idea too. She could never go back to the life that she had with Stacey before, but, on the other hand, with Stacey in town, she would have an ally, someone who she could count on if an interesting situation presented itself. She warmed inside at the thought.

Stacey frowned. "What about our plan? We were supposed to marry well, end of story. Jack is not nearly as rich as Richard is."

Liza wasn't concerned. "Like I said, I think that Jack is doing much better financially. After all, his crew has trucks out everywhere. I know he's not as wealthy as Richard, but..." she smiled smugly, "you don't have to stay with Jack forever. When another opportunity presents itself, then you can go for it!"

Stacey's chest burst with happiness and she was flooded with relief. She'd been so worried about having another child with Richard, and besides she just hated living in Nevada. Besides, if she remembered correctly, Jack shouldn't be so hard to lure in. Before she had him following along behind her like a little puppy within days of meeting her.

Stacey reached over and squeezed Liza's hand. "Oh, Liza, I'm so excited. This sounds like it could be a great plan. Let's figure this all out together while we're here this weekend, okay?"

Liza agreed. Then she noticed two gentlemen at the bar who were gazing at them. She sent a seductive smile their way. "Stacey, hon, don't worry. We'll figure it all out later, but right now, I see some hot prospects at the bar." Stacey's eyes lit up.

Liza stood, adjusted her dress and seductively headed over to the bar. She had the immediate attention of both the men who had been eyeing them. Liza knew that Stacey would be behind her. They both knew their roles. Stacey retouched her lipstick, checked her hair, and then stood and sauntered over towards the men.

The hunt had begun.

Chapter Twenty-Four

Jack ran around to the other side of the car and opened the door for Cassie. With a smile and a bow, he took her hand. Cassie took his hand and stood up.

"Why thank you."

"You're welcome. How did you like the ride?"

Cassie laughed as she combed through her hair with her fingers. Jack had rented a convertible for the day, since they decided to drive to the Harvest Festival and then to the coast. Jack thought she'd endured his bumpy old truck enough when they went to dinner and she deserved to have a comfortable ride. Actually, Cassie didn't mind riding in the truck. She was sitting next to Jack while she was in it and that's all that really mattered to her.

As they looked towards the entrance to the Harvest Festival, Cassie took Jack's hand and their fingers entwined. "I'm excited to be at the festival with you."

Jack squeezed her hand tightly. He was too. Jack smiled at her and kissed her quickly before they walked in.

They'd seen each other almost every night this week. Cassie's home cooked dinner was spaghetti and Jack declared that he had to reciprocate, so two nights later he brought takeout from Trebbiano's. Then they both teased that they would be way too tired to cook at the end of the week, so on Friday night, Cassie picked up a pizza and Jack came over. They woke up together this morning.

There was a cool crispness to the air and autumn was definitely upon them, but it was still a beautiful day and Cassie only needed to wear a light cardigan. Still, Jack dropped her hand and put his arm around her instead.

"Are you warm enough?" Cassie snuggled in closer to Jack as they walked. "Now I am."

As they walked towards the festival, Jack and Cassie were both thinking about how well they fit together. After another night of fantastic lovemaking, they finally gave in to sleep. Jack spooned Cassie and it was a perfect fit. She fell asleep instantly as Jack cradled her. Jack wondered how it was possible that another body could fit his so well. Cassie had snuggled her back into Jack's chest perfectly, her butt into his groin and their legs lay side by side.

When Jack slept next to Cassie, he was able to forget about all the sleepless nights when he had been in his own bed, tossing and turning, wondering if Charlie was sleeping, getting enough to eat, being snuggled or held and if he was ever told that he was a good boy or that he was loved. Jack had lived with Stacey long enough to believe that most of Charlie's needs for food, baths and shelter were being met, at least on the most basic level, but he was highly doubtful that Charlie was ever told that he was loved or wanted. Jack had thought so many times, what he wouldn't give to tell that little boy how much he loved him or how much he was wanted by Jack.

Each moment that Jack spent with Cassie, he was getting closer and closer to telling her about Charlie. He realized recently that it was never about him not trusting her with the truth. Somehow since he'd met Cassie, he felt like he could tell her anything, but it was facing the horrors again that were so hard for him. He couldn't tell her everything without sharing all his feelings, his confusion about being Charlie's Dad and the longings he still had to find Stacey and Charlie, so that he could learn the truth. There was no way he could tell Cassie all this, without letting himself live and feel the nightmare again. He was starting to feel strong enough to share all that with her. He knew he wanted to tell her soon, and he promised himself he would.

Right now, he wanted to enjoy the freedom of the pain for a little longer. He'd been living with the nightmare day and night for a little over two years now. Now, with Cassie in his life, he still never forgot about Charlie, but he could focus on someone else and he could make her laugh and when he did that, he felt light and happy.

With Cassie in his life, he no longer felt starved of any physical contact and genuine affection. In the months before Stacey left, Jack had been unwillingly to touch her. Stacey wasn't his, she had never been his. She'd given her body to too many others and apparently her heart to the man she claimed was Charlie's father. Jack's gut still tightened at the thought of another man being Charlie's Dad.

As he and Cassie walked through the festival gates, he looked at Cassie and her eyes lit up like a kid in the candy store. A smile broke out on her face, as she could see all the scarecrows in the field, the kids, carnival rides, pumpkins and bales of hay for benches. He just couldn't resist her face or her smile and he was struck so suddenly that he just couldn't imagine ever wanting to not kiss Cassie, or not see her dimpled smile.

When they were at work, they still snuck in kisses in her office or behind a book shelf, but it was later, when they were alone that he would lose himself in her kisses and in her touch. Two years ago, he would have bet his last dollar that he would never surrender to another woman's touch again, but he had and the newfound passion and trust was all because of Cassie.

As they walked through the Harvest Festival, they both noticed the hay ride and pointed to it at the same time. Jack boosted Cassie up onto the wagon and they joined several couples and lots of kids. Jack winced once inside when he looked at the children pointing to the scarecrows that they passed along the way. Charlie was at the age now where Jack was sure he would absolutely love going to festivals. He pushed the thought out of his head and focused on Cassie. They laughed at the scarecrows that were adorned not only in traditional scarecrow clothing, but some were dressed up as nurses, doctors, fireman, in military gear, cowboys and baseball players.

After a bumpy ride, they got out of the wagon and headed towards the corn maze. There were two entrances and one exit, so Jack challenged Cassie to a race to the finish line. The last one out of the maze and waiting at the exit was buying the other one a hot apple cider and a roasted ear of corn on the cob. Later on, as Jack raced through the corn maze, positive that he would be the first one out, there stood Cassie, wearing a hat from one of the scarecrows and a smile.

Jack was breathing hard from his rush to finish the maze before Cassie, but when he spotted her, he couldn't help but laugh. He threw his hands up in the air. "How the hell did you do that so fast?" Cassie didn't even answer him; she just laughed as she popped the straw hat onto his head.

Jack took her into his arms and held her tightly before giving her a kiss.

"I'm a sore loser." Jack pretended to pout as he nodded his head towards the barn that was to the left of them. "So how about we sneak into the barn and you can console me?"

Cassie burst out laughing and swatted him lightly on the chest. "Oh, what a tempting offer that is, but, hmmm," she looked into his eyes, "what if one of the little scarecrows happen to walk in?"

Jack pulled her even closer to him. God, it felt so good to have her in his arms. "I'm willing to risk it."

Cassie chuckled. "How about I give you a rain check to console you? Maybe we can go someplace where straw won't go where straw is not supposed to go."

Jack was gleefully intrigued. "Perhaps, we could work something out."

Cassie again swatted his chest softly. "Good, now pay up. You owe me a piece of corn on the cob."

They spent a few more hours are the Harvest Festival, exploring the craft fair items, guessing the weight of the pumpkins and listening to local country bands. Jack bought Cassie a porcelain figurine of a scarecrow at one of the craft booths. He could see her looking at it and touching it gently.

"Do you like that one Cassie?"

She nodded. "I do. There's something about it that I like so much. I think maybe it's the sweet smile that's painted on its face."

Jack pulled out his wallet and handed the money to the cashier.

When they got into the car to leave, Cassie looked at the scarecrow again before putting it back in its packaging.

Jack hadn't started the car engine yet. He turned and looked at Cassie. She looked into his eyes. "I think I was a lot like that scarecrow before I met you." Cassie urged him on with her eyes. "For a long time, I was just a shell of a man with some expression painted on my face."

Cassie touched his cheek with her finger. "Do you still feel like a shell of a man?"

Jack hooked her chin with his finger and pulled her towards him. "Not since I met you." Then he kissed her softly.

A small tear formed in Cassie's eyes, but it didn't spill over. She stroked Jack's cheek again. "I feel the same way about you." Jack looked more closely into her eyes and saw that they were shimmering with wetness, but he could tell that she wasn't sad, not at all. Neither one of them were sad now.

"What do you say we head towards the ocean now? We should be able to make it before sunset."

"That's sounds great. Let's go!" With the wind in her hair and the scent of the sea in the air, they headed out together.

****

Jack and Cassie got to the beach with enough time before sunset to take a stroll along the water. With the temperature in the air starting to cool off, they both put on a heavier jacket. Still the temptation to walk in the water was too great. They both took off their shoes and rolled their pants up to their knees. The tide was starting to come in and the waves were growing stronger. The first few times that the ocean water hit them, they both gasped at the coolness of it and ran back to the dry sand. There was nothing more beautiful than the bluest blue of the Pacific Ocean, but it was also so cold. Yet it called to them and they were right back along the water line and the waves were splashy gently over their feet and calves. Cassie breathed in the smell of the ocean air. Its crispness filled her lungs and invigorated her spirit.

They stopped and looked at the rolling waves that were headed towards the beach. Jack pointed out a sea otter that was floating on his back. Suddenly he was gone, probably looking for food. A minute later, it was Cassie who spotted him again. It was dinnertime for the marine life and some of the seagulls were diving into the sea while other seagulls had found their dinner on the beach, in the leftovers from the beach goers.

Jack and Cassie strolled slowly, hand in hand, down the length of the beach. They stopped occasionally to pick up a seashell and inspect its colors or shape, or to look at an odd shaped piece of driftwood. Most of the beach goers were packing up for the day, but a few remained. A fisherman or two had a pole out in the sea and was hoping for a final catch of the day. Jack and Cassie quietly said hello to the people they passed or responded to comments of "it's a nice evening tonight isn't it?"

Finally, they turned around and headed back in the direction of their car. Jack had spotted a very large piece of driftwood a ways back and it would be the perfect place to watch the sunset. When they got to the log, Jack spread out a beach towel down in front of the log, so that they would stretch out their legs, but still lean back on the log like a chair. Once they were seated and settled, Cassie leaned her head on Jack's shoulder and he took her hand into his.

"Are you warm enough?"

"I am. This is just so perfect here." Cassie looked up at Jack. "Thanks for bringing me to the festival today and to the beach." She looked out at the ocean and the sky that was starting to paint itself orange, violet and a darker blue as the sun set in the distance.

"I think that sometimes life just gets so busy, that we forget that we need to take a moment like this," Cassie looked at Jack again, "especially with someone that's special to you."

"I couldn't agree with you more." Then Jack looked at her tenderly. "Cassie, I hope you know how special you are to me."

Cassie nodded that she did.

"I don't know if I'm very good at showing you, but you mean so much to me."

Cassie swallowed a lump in her throat. *She was in love with Jack.* It hit her at some point today. She didn't know if it was on the hayride, or when Jack helped a little boy pick up a heavy pumpkin, or when they walked along the beach, but today, time after time, her heart kept telling her *"you're in love with Jack"* and she knew without a shadow of doubt that she was head over heels, madly, passionately, forever in love with Jack Shaw!

Her lips touched his slightly. "I know how much you care and you do a great job of showing me." Jack smiled at her comforting words and Cassie continued. "Neither one of us are kids. We've both been hurt before, but I want you to know that I want to be with you. There's no rush to…" Cassie was searching for the words she wanted to say, but she couldn't find them. Jack found them for her.

"Cassie, please don't think that I need more time to get over Stacey." Cassie looked up at him wide eyed and listened. He knew exactly what was worrying her when she didn't even know it completely herself. Once he said the words, she knew that she had been concerned about it.

Jack continued. "You're the one I think about when I wake up each morning." A flood of happiness washed over Cassie.

"There were some things that happened in my divorce that were extremely painful." Jack looked at Cassie and saw nothing but concern for him in her eyes. "I want to tell you all about it. I really do," Jack paused, "but not today."

Jack looked at the darkening sky and a dim, twinkling star could be seen. "Tonight I want to watch the rest of the stars come out with you, then take you home and spend the night with you."

Cassie couldn't possibly know it, but sharing the day and the night with her, gave Jack the strength he needed to tell her all about Charlie.

"I'm here when you're ready to tell me whatever it is that you want to talk about." Jack just pulled her closer to him and she embraced his warmth. There was no rush. Jack was right. Today needed to be this glorious day that they shared together. They were creating memories together and it was feeling very magical to Cassie. Her heart was filled with joy in realizing that she was in love with Jack and the feeling of this new love warmed her.

Chapter Twenty-Five

Jack and Cassie were both in his truck and they pulled up in front of the Pueblo Playhouse. There were boxes of clothing in the back of his truck that they had brought over from Cassie's Closet and from the seamstresses house. Jack knew that Cassie was going to a meeting at the playhouse and he offered to take her.

Earlier in the day, they had talked about it. "Are you sure you want to go with me?" Cassie looked into Jack's eyes.

"There's not a rehearsal today, but I can't guarantee you that Liza won't be here today."

Jack appreciated her concern, but shook his head no. "I promised Colleen that I would help her with the wall, so I need to talk to her and get an idea of what she wants."

Cassie smiled. "You know, Colleen has a bit of a crush on you."

Jack grinned. "Yeah, I think I figured that out when I renovated the theater. I just hope that Kevin doesn't attack me with a baseball bat when I'm not looking."

Cassie leaned in to brush her lips against his. "I think you're pretty safe from Kevin. He told me once that a crush was no fun, unless you could tease your spouse about it."

Jack put his arm around Cassie's waist and pulled her closer to him. "Kevin will be happy to know that his wife is safe with me."

He leaned in and smelled her hair. "Besides, I think I have my own crush."

After they pulled into the parking lot, Cassie took a quick look around for Liza's car and didn't see it. She let out a silent breath of relief. Cassie found Jack's willingness to help Kevin and Colleen, even knowing that there was a risk of running into Liza, very admirable, but her first priority was Jack and she didn't want Jack put into an uncomfortable position.

On the drive over, Cassie had contemplated asking Jack to attend opening night with her. It was an event that she usually attended and she always looked forward to it. But she knew in her heart, that as much as she would like to attend with him, how could she possibly ask the man that she was in love with to endure watching his ex-wife's best friend, especially under the circumstances of their divorce? So she'd made up her mind and she wasn't going to invite him. Jack was incredibly giving and he would want to do it for her, but it would be so unfair of her to ask him.

Jack loaded the boxes onto the dolly and they walked towards the theater. Cassie looked over at Jack. "I can't believe how fast time is flying. The project at Cassie's Closet will be done in a matter of weeks, the play is almost here and next month is Thanksgiving."

Jack nodded in agreement. "Will Brett be coming home for Thanksgiving?"

Cassie's smile grew as she looked at Jack. "He will be home then and I'm so excited. This is the longest time that I've ever gone without seeing him."

Jack stopped walking and looked at Cassie. "I would like to meet Brett," he paused, "if that's okay with you."

Cassie was delighted at the thought of the two men she loved so much meeting each other. "I would love for you to meet my son." She had already planned to ask Jack to come and join them for Thanksgiving dinner. Even though Thanksgiving was right around the corner, for now she was dealing with the construction issue at work and the play was going to have its opening night in two weeks.

Jack smiled and started walking again. He'd thought about meeting Brett and he felt good about it. Although not too proud of it, he remembered that in the past, he'd been a little envious when someone would talk about their child. Recently it hit him that not only was he ready to meet Brett, he was eager to meet Cassie's son, to know the guy behind the stories and learn more about the young man that held a huge piece of Cassie's heart. He would not and could not begrudge Cassie's love for her son.

Colleen must have seen them coming, as the back door opened quickly. Colleen reached over and hugged Cassie and then looked at Jack with accusation in her eyes. "I've heard the rumors that you have found another. Now seeing the two of you together, it must be true."

Jack laughed and leaned in close to Colleen. "Shhh, Cassie must never know about us."

Cassie put her hands on her hips and feigned annoyance. "Hey, I can hear you two!"

They all laughed as they entered the storage room and Colleen pointed Jack in the direction of the dressing room. After he unloaded the boxes, Colleen put her arm through Jack's and told Cassie that she was taking him away from her. Cassie knew they were headed in the direction of the stage and Colleen would have him to work in no time.

Cassie started unloading the boxes and put a name tag on each costume for the character who was supposed to wear it. She hung up each piece and got the steamer warming up so that the items could be steamed before the final fitting. Then she looked through the accessory boxes and matched everything that she could. She'd been working for about hour when she got hot and a little dizzy. She decided that she needed to get some air.

When she was outside, with a bottle of water in hand, she started to feel better. Abby pulled up and walked towards her. She looked exhausted.

"I'm surprised to see you here." Cassie had talked to her on the phone the day before and knew that another delivery was happening soon, as Abby was heading over to the expectant's mother house.

"I'm exhausted. It was another all-nighter." Then she looked at Cassie. "You look kind of wiped out too. Are you okay?"

"I'm okay. I was just steaming all the costumes. I got hot and felt a little dizzy." She held up the water bottle. "A little water and fresh air is doing the trick. I'm feeling better now."

Abby leaned up against the same building that was holding Cassie up. "I'm not staying long. Kevin asked me to work my magic with the glue gun and add some sequins to the high heels."

Cassie added. "I can help you with that, so you can get out of here faster."

Abby shook her head no. "I appreciate it, but I'm just going to grab them and take them home. I'll take care of the sequins after I wake up."

Abby looked around and didn't see Cassie's car. "Do you need a ride home?"

"No. I'm here with Jack. He's helping Colleen with the moveable wall for the stage."

Abby brightened up a little bit. "Oh, good! I'll take a swing by the stage and get a closer look at him."

With her saying that, Cassie was reminded that Abby hadn't met Jack yet. "I totally forgot that. Come on, I'll introduce you."

As if on command, Jack walked out the back door and was headed for his truck when he spotted Cassie and Abby. Cassie signaled him over and made the introductions. They both said that they were happy to meet each other and chatted easily for a few minutes. Then Jack excused himself and walked towards the truck. Abby looked over to Cassie and silently mouthed "oh my God, he's gorgeous!" As Cassie chuckled, Abby retreated inside to get the shoes.

On his way back, Jack stopped in front of Cassie. He sat his tools down briefly and leaned down and gave her a kiss.

"Are you okay?" Cassie told him the same story that she had Abby. "Then Abby showed up, so I was talking to her."

"Abby is your best friend that you've told me about, that did so much to help you raise Brett."

"One and the same." Cassie said with adoration.

"She seems nice."

Jack leaned over towards Cassie and gave her another kiss. He didn't know why he needed to kiss her so much. He couldn't seem to stop himself. He'd never considered himself particularly affectionate with women, but with Cassie, he literally felt like he was running low on energy if his lips didn't touch hers every hour or so.

Cassie returned the kiss. "We better get in there and finish up our work."

Jack sighed. "I suppose you're right." But then Cassie lightened his spirits. "When we're done here, the rest of the night is ours." Jack's eyes brightened. "Now you're talking."

This time it was Cassie who swatted his butt lightly and they both walked back in.

Liza sat in her car and watched Jack and Cassie together. She had pulled up while Abby was there and no one seemed to notice her. She thought about getting out of her car and making her presence known, but decided against it. Something told her that she needed to stay there, be quiet and watch. She was glad she did, as she was able to witness Jack kissing Cassie and Cassie's affectionate swat on his butt.

She pondered the situation for several minutes. This was a startling bit of news and she wasn't happy about it. She didn't think that Jack was seeing anyone. She was surprised that it was Cassie too. Personally, she considered Cassie so blah and she couldn't imagine what Jack saw in her, especially after being with someone as vibrant and sexy as Stacey.

During her weekend stay with Stacey in San Francisco, they had planned out the whole scenario for Stacey's return. Since that weekend, Liza had become more and more excited. Having Stacey back here was the answer to all her prayers. There was absolutely no one that she trusted more than Stacey.

Liza was still fully aware that she would not risk Tom finding out about any indiscretion, but after spending time with a few men friends in San Francisco, Liza was reminded just how desperately she missed that part of her life. She needed to find a safe way to make it a part of her life again and Stacey was the only tool that could help her with that.

Liza stared at the back wall of the theater. Would Jack dating Cassie change their plans? She thought long and hard about it. She considered it from all angles and then came to the conclusion that nothing would change. She didn't even think she'd tell Stacey about Jack seeing someone. There was no point in Stacey losing confidence or making her believe that there had to be a change in their plans.

After all, it wouldn't matter. Once Jack discovered that Stacey was back in town, he'd fall head over heels in love with Stacey all over again. In fact, Liza reassured herself, he was probably still in love with Stacey. Stacey was certainly younger and sexier that Cassie. Besides, Liza reminded herself, she couldn't let herself forget about Charlie. He was their ace in the hole. The bottom line was that all Stacey needed to do was tell Jack that she wanted them to be a family again. Cassie would be out of the picture instantly and their plan would remain in place!

Completely satisfied with where her analysis took her, Liza turned the key in the ignition and the engine silently purred. She wasn't going to go into the theater after all. There was no point in Jack seeing her today. She was just going to let the whole scene play out, just the way she and Stacey had planned it.

Chapter Twenty-Six

Cassie was so nervous. She had butterflies in her stomach. She and Jack were about to arrive at his parents' house. This is the first time that she would be meeting them and she desperately wanted them to like her.

Cassie recalled the conversation with Jack a few evenings ago. When they were at Cassie's house, Jack built a fire in the fireplace while they were watching a movie on DVD. After it was over, they were both very relaxed and enjoying the dancing colors of the flames in the fire.

"Cassie, would you like to come with me to my parents' house for brunch this Sunday?"

Cassie looked up at Jack, both surprised and delighted at his suggestion. "I would love too." Cassie knew in her heart, that like any man, at any age, when they asked you to meet their parents, it's an important step. It was telling about the status of their relationship and Cassie's heart leaped in her chest.

Jack pulled her closer to him. "Good. They're looking forward to meeting you," Jack paused, "besides I want them to meet you before opening night of the play." Opening night was a week away.

Cassie's head quickly turned towards Jack. "Your parents will be at the play?"

Jack nodded yes. "They're big fans of local theater, even more so now, knowing how involved you are." Cassie was genuinely touched.

"I think it would be awkward for me to introduce you to them there."

Again Cassie's head turned quickly towards Jack. She hadn't even mentioned him attending the play with her.

"You'll be there too?" Jack said yes and Cassie shook her head no. Jack teased her. "What? You don't want me there?"

"Jack, you are so sweet to want to go with me, but what about Liza? I can't imagine how it would make you feel to watch her on stage."

Jack had thought about it for days before he volunteered to go. He'd gone back and forth in his head about whether or not he could actually attend any play that Liza starred in. Finally, he knew his answer.

"Cassie, what I feel about you is far more important than what I think about Liza." Jack continued to gather his thoughts for a moment before continuing. "I'd be lying if I said it will be easy to watch her on stage, but I want to be there with *you*." Besides, Jack sensed that it was time to face certain demons from his past.

Cassie jumped up, turned herself around and sat on Jack's lap and smothered his face with kisses. When she was done, Jack chuckled. "However," he teased, "you'll need to resume this position, and possibly others, as soon as the play is over." Cassie happily agreed.

Now as they pulled up in front of Jack's parents' house. Cassie let out a slow breath. She looked at the bouquet of flowers she had picked up for his Mom and readied herself to go in.

Jack leaned over and whispered, "Remember that my Mom is just as nervous as you are. It will be okay."

Jack opened her car door and led her towards the back gate that led into the backyard. "We'll go in this way. My Mom wanted to do brunch in the backyard today, since this will probably be the last nice weekend we have weather wise for a while."

As they walked through the backyard and around the corner, Cassie could see the lovely yard with autumn flowers growing along the border and a small, but very green vegetable garden in the corner. A beautiful redwood deck extended out onto the yard and a large table with several chairs sat in the center of the deck. Several people were either casually seated or standing around talking. Cassie recognized Jon and he smiled at her.

Jack's parent's approached them. "Cassie, I'd like you to meet my parents. This is my Dad, Will, and my Mom, Barbara."

Cassie could see Jack's strong resemblance to Jack's father. Will, too, had dark hair, or at least he did when he was younger. Now it had more gray than dark, but he had Jack's same dark, shining eyes and soft smile.

He was the first one to speak. "I'm so happy to meet you. My, but you are a pretty one." Cassie smiled. Now she knew where Jon got his flirtatious streak from.

It was Barbara's turn to speak. She leaned towards Cassie. "We hug in this family." Cassie leaned in for Barbara's hug. The butterflies left both their stomachs. "We're so happy that you're joining us today."

Cassie couldn't possibly know how eager Jack's parents were to have Jack finally meet someone special enough that he wanted them to meet her. During the last two years, they often wondered if Jack would ever forgive himself for the mistake he made in choosing Stacey, and then, more importantly, letting himself open his heart to the mere possibility of letting someone else in.

"I'm happy to be here too. Thank you for having me over for brunch today." Cassie handed Barbara the flowers.

Barbara beamed. "Look at these, Will. Aren't they beautiful? Thank you, Cassie. I'm going to go put them in a vase right now and they'll be a beautiful centerpiece for our table today."

As Barbara did that, Jack took Cassie's hand and headed towards Jon. He embraced her with a welcoming hug. "Nice to see you again, good lookin'."

Cassie smiled at the compliment. "Hi Jon, it's nice to see you again too. Jack wasn't sure if you would be on duty and could make it today."

Little did she know, but absent a hostage situation, Barbara had absolutely demanded that he be present today, although Jon didn't object to her demand. It was rare that she demanded anything, so when she did, all of the Shaw men took it to heart. It was no secret that Barbara wanted the immediate family all present for today's brunch. After all, it wasn't every day that Jack brought someone home to meet them.

Jon grinned at her. "I wouldn't miss a brunch if you're going to be here." Cassie truly enjoyed his good natured friendliness.

Jack gently took her elbow and guided her towards his brother Jeremy. Jeremy leaned over and gave her a quick hug. "It's nice to see you again, Cassie."

Cassie had met him once, briefly, when she was signing the contract for the remodeling at Cassie's Closet. "You too, Jeremy."

Jeremy was very similar in looks to Jack and Jon, but he was lighter colored, with light brown hair and milk chocolate colored eyes instead of Will and Jack's dark, almost black-colored eyes.

Cassie could sense just the tiniest bit of sadness in Jeremy's eyes, but it was probably because Jack had told her that Jeremy's girlfriend of six months had recently left him. Jeremy wasn't one to get serious too often, so he was disappointed and struggling to get over the break-up. Cassie thought to herself that he was so good looking and if he was as loving and attentive as his older brother, then he'd find another woman in no time at all.

Barbara returned from the kitchen with the vase of flowers in her hands, which she immediately put in the middle of the table. They really did look beautiful.

"Barbara, is there anything I can do to help you?"

"No, thank you. I have everything taken care of. Will, did you get Cassie a drink?"

Will had been so busy watching Jack and Cassie's interactions together that he forgot his manners. Barbara knew immediately what he had been doing and smiled her okay to him.

Will stood at attention close to Cassie. "Cassie, dear, what can I get you to drink? We have coffee, hot tea, iced tea or water."

"Iced tea would be great, thank you."

As drinks were served, they all stood around and talked about the project at Cassie's Closet.

Barbara jumped in. "I like your store very much. I've been there several times."

"Jack mentioned that. I'm so glad that you like it. I'm very lucky to be able to own such a unique store. I enjoy going to work every day." Cassie looked briefly into each person's eyes as she continued talking about Cassie's Closet.

"I have very loyal customers, but I also get a lot of visitors from surrounding cities and they are starting to come back more and more often. I can't believe how much it's grown in the last ten years."

Will asked when she bought it and Cassie told them about her history with the store; how she had worked there for many years for the O'Connell's and when it was time for them to retire, they had offered it to her.

As they all talked, Barbara watched Jack with Cassie. Jack kept his hand on the small of Cassie's back and he looked at her tenderly and often. Cassie's eyes diverted towards Jack's eyes often too. Whenever Jack smiled and looked at Cassie fondly, Barbara's heart did a double beat! Her son had almost been destroyed by that evil woman, Stacey. It was unforgiveable what she had done to Jack; to all of them, but now Jack was standing here with a beautiful, delightful woman and Barbara was beyond thrilled.

Finally, it was time for brunch to be served and they all sat at the table. "Barbara, the frittata smells and looks delicious."

Barbara sighed in relief at Cassie's compliment. She had agonized over what to serve for brunch. Will had tormented her terribly. "Barb, the President isn't coming over." Barbara shushed him. "I know that, but someone *even more important* is coming over, our son's new girlfriend!"

Through brunch they all chatted easily. Jack, Jeremy and Jon had Cassie in stitches laughing over all their antics growing up. Barbara and Will joined in often with their own stories about raising three boys, the emergency room visits, calls from the school principal and an occasional call from a neighbor complaining about one or all of the boys. Barbara pointed to her gray hair. "See these," then she pointed to each son, "each and every one is because of all of you."

After brunch was consumed and they rubbed their full stomachs, they all continued to sit around the table and talk. It was so nice for Cassie to hear all of them share with each other about their week or listen to their bets about who was going to win the World Series. As she looked from person to person, she could tell what a wonderful family Jack had. It was more than obvious that they all loved each other dearly. There weren't a lot of families that continued to live in the same community as their parents and be willing to spend most Sundays with them. Cassie hoped that was something that Brett would consider when he was older. Would Jack still be in her life then? She glanced over to him as he sat by her side. She certainly hoped so.

When it was time to clean up, Barbara finally agreed to let Cassie help her. It would be a chance for just the two of them to talk without all the men around. As they were loading the dishwasher, both of them could see out the kitchen window. All the Shaw men were huddled around each other, talking and laughing. As Barbara's eyes landed on Jack, she felt a lump form in her throat. The light had been turned back on in her oldest son's eyes and he was laughing again. She couldn't be happier at this moment.

Barbara could see Cassie smiling as she looked out the window too. It was hard not to watch them together and not see what a good time they were having.

"Jack tells me that you have a boy too, that's in college."

Cassie smiled at the mention of Brett. "I do. His name is Brett." Barbara could hear the pride in her voice about her son with just those few words.

"What is Brett like?"

"Brett is a great kid," then she reconsidered, "I guess I shouldn't call him a kid anymore. He's away at college and living on his own, but it's hard for me to believe that sometimes. It's much easier to remember him as a little boy."

Barbara nodded in complete understanding. "Even with my boys as old as they are, to me, they will always be my kids and I think I'll always worry about them."

"That's true. I don't think I'll ever stop worrying about Brett. It was just the two of us for so long. Even before Brett's dad and I divorced, Brett's dad's work kept him away most of the time, so we just had this pattern of how we did things and it was mostly the two of us."

Barbara was listening closely. "How long ago did the two of you divorce?"

"More than ten years ago. It was around the time that the O'Connell's wanted to retire and they offered the store to me. It was a lifesaver for me in so many ways." Cassie paused to remember that time. "Not only did it give me something to do and think about every day while I was going through the divorce, but it gave me some financial security for Brett."

Barbara patted Cassie on the hand, but just let her speak. "I was very young when I got pregnant, still in high school." Cassie looked into Barbara's eyes and saw no judgment there. "So I didn't have any real skills except for being a Mom. The O'Connell's gave me such a gift when they entrusted their store to me."

This time it was Barbara's turn to speak. "You should be proud of yourself. You are obviously a caring and loving mother. Unfortunately there are some women out there that don't care about what's best for their child, or who are willing to work as hard as you did, to give them what they need." The thought of Stacey flashed through Barbara's mind as she spoke.

Cassie was genuinely touched by what Barbara had to say to her, not only because she was Jack's mom, but because she was a mother and she understood just how hard it is to take care of all of your kid's needs. To sense that Barbara respected her was very satisfying.

"I'm so happy that I was able to meet you and the rest of your family. I can see now why Jack is the kind of man that he is."

Barbara was touched by Cassie's comment. Cassie could see how special Jack was and that's what Barbara had always wanted for him. Jack needed someone who honored him with all the love and respect he craved. Barbara could see that love for Jack in Cassie's eyes whenever she looked at him. Barbara knew their relationship was in its early stages, but she wasn't concerned. She could see that Cassie wasn't immature like Stacey. She correctly assumed that Cassie wouldn't enter into a relationship casually. It would have to mean something to her. By the way she looked at Jack, he mattered to her.

"Barbara, can I use your restroom?"

"Of course, it's down the hall, the first door on the right."

After Cassie finished up in the restroom, she walked down the hall towards the kitchen and noticed a wall full of pictures. There were pictures of Will and Barbara on their wedding day, pictures of the boys at different times through elementary school and high school, Jon's police academy graduation photo and Jack in a tool belt when he was about six-years old. Cassie slowly looked at the pictures and smiled at the devilish looks on the boys' faces, the rumpled hair and obvious scratches or dirt smears. One of them even had stitches on his eyebrow in one school photo.

Towards the end of the hall, Cassie noticed a more recent picture. It was of Will, Jeremy, Jon, Jack and a sweet-faced toddler that was about two-years old. The toddler had the cutest speckling of freckles across the bridge of his nose and he had a smile as big as the sun. Jack was holding the toddlers' hand and they were all standing up in a boat, holding a fish that one of them had caught. Barbara entered the hallway and saw Cassie looking at the pictures.

"Barbara, this is the sweetest collection of pictures of the Shaw boys. You're wedding picture is so lovely too." Barbara smiled and thanked her.

Cassie commented on several other pictures and then moved back towards the picture of all the men and the toddler in the boat. "Who is the cute little toddler in this picture?" Barbara's breath caught in her chest and no words would come out.

After a silent moment passed, Cassie became aware that Jack had appeared in the hallway. He walked towards the picture and looked at it for a brief moment, before turning towards Cassie and saying softly, "that's my son."

Chapter Twenty-Seven

Jack and Cassie were silent on the drive home. Cassie's mind was reeling. Jack had a son! There is no way that the man she had come to know and love would ever give up complete custody of a child to his ex-wife. Did they move out of state? Had the little boy died? Her heart felt heavy at the thought of it.

Cassie glanced over at Jack and his face was drawn and he was deep in thought. He didn't look angry, but he was clearly reliving something in his mind.

Finally they pulled up in front of a house. Cassie assumed that it must be Jack's house. She'd never been to his home before; he'd only spent the night at her house and he always picked her up there or at Cassie's Closet.

Once in the house, Cassie looked around. It was neat and clean, but Cassie noticed right away that it lacked warmth. There were no pictures hanging up, no soft pillows on the couch for a nap, no books, DVD's or any sign that one could seek comfort here. It was obvious that it met his basic needs for eating, showering and a bed to sleep in after work and that was it.

Jack pointed to the couch and asked Cassie if she'd like to sit down. He looked towards the kitchen. "Do you want something to drink?"

"No, thank you."

Jack was still standing and stood near the arm of the couch. He looked over at Cassie.

After another moment, he began. "Remember that I told you that there were things about my divorce that I wanted to tell you when the time was right?" Cassie eyes told him yes.

Jack took in a deep breath. "I don't even know where to start." He rubbed his hands through his hair. "At the beginning, I guess."

Cassie waited patiently while Jack gathered his thoughts. "I waited a long time to get married. When I was in my twenties, it didn't feel so urgent. I enjoyed being a single guy, but as I got into my thirties and then mid-thirties, I realized that I wanted to meet someone that I could settle down with and maybe even have a kid or two."

He paused. "I wanted what my parents have." Cassie could understand that. She'd always wanted that herself.

"When I met Stacey, she said she wanted all the same things that I did. It seemed like she was crazy about me, and I admit that I fell for her pretty quickly." Jack shook his head as if to shake off the memories.

"We had a super short courtship, but even before we got married, I can see now that I chose to ignore her self-centeredness. Obviously, I feel so angry at myself now, but I didn't want to see that she was very self-involved and immature."

Jack continued to explain. "There was close to a fifteen year age difference between us, but Stacey quickly reassured me how much she wanted a life with me. On her promise, I let myself believe that once we got married, we would just settle into this nice, happy life."

Jack looked at Cassie, but then sunk back into his memories. "We got married at City Hall about a month after meeting. Within weeks, we found out that she was pregnant. We thought it was a 'honeymoon baby.' I was overjoyed. Stacey, on the other hand wasn't so overjoyed. She hated being pregnant. She was sick all the time and she definitely hated gaining weight. I tried to do what I could to make her comfortable, but I don't think anything I did made her feel any better. She absolutely could not wait to have the baby, so that she wouldn't be pregnant anymore. She swore a thousand times that she would never, ever get pregnant again." Jack's eyes were downcast at the memories.

Cassie quickly thought back to her own pregnancy. She, too, was so young, but she loved being pregnant. She would sit on the couch and watch as Brett moved inside her and wonder what he would look like and how it would feel to hold him. She would sing to him in her belly and make up silly stories that she would tell him before she went to sleep at night. She'd spend hours in his nursery and imagine him sleeping in his crib or rocking him to sleep with the sounds of the lullabies playing softly next to him.

Cassie was pulled back from her memories as Jack began to talk again. "Finally, the baby was born." Cassie could see the pride reflected on Jack's face, as he remembered his son's birth.

"Stacey didn't care what we named him, and I liked Charlie. Besides my Dad's middle name is Charles and it's also my Mom's maiden name. I thought it would be nice for Charlie to be connected to his grandparents like that." Cassie nodded in agreement. Family connections were important, which is why Brett's middle name was the same as her own father.

Jack had a faraway look in his eyes and then he smiled. "When Charlie was born, it was the happiest day of my life. I looked at him and I didn't think it was possible to love someone so much."

Cassie's eyes filled with tears at Jack's expression of love. "But I was so wrong, Cassie because I grew to love Charlie more and more every day. I had never known I could love like that." Jack's voice choked. "I was so honored that this precious little boy was mine and that I was his father."

Cassie could not only see the love and affection for Charlie in Jack's eyes, but she could feel it from every pore in his body. She so desperately wanted to stand up and hold him, but she knew he needed to tell her his story, in his way, so she sat patiently and listened to every word he said.

"I thought that after Stacey wasn't pregnant any more, that she would be happy to be a mother." Again Jack slowly combed his fingers through her hair. "I was wrong again. Stacey wasn't happy being a mom at all. Within two or three months of Charlie's birth, she'd had enough of staying home and she wanted to be gone all the time. Even if she wasn't gone, she was on the phone or surfing the web, shopping or playing games on the computer."

Jack waited a minute and collected his thoughts. "I can't tell you how many days I'd come home from work, and my Mom would be watching Charlie, because Stacey needed to go out."

Jack looked over to Cassie. "As you probably guessed, she was usually out with Liza." He shook his head slowly from side to side at the memory.

"She always had some lame excuse. She needed girlfriend time or time at the mall, or that Charlie was such a handful, she needed a break." Jack looked over at Cassie, "My mom had a good idea of what was going on. Remember I told you that she even confronted me about it later on?" Jack didn't wait for Cassie's answer.

"Like me, my Mom was hoping that Stacey would come around and realize what an incredible baby Charlie was. I think we all naively thought it was some kind of post-partum blues that Stacey was experiencing."

Jack thought back to those days. "I was worried about it and even read articles on the internet that some Mom's don't feel an instant bond with the baby and it makes them feel inadequate, so I did everything I could think of to make her happy, to make her want to be home more, to want to be with Charlie."

He sighed. "Nothing worked."

Jack then told her about the men, the rumors and admitted his own denial of what Stacey was doing.

Jack was silent for several minutes before he continued. "I was the exact opposite of Stacey. I loved spending every second with Charlie and

I couldn't get enough of it." His voice caught again, "there wasn't anything that I didn't like to do with him. It didn't matter if we were playing with his toys, out in the yard, coloring, playing with stuffed animals, bouncing balls or watching cartoons."

Jack looked at Cassie and his eyes were rimmed with tears. "Some of my favorite memories are on Saturday mornings, just us guys." Jack's mind went back to those days. "When Charlie would wake up, I'd get him out of his toddler bed and we'd come right here, into the living room." Jack pointed to the spot where Cassie sat.

"I'd let Stacey sleep, but Charlie and I would lay on the couch, all covered up with blankets. Charlie usually sat on my chest and I'd turn on cartoons."

Jack's mind drifted back to those mornings. "Charlie would hide under the blanket. I would pat my hands all over it and pretend to search for him." Jack eyes glistened with tears at the memory.

"I would tease him and ask 'where's my Charlie boy? He was just here. Where did he go?' Pretty soon, Charlie would climb out from under the blankets and get right in my face. 'I here Daddy!' Then he'd be back under the blankets and the game would begin again."

Cassie could visualize it all so easily; the freckled nose of the toddler, still wearing his sleeper pajamas and popping his head out with giggles and hugs, before hiding from his dad again.

"I hated what Stacey was doing to me and even more so to Charlie, but I just couldn't face a divorce yet. Trust me, by then, I wanted a divorce, but I was also scared to death, not for me, but for Charlie."

Jack looked directly into Cassie's eyes. "If we got a divorce, I knew that Stacey would want Charlie." Cassie looked at Jack in surprise and he elaborated. "It certainly wasn't out of any desire to be with Charlie, but it would be to spite me because she knew that I loved him so much and that I worried about him so." A small tremor traveled down Jack's spine as he remembered the cold and callous side of Stacey.

Jack looked into Cassie's caring eyes. "With good reason, I was genuinely scared that she wouldn't take care of him properly. Obviously she never physically hurt him, but she was so lax about most of his needs. At first, I'd come home and ask her what Charlie had for lunch and she'd say a banana or a teething biscuit and that would be all he would have had all day. It got to the point where I came home every day early in the afternoon to make sure he had been fed, that he had on a dry diaper and that he was okay."

Jack took in a deep breath. "I had a plan. I was just trying to hold on the best I could, at least until Charlie started kindergarten. That way, I knew he'd be in school several hours a day and I wouldn't worry about him being with Stacey so much of the time. After school was out, I knew I could adjust my work hours to finish by the time Charlie got out of school. That was the only thing that made sense to me at the time."

The anger was rising in Cassie about Stacey's lack of responsibility for her child's most basic needs. How could she! Cassie just didn't understand. Babies and toddlers are so little and sweet and they rely on you completely, but in the most wonderful way. How could Stacey not care for him properly? She thought of Brett as a toddler and remembered that she got so much in return when she did all those things for Brett. She'd laugh herself silly over Cheerios in his hair and they'd play for hours together, oftentimes until they were both exhausted and napped together, side by side. She wouldn't trade those moments for anything in the world. How could a mother want to miss out on so much with their child?

Cassie's heart bled for Jack. She remembered feeling like she needed to compensate Brett for his dad's absence so much of the time. As if reading her mind, Jack said to her, "I was trying so hard to give Charlie everything he needed." He looked at Cassie. "You know how hard it can be, but I thought it was working. Charlie was such a happy little guy and we laughed together every single day and just enjoyed being together.

Honestly, I felt like the luckiest man in the world to have Charlie as my son."

Cassie could see that Jack looked exhausted and terribly sad. He was now sitting on the arm of the couch and he looked at the front door. Intuitively Cassie knew that another important part of the story was coming.

Jack began. "I had a big job that I needed to do, which would keep me away from home for a few days. I had talked to Stacey about it and she swore she would stay home. My parents were going out of town to visit friends, so I was doubly worried that Stacey wouldn't have my Mom as a back-up."

Jack looked over towards his front door. "I was worried about Charlie, for all the usual reasons, but we'd celebrated his second birthday a few weeks before that and he must have caught a cold from one of the kids at the party, so he wasn't feeling a hundred percent. It made it even harder to leave for the job, but I knew I needed to go. I'd delayed that project for far too long. Stacey reassured me and told me to call her on her cell phone anytime and I could talk to Charlie. She seemed eager for me to go and I stupidly thought she might enjoy having some time with Charlie."

"I called a couple of times. Stacey was always in a rush, but she'd put Charlie on the phone and I asked him how he was feeling and he told me 'all better daddy!'"

Cassie could see the anger rise in Jack and he was on his feet again, pacing in front of the fireplace. "You know, when I looked back afterwards, I remembered Charlie talking about riding in a truck, but I thought that he was talking about going for a ride in *my* truck because he loved to go for rides with me." Jack shook his head in disgust. "It was much later when I figured out that he must be riding in a moving truck."

Cassie interjected. "There's no way you could have known that. No rational person would ever even consider that."

Jack agreed with her now, but in the days following Stacey's departure, he tortured himself with doubt.

"When I left for the work project, Charlie was standing at the door and blowing kisses to me. I was pretending to catch them and I put them in my pocket."

Lost in thought, Jack paused, "I pulled out of the driveway and that's the last time I saw Charlie." Jack shuddered at the memory, his face pale and laced with pain. The knot in Cassie's stomach tightened.

"When I returned home and saw that they were gone, I tried to call and Stacey's number had been disconnected." Jack shook his head in disgust. "I had talked to Charlie just the day before on the phone, but it all changed overnight."

Cassie raised her hand to her heart. "Oh no, Jack, no." Cassie recalled once when Brett was about four years-old and she had taken him to an amusement park. He went to the top of a four-sided slide and he didn't come down the slide he said he was going to. Cassie ran to the end of each of the other slides and he wasn't there. As her panic grew, she thought her heart would beat out of her chest. When she called for Brett and he didn't answer, there was such a fierce sense of urgency inside her to find him that she was almost paralyzed with fear. Suddenly, out of the corner of her eye, she spotted his bright blue shirt a hundred yards away. She went running towards him. When she got to him, she was hugging him, crying and yelling at him to never leave without her again. She would pull him into a tight hug and then hold him outstretched in her arms, as if making sure she was really holding her son.

The scene at the amusement park had given her nightmares for several nights afterward. It was the most horrible feeling to think that your child was gone. She found her son within minutes, but Jack still hadn't found the child that he loved so much. Now it was her turn to shudder at the thought.

Jack shook his head in disgust. "I told you that when Stacey left, she took everything." Jack was angry and frustrated and clinched his fists. "I didn't give a crap about anything in this house," he pounded his fist on the mantel, "except Charlie. She could have had it all and I would have never cared. I just wanted Charlie with me and to know he was cared for and loved."

Cassie sat there in stunned silence with her hand on her heart. How could Stacey do that? It was unforgivable. When she was angriest with Peter, she never considered for a minute taking Brett away from him. Peter was his father. What kind of woman could do that to her child or their father?

Jack had returned to the arm of the couch and sat still for several minutes, with his head bowed down into his hands. Cassie rubbed his back, but he probably wasn't aware of it. She could tell he was deep in thought. He finally sat up and turned towards her to and looked deeply in her eyes.

He spoke softly and his voice caught several times. "The worst part, besides losing Charlie, was when Stacey left. She left me a note on the kitchen counter saying that she'd left to be with the love of her life, *Charlie's father*." Cassie's eyes darted from side to side and then back to Jack. She didn't understand. Jack was Charlie's father!

"Jack, I don't understand."

Jack shook his head too, still confused after two years. "Along with the note, she left the results of a DNA test, which said that the likelihood of me being Charlie's dad was less than one percent. I don't know if she took a hair sample or a cheek swab while I was sleeping or what. I don't even know if the sample was really from my body." Jack shook his head from side to side. "I just don't know."

Cassie was in shock and trying to take it all in.

"I went every place that I could think of to try and find them, I filed a police report, I put Charlie's picture on the National Center for Missing and Exploited Children, I did everything that could legally be done through the courts, but he was gone. Vanished! I looked every day. I'd go to the library and scour newspapers for articles to see if there was anything about a young boy left home alone or unidentified accident victims." Remembering all he did, Jack stared off into space for a while.

"I was desperate to find him. I was in constant contact with Jon, who was using every resource he had at the Sheriff's office. Charlie was too little to go to school, so I couldn't check school registrations. I ran out of places to check. Everywhere I looked, it turned into a dead end."

Cassie stood up, facing Jack. She put both of her arms on his shoulder.

"Do you believe Stacey that you're not Charlie's biological father?"

Jack had asked himself that question no less than a thousand times since Stacey left with Charlie. "I just don't know for sure. It torments me, Cassie. We married so quickly after meeting each other. She could have been with someone else right before me. I thought we were together most of the time when we met, but I still had to go to work during the day. Now that I know the type of person she is, she could have easily been cheating then too while I was at work." Jack's shoulders slumped a little bit. "I think she was just using me."

Jack stood up and started pacing. "I'm so confused by it all. I don't have any clear answers and now I don't know if I'll ever have any answers."

Then he turned and looked at Cassie and with complete and total honesty, he told her, "I wouldn't have cared if Charlie was my biological son, if she would have told me the truth. I was crazy in love with that little boy and I would have adopted him in a heartbeat. Stacey didn't want him. I did," he paused, "I still do."

Jack remembered Cassie's question of 'do you believe Stacey?' "Charlie could be my biological son. I could be wrong, very wrong because Stacey could have easily been with someone else before me that got her pregnant and they reunited. Up until she left, I never had a reason to question that I wasn't his dad. Stacey never let on once of anyone else being Charlie's father; not during a fight, not ever."

Jack's shoulders drooped. "Maybe what I want to believe isn't the truth after all. I may never know the truth and that torments me."

The tears were running down Cassie's checks and she pulled Jack closer towards her. Cassie stroked his cheek with her hand. Then she held his chin in her fingers and lifted his bowed face until their eyes met. The tears still clung to her wet cheeks. She was absolutely heartbroken that the man she was in love with had been so betrayed, so hurt and was still in so much pain. Even in all that pain, it reminded her just how deeply she had fallen in love with him. She shared his pain now. He hurt, therefore, she hurt with him.

Jack pulled Cassie tightly to him. He allowed himself to feel her warmth, to feel the gentle strokes of her hand on his cheek and to listen to her heart beating against his. He softly choked out the words that had been in his throat for over two years now.

"I miss my Charlie. I just miss him so much." Finally willing to let his emotions escape, to let the pain and the loss out, to share it completely with Cassie, Jack released the pain that had been building inside him since the day he tucked Charlie's pretend kisses into his pocket and waved goodbye.

Chapter Twenty-Eight

It was opening night of "Dig It, Dudley" and the entire cast, crew and all volunteers were all on deck. Colleen and Kevin had been at the theater since about nine o'clock that morning and everyone else had arrived in the afternoon. Showtime was at eight o'clock; now a mere hour away. Cassie was no exception. She'd arrived earlier in the afternoon. Colleen told her that she didn't need to arrive so early, as she knew that construction was nearing the end at Cassie's Closet and Cassie needed to be there.

Colleen also now knew the story of Jack and her heart had broken into a million pieces when Cassie told her and Abby about his history with Stacey and about losing his child, or at least the little one that he considered to be his child, so unexpectedly.

Cassie had Jack's okay to share his story. He was never opposed to her telling the people she was closest too, but it was too hard of a story for him to tell casually or in passing. He trusted Cassie to tell his story in the way he would have told it.

Normally, Colleen always tried to look at the bright side of things, but as Cassie told her about what happened to Jack, she found the tears silently rolling down her cheeks. It was difficult to find any kind of silver lining to Jack's loss.

Colleen had promised herself that she wouldn't treat Jack any differently. She'd always liked him and now the more she got to know him, she liked him even more. Besides, one of her best friends had fallen in love with him. Colleen knew in her heart that Jack was a good man, otherwise Cassie wouldn't have fallen so hard and so completely for him.

As it turned out, Colleen did run into Jack a few days later at Cassie's Closet and contrary to her promise to herself, she grabbed him in a too-tight hug and didn't let go of him for several seconds. When she finally let go, there was a hint of moisture in her eyes. Jack could tell that she was feeling very emotional about his situation and he genuinely appreciated her affection for him.

When Jack saw the tears that were shimmering in Colleen's eyes, he decided that it was his turn to make light of the moment and make her smile. He leaned down close to her ear and in a low voice whispered, "Cassie isn't looking now. How 'bout we sneak out of here. I hear the blue waters of Aruba calling our name?"

Colleen broke into a huge smile and grabbed him by the elbow and teasingly took two steps towards the door. She stopped and turned to Jack, and bantered back to him with her usual flirtatious jokes.

"Sounds like a plan. I just need to go home, pack my bikini and I'll meet you at the airport later tonight."

Jack grinned. "It's all set then. I'll see you at the airport tonight at midnight and we're off to paradise." He winked at her before walking back to the construction zone.

It had taken a few days after Jack told Cassie about Charlie, but he had finally gotten over the emotional hangover of telling her everything. He was feeling uplifted about sharing it all with her. It was no longer a burden that he carried alone. Cassie stood by his side throughout and held him tightly. There was nothing that she didn't know now.

Now it was days later and Colleen was in the theater office and the clock told her that there wasn't any more time for remembering or lounging. She had a dozen things to do before the show. One of those things was to do her best to make sure that Liza and Cassie were miles apart. She knew that Liza was here. She'd heard her demands through the crew, but, fortunately, Liza wasn't the type to mingle and routinely she stayed in her dressing room before a performance.

Cassie told her that she would be okay being around Liza. Cassie didn't like Liza before and she certainly liked her a lot less now, but as they say in show business, 'the show must go on.' Cassie wasn't going to create any kind of scene on opening night. Besides, she told Colleen, there was no reason for her to even have to be around Liza.

Colleen had checked back stage and briefly talked to the director. There was a chorus of activity, as sets were still being worked on, some of the cast was rehearsing and others helped each other with their stage make-up. Colleen looked around to see if she could see Liza and Cassie. Negative for both, so that was a good thing. She passed Kevin in the hallway. He was walking quickly with the orchestra conductor and they were deep in conversation. As they passed, he quickly leaned over to her, with a brief kiss and a "love you, darling" before continuing down the hall.

Colleen peaked inside the conference room and Cassie was there, talking to someone on the telephone. She signaled to Colleen that she would be hanging up in just a second.

"How's it going? It looks like crazy town out there." Cassie inquired as she hung up the phone.

Colleen took a deep breath. She had a love-hate relationship with Opening Night. She hated all the chaos, the last minute emergencies, all the work that needed to be done, and yet, she absolutely adored Opening Night. When the cast was in place and the audience was full, she always stood on the wing of the stage and watched as the conductor lifted his baton and stayed in that position until he gestured for the curtain to rise. As the music began to swell and the curtain rose, Colleen's breath always caught in her throat as the stage lights brightened and the magic of the performance began.

Colleen threw her hands up in the air in mock exasperation. "You know how it is on Opening Night?"

Cassie nodded. "That I do. So I've finished everything that I needed to do for the costumes. What do you need me to do now?"

Colleen thought that Cassie had already done enough for her, especially after the week she'd had learning about Jack's situation. Colleen knew that Cassie had been exhausted from restless sleep. Cassie told her that when she slept, she dreamed of a freckle-faced little boy running away from her and Jack. She woke up each morning feeling tired and groggy.

"No, you've done enough and I thank you. You look tired, why don't you go freshen up before Jack gets here?"

Cassie smiled. There was still about a half an hour before Jack arrived, so she was willing to do whatever she could to help out Colleen.

"No, it's okay. Jack is going to meet me by the box office a few minutes before show time, so I have some time to spare."

Colleen's eyes popped at the mention of the box office. "Crap! I haven't made it to the box office yet. Would you mind heading up front and find out if there's any problem with ticketing? If there is, call me right away, okay?"

Cassie headed out the door. "No problem, I can wait for Jack there too."

Colleen thanked her and started to leave when she suddenly remembered something.

"Don't forget that Trebbiano's is delivering some appetizers after the show. The cast and crew will be there and Kevin and I want you and Jack to stop by."

Colleen lowered her voice. "I honestly don't think you-know-who will be there. She always leaves with her husband and their friends and they celebrate somewhere much nicer than backstage."

Cassie nodded. Colleen had mentioned the after-party to her before, but she didn't plan on going. It was already so big of Jack to be willing to come to the play tonight when Liza was starring in it; she wasn't going to put him in a position to potentially see her or even risk having him hear how wonderful of a performer Liza was.

Besides not being willing to do that to Jack, she had been so nauseous ever since Jack told her about Charlie. It just broke her heart for Jack, for Charlie, for their loss – just everything. It was too difficult to keep much food down the last few days, not that she had much time to eat with construction ending within days and the play opening tonight.

Cassie stopped by the restroom, ran a comb through her hair, touched up her lips with some gloss and headed out to the box office area. She couldn't help but smile, knowing that she would see Jack soon.

****

Jack finished taking one of the quickest showers of his life. He arrived at his house late and he was running behind. He had been working at Cassie's Closet and the work went on longer than he expected. The project was so close to coming to an end. They had a few days' worth of work to do and another day or two of clean-up. It was bittersweet for him.

On the one hand, he was so proud that he had been able to bring Cassie's vision to life. On the other hand, Jack knew that he would miss seeing Cassie on a daily basis. Jack quickly brushed aside the thought of not starting each day without seeing Cassie blowing softly on her coffee mug or hearing her say softly "good morning, Jack" as he approached her.

Instead of entertaining that depressing thought, Jack let his thoughts drift mindlessly back to the work his crew had done. Cassie's Closet looked amazing and turned out even better than he expected. Jack had a sneaking suspicion that when other large thrift stores discovered how practical and customer-friendly it is to showcase key areas, that more shops would follow suit with similar ideas. He was proud that Cassie's idea would likely shape other stores in the future.

Jack smiled once again at the thought of Cassie. Not only was she beautiful, sweet, kind and sexy, but she was more loving towards him than anyone had ever been to him in his life. Before he told her about Charlie, he had so many worries. Initially, he didn't know how to tell her, how to explain to her how he felt, what the loss did to him, or how it changed him. Could she deal with a man that had been so broken and betrayed by another?

How wrong he'd been to worry. Cassie had been incredible. He'd never cried in front of a woman before, at least not since he was a young boy in front of his own mother. Much less would he let himself feel all his pent-up emotions and share them with someone to the depth he had. She cried with him. It was obvious that she was experiencing his pain, confusion and loss. He was no longer experiencing it alone. After he told her everything, they talked for hours and hours, until they could barely keep their eyes open.

When they woke the next morning, he was worn out emotionally, but he took one look at the woman lying next to him and he needed her desperately. It wasn't the intense urge he usually had when he needed to make love with Cassie. Instead, that morning, he gently woke her up with soft kisses. Most of the time, their lovemaking was powerful, sexy and urgent. It seemed like it was feeding an insatiable hunger that they both had for each other.

However, that morning their lovemaking was quiet, yet soulful and their hunger was only about touch; touching as closely as they could. There was no foreplay, but there didn't need to be that day. His unexplainable need for her had grown simply because she now knew who he was. Cassie's own need for Jack had grown by the intense emotional intimacy they had shared the night before. The comfort they needed to give each other that morning came simply from the sharing of such raw emotion.

Jack remembered how Cassie eyes were still closed as he awakened her with kisses along her throat. Jack pulled himself on top of her and touched his mouth to hers. As her tongue discovered his, she moaned and Jack lost all awareness of anything except that he needed Cassie, more at that moment, than he needed air. As their bodies met each other's tempo, a shared passion spread through their bodies.

Jack was trying so hard to wait until Cassie reached her peak, but it was becoming too difficult. His need was too potent, too strong. Suddenly, he could feel Cassie's approaching climax. Her own hips thrust him deeper into her and she arched her back as the sensations built and rumbled on the edge of her eruption. No longer able to control his own oncoming release, Jack let himself go, and when he did, the two of them simultaneously exploded into each other. Jack collapsed onto her and they held each other more tightly than they ever had, long after the rapid breathing had stopped, long after their heartbeats returned to normal. They just held each other.

At the memory of their lovemaking, Jack smiled to himself and pulled up his pants, zipped them and buttoned up his shirt. When he put his second boot on, his cell phone rang. Without looking, he reached over to answer it. No doubt that Cassie was wondering where he was, since the play was supposed to start in about twenty minutes.

Jack grinned as he picked up the phone. "I'm walking out the door now." Jack put his wallet into his back pocket and picked up his keys.

Jack expected to hear Cassie's happy relief that he was on his way. Instead, he heard a soft, trembling female voice.

"Jack," then a brief pause, "its Stacey."

Jack's keys dropped from his hand. The sound echoed throughout the house.

Chapter Twenty-Nine

Throughout the first act of the play, Cassie was trying not to squirm and she kept glancing over her shoulder towards the entrance. Jack still hadn't arrived and she was starting to get concerned. She was trying hard not to worry about him, but it was difficult not to. It wasn't like Jack to not show up. Then again, she reminded herself, maybe he realized that he just couldn't watch Liza perform after all. She couldn't blame him. She's not sure that she could do it under the same set of circumstances. It was very big of Jack to even offer to attend with Cassie, but she acknowledged to herself that some things were just too hard to face.

At some point after the play started, Abby arrived and scooted in next to Cassie. Abby mouthed "where's Jack?" and Cassie whispered back that she wasn't sure. By now Abby knew Jack's story and she nodded in understanding.

During intermission, Cassie turned her phone back on to see if there was a message from Jack. There wasn't a voice mail, but she was relieved when a single one-lined text popped up from him.

"I can't be there tonight. I'll explain later."

As they stood in the lobby, Cassie relayed the message to Abby. Cassie felt better knowing that Jack wasn't hurt or that some other terrible thing hadn't happened, but she still felt a little curious to know what it was that he needed to explain and said that to Abby.

Abby wasn't concerned. "I'm sure that Jack decided that he just couldn't be here tonight and he probably feels a little bad about it, thinking that he disappointed you or something." Abby took a sip of her soda and continued. "It's just too much to text the explanation."

Cassie shrugged her shoulders slightly. "You're probably right. I know he's okay now and that helps, but I just have this funny feeling that I can't explain." In saying it, Cassie realized that she did have an odd feeling that she just couldn't quite shake. That nagging, lingering feeling wouldn't quite go away. What was it that she was sensing?

Cassie looked around the lobby to see if she could see Jack's parents and she spotted them standing near the concession stand. When the play started, she had waited for Jack for so long, that she hadn't been able to find his parents and talk to them. As it was, she slid into her seat quietly after the first act started. Jack had his own ticket, so she knew he'd be able to get in as soon as he arrived.

Cassie indicated to Abby where Jack's parents' were standing. "Come on. I want you to meet them."

As Cassie and Abby approached Barbara and Will, Barbara caught sight of them. She broke into a huge smile and nudged Will to get his attention.

Barbara had felt so bad about Cassie finding out about Charlie the way that she did, that she'd called Jack and apologized. It had just never occurred to her to take down family pictures. Besides, there were times when she'd look at Charlie's picture and allow herself to dream about what it would be like to be his grandmother again.

Naturally, Jack wasn't upset with his mother. By the time Barbara reached him on the phone the next day, Cassie knew everything. Jack was relieved to have told her and happy that she'd been so understanding about his situation.

When Jack told his Mom that they'd talked about Charlie for hours and hours, she was beyond excited that Jack had found someone to share his thoughts and feelings with. Throughout this whole drama with Stacey, Barbara knew that Jack had held almost everything inside and that had concerned her immensely. She knew that kind of pain, without any release, could be very damaging to the mind, body and soul.

Barbara's arms were outstretched as Cassie approached her. "Cassie, dear, it's so nice to see you again."

Cassie hugged her back. "It's so nice to see you too." Then she headed towards Will. "And you too!"

Cassie motioned that Abby was standing beside her. "I would like to introduce both of you to Abby, my dearest friend. These are Jack's parents, Barbara and Will." They both responded to Abby that it was nice to meet her.

Barbara remembered a conversation she'd had with Cassie during brunch. "So, Abby, you are the friend of Cassie's who's known her since school and helped her so much with Brett?"

Abby smiled at the statement. "I am. We've known each other since we were young girls." Abby then smiled at Cassie and looked back towards Barbara. "Cassie is more than my friend; she's like a sister to me and Brett, is…" she looked for the words. "Well, they're both like family to me."

Barbara was happy to hear it. It said a lot about Cassie in the company that she kept. It was difficult not to compare it to the company that Stacey kept in Liza.

Will offered to buy Cassie and Abby a drink, but they both declined the offer with thanks.

Barbara lowered her voice slightly and leaned in towards Cassie. "I thought Jack was going to attend with you tonight?"

"I did too, but something came up." Cassie explained about the text message that he left on her phone and her thoughts on why he didn't attend. She then added, "I don't blame him at all."

Barbara concurred with Cassie's thoughts. She, too, could understand. Normally they didn't attend the performances when Liza was starring, as there were too many times when Barbara showed up to babysit Charlie and Liza would be outside in the car waiting for Stacey, dressed to the nines in very revealing clothing. Barbara shivered a little at the memory. Her only consolation when Stacey and Liza went out together was in knowing that Charlie was now safe in her care. Besides, at the heart of it, Liza couldn't be held accountable for Stacey's choices, but Barbara had little doubt that she highly influenced Stacey in those decisions.

The four of them continued to talk until the lights dimmed indicating that intermission was almost over. After quick goodbyes, they all returned to their seats.

After the performance ended, Cassie turned back on her phone. No other message from Jack. She sighed. Abby was right; it was too much to say on the phone. Hopefully he would call her when she got home, or maybe even be parked in front of her house. She smiled at the thought of that homecoming.

Cassie knew that Colleen wanted her to go backstage and have an appetizer. She'd rather go home to see if there was any news from Jack, but she wanted to at least go and congratulate Colleen and Kevin for another stunning production, although she didn't intend to stay long.

Cassie and Abby walked backstage and it was a bustle of activity and sounds. A lot of the cast members were still standing in their bell bottoms, jumpsuits and psychedelic-patterned shirts. They were high-fiving each other and chattering away. They still wore the heavy stage make-up that made them look a little cartoon-like when you stood close to them. Cassie knew most of them and she congratulated them on their performance. Fortunately, Liza was nowhere to be seen. She hoped that Colleen was right and that she would leave with her husband quickly.

After stopping to talk to several cast members, Cassie and Abby finally found Colleen and Kevin.

Both of them were full of high spirits after a terrific opening night. A highly receptive packed house on opening night held the promise of word getting out that it was a great performance and the remaining tickets for upcoming shows would be sold quickly.

Kevin was particularly excited. He'd taken a little bit of a risk putting on a show that wasn't a commonly known production, but he'd fallen in love with the script and he knew the music from the seventies was full of energy and excitement, so he hoped the audience would approve. By the long ovation, it certainly seemed as though they did and he was thrilled.

He raced towards Cassie and embraced her in a big hug. "Thank you, thank you, darling, for all your help with this production."

Cassie smiled and waved her hand in front of his face. "You know there's nothing that I wouldn't do for two of my favorite people."

This time it was Colleen who hugged her. "We appreciate it so much." Colleen was still flying high too. "Did you hear the audience laughing throughout the show?"

Cassie laughed. "Are you kidding me? I was out there with them. It was a terrific show."

Both Kevin and Colleen also gave Abby a big squeeze and thanked her again for all of her help.

Colleen shooed them towards the conference room. "Go get something to eat. We'll be in there in a few minutes to join you."

Cassie wasn't particularly hungry, but Abby had just said that she was, so they headed towards the conference room.

When they walked in the room, there were hot plates that held stuffed mushrooms and meatballs and a table full of fruit, veggies, crackers and cheese.

Cassie and Abby both fixed a small plate and made their way to a corner where there was a little more room to stand, as the minimal seating was already taken. They were almost finished eating, when suddenly Liza walked into the room. She had changed from her last costume and had removed her stage make-up. Now her face was fresh with the newly applied evening make-up. She went up to a few of the other performers and kissed them on both checks. Cassie couldn't hear what she was saying, but she could see by the looks on their faces, that they were eager to get away from her. Liza may have had fans in the audience, but Cassie got the impression that she wasn't well liked by too many of the cast and crew.

Cassie had thrown her plate in the garbage can and was about to leave, when she heard Liza say, "Cassie, I want to thank you for the costumes you helped with."

Cassie was eager to respond quickly and get out of Liza's way. "You're welcome, Liza, but it was more the seamstress than me."

"Oh no, Cassie, you found these wonderful clothes. I had my doubts about some of the pieces, but I should have trusted your vision."

Abby was talking to one of the cast members and Cassie was trying to get her attention so that they could leave.

In a sudden surprising move, Liza leaned over and gave Cassie a quick hug and then released her.

"Oh, this is such a happy night for me. I just put on an incredible performance and the audience went wild." Liza had a broad smile and spread her arms out as she spoke. "Now, my handsome husband went to get the car and he's taking me and several of our friends out to dinner to celebrate."

Cassie couldn't even pretend to be nice to her. She remained silent.

Liza leaned her head closer to Cassie and in a lowered voice almost whispered, "The icing on the cake is that I heard from my oldest, dearest friend, Stacey, today and she's back in town."

Stacey's back in town! Cassie's heart dropped to her now queasy stomach.

Liza continued talking to Cassie in a lowered voice, with her face very near to Cassie's. "You know, Jack, the contractor that's been doing the work at your place." With excited glee, Liza continued, "Of course you do! Well, that's Stacey's ex-husband." Cassie's mind was racing. Stacey was back. Oh God! The sick feeling that she'd been feeling all night suddenly increased.

In the midst of the fog that was now in her brain, all she could hear was Liza telling her, "Stacey knows she made a terrible mistake in leaving and she wants to make things right with Jack. She wants all three of them to be a family again!"

Liza clapped her hands. "I just love a happy ending. Don't you?"

Without waiting for an answer, Liza announced, "Well, I must go. I'm sure Tom is out front with the car now."

With an arrogant smile on her face, Liza turned away from Cassie and left the room.

Once Liza was gone, Cassie was left with the wall holding her up.

Chapter Thirty

A stunned Jack sat back down on the arm of the couch. His legs had temporarily gone out from under him. He kept staring at the phone and found himself concentrating on breathing. *Stacey called him.*

When he first heard her voice, he thought he must be in some parallel world. He thought that this couldn't be happening. His first reaction was to hang up on her. He literally had to stop himself from hitting the 'end call' button. Fortunately, he was able to remind himself to just keep his cool.

Jack went over the conversation in his head again.

"Jack, are you still there?" Stacey waited a minute before Jack's response.

"Where are you and Charlie?" Jack had had to center himself and calm himself down before he even said that. His first reaction was to scream out 'where the fuck is Charlie?' but he reminded himself immediately that it was much more important to keep calm and not have Stacey hang up on him.

"Jack, I need to talk to you." Stacey waited and then in her most serious voice said, "It's really important."

Jack struggled to keep his emotions intact and with Stacey's reference that it was important, Jack was filled with dread. "Is Charlie okay?"

On the other end, Stacey thought quickly. Her only goal for tonight was to talk to Jack in person. She had to get him to agree to that. She knew that everything would go so much smoother if they were face to face. She had no control if she wasn't talking to Jack in person.

Stacey exhaled. "Charlie's here, Jack, in town, but I want to see you first."

Charlie's here! In town? Oh God. Jack's hands were shaking and he could barely hold the phone. Once again, Jack reminded himself to keep his cool. It took every ounce of control to keep his composure.

Jack was having a difficult time controlling his voice, but he managed to somehow. "When and where? I'll be there."

On the other end, Stacey let out a silent breath of relief. Thank God Jack had agreed. He wouldn't be able to resist her in person. Besides, like Liza pointed out, there was no way Jack could resist Charlie too, although she had no intention of bringing him to the first meeting with Jack.

"Is Hank's Diner that we both like so much still there?" Jack told her it was.

"I'll be there in an hour, okay." Jack told her okay and was about to hang up when Stacey remembered one other thing. She would always look out for herself first.

"Jack, don't call the police," she stopped, "if you do, I won't tell you where Charlie is and I'll leave immediately and never return again."

"Agreed. I'll see you in an hour." Jack hung up and then looked at his phone again, but Stacey's number wasn't showing on his phone. It just said "private number."

Having re-thought the conversation in his head several times, Jack was calmer now and mostly collected. He knew what he needed to do. Finding out how and where Charlie was, was his first priority. Everything else from there, he would take one step at a time. He would be very careful when it came to Stacey.

Suddenly remembering that he was supposed to meet Cassie, he typed the quick text that he couldn't make it and that he'd explain later. There was no way he could explain Stacey's return in a text, besides, he wanted to meet with Stacey first and find out as much as he could. Then he would tell Cassie.

No doubt that Stacey was worried about the police showing up. He wasn't going to chase her away, but he wasn't going to be stupid either. He picked back up his phone and hit Jon's cell number. Jon picked up on the second ring.

"Hey Jack, what's going on?"

There was no way to dance around it and he didn't have time. "Stacey's back and I need your help."

Instantly Jon was sitting upright in his patrol car seat and listening to his brother closely. Stacey was back and a fire was starting to burn in Jon's belly.

"Talk to me, Jack. Tell me everything." Jack relayed every word of the conversation he'd had with Stacey from beginning to end. He left out nothing. Jon listened with his sharp cop ear for details.

When Jack was done talking, Jon started. "Forget her, Jack. She doesn't want any police. She doesn't get any say in this."

Jack interrupted him quickly. "No, Jon, there's nothing I'd like more, but I can't risk Charlie." At that comment, Jon, too, remembered her threat. He couldn't risk her slipping away again with Charlie either.

Jack continued, "However, I won't be stupid either. She'd recognize you, but would any of your buddies be willing to go undercover and hang close to the diner? I want to know where she's going when she leaves and who she's with."

Jon looked at his watch. "Consider it done."

Jon confirmed the time and location of the diner. "Don't worry Jack. These are guys I trust. I know I'll be able to count on some of my buddies. Besides, I'm going to get an unmarked police car from the garage and stay back from the diner, but close enough to see her. Stacey won't get away from us this time."

Jack was relieved. "Thanks, little brother. I owe you."

Jon shook his head in disbelief. His brother didn't owe him a thing. He'd been itching to find Stacey and Charlie since the day she left. He hadn't been able to find them. Now, there was no way she was going to slip through his fingers.

Before hanging up, Jon told him, "I'll call you the second I know where she's at after she leaves the diner and we'll go from there. We need to make sure that Charlie is really with her."

The brothers hung up.

Until it was time to go and meet Stacey, Jack sat and collected his thoughts. He needed to have a Plan A, a Plan B and maybe even a Plan C. He wanted to be prepared for any situation.

When it was time to leave, Jack clicked off the living room lights and had a flashback to when he came home to a darkened house and Stacey was gone. Now, he just might learn the truth and all the darkness that had been cast upon him since then could be removed.

*****

Jack pulled up in front of the diner. It was a glass structure that allowed you to easily see in or out. Jack looked inside. Stacey wasn't there yet. He walked in and looked around. A few couples were in there, a family with two young girls and two single men. One was dressed like a trucker and another was reading a newspaper and drinking coffee. Jack looked at the man who was reading the newspaper and they briefly caught eyes. Jack looked away assuming that it was Jon's buddy. He ordered a cup of coffee and chose a booth and sat where the seat was facing the front door. At the first sip of the coffee, his stomach pitched and rolled.

Jack looked at the clock. It was one hour on the dot from when Stacey called. *What if she didn't show up after all? What would he do then?* He looked into the parking lot and could see the headlights of a car enter the parking lot. He watched in agonizing anticipation until a woman stepped out of the car. He let out the breath that he didn't know he was holding; it wasn't Stacey. He tried to force down another sip of coffee and reminded himself to settle down. He held tightly to his coffee cup, which made it easier not to shake.

Jack looked up to see another car's headlights entering the parking lot. A woman got out and started to walk in. Although her hair color was significantly lighter now, Jack knew instantly that it was Stacey. She was wearing a knee-length dress, which Jack quickly remembered was unusual for her. She always wore a mid-thigh dress, or shorter, when she went out. She caught eyes with Jack the moment she walked in the door. Then she broke eye contact and looked around quickly. Apparently, feeling satisfied that the police weren't there she quickly walked to the table.

Jack couldn't take his eyes off her. He'd imagined seeing her again one day but nothing he imagined could have prepared him for the multitude of emotions swirling inside of him at this moment.

Stacey looked about the same, except for the hair color. She had carefully applied her make-up, but it wasn't overdone. She slowly smiled at him. Jack was still stunned that he was finally face to face with her.

"You look good, Jack." She pointed to the seat. "Can I sit down?"

Jack indicated with his hands for her to sit down. He was having trouble finding his voice at the moment.

The waitress came over and Stacey ordered a diet soda. When she returned with the soda, Stacey finally spoke.

"I'm glad you agreed to meet me."

Jack's voice was back and he said the first thing that came to mind. "I need answers Stacey."

"I know you do." Stacey's voice shook. "I want to tell you everything, but I have to start off by saying that I made a terrible mistake. I want you to know that before anything else."

Jack couldn't help but to roll his eyes at her little speech. Stacey noticed his eye roll and was desperately trying to get him to listen to her before he got up and left the diner.

"You have every right to be upset with me Jack."

Stacey looked at him for some response. Seeing none, she continued. "I'll tell you everything, but I need you to hear me out with an open mind."

Jack knew there was nothing that she could say to make it understandable or right, yet he had no choice but to sit there and listen.

Still, he couldn't help but be sarcastic just once. "What, did 'the love of your life' get tired of your bullshit and throw you out?"

His comment irritated Stacey, but she couldn't let it show. She had practiced dozens of times what she was going to say to Jack to convince him to take her back. Besides, her situation had recently changed and there was a certain amount of truth to that statement, but she couldn't let Jack know that.

"For your information, he did not." Stacey let out an exasperated sigh. "I took the chance to come into town to see you because I realized what a terrible," Stacey paused and looked sincerely at Jack, "just what a terrible mistake I made when I left you."

Stacey looked down at her soda and gathered her thoughts. When she looked up, she met Jack's eyes and a tear slid down one cheek of her face. "I finally came to my senses and realized that it was you, Jack, who's the love of my life."

As if to punctuate the truth of her statement, she quickly added, "I even met Liza in San Francisco a few weekends ago and asked her if she thought it was possible for us to get back together."

Stacey could never begin to understand that her statement about meeting Liza infuriated Jack, when she naively hoped it would be some kind of confirmation to Jack that she was sincere because she had approached her closest friend about her desire to come back.

Fury burned within Jack. He wanted to vomit it at the mention of the two of them together in San Francisco, but he continued to hold it together. Some things were more important than reacting.

Stacey stopped talking and stared at Jack. Again there was no response, so she continued, "She helped convince me that I just *had* to come back, that we were meant to be together. All of us – you, me and Charlie, as a family."

Stacey reached over and touched Jack's forearm and stroked it gently. "I don't expect you to forgive me yet, but I hope you'll give me the chance to make it right."

She stroked his arm more firmly now. "I think we owe ourselves the chance to at least try." To drive her point home, she added. "For Charlie's sake."

Jack didn't believe a word she said. He thought to himself that his first instinct was right. Whoever Stacey had left with, had tired of her ways and kicked her out. If it was just Stacey, he'd leave her twisting in the wind, but there was one more element to this whole picture that he couldn't ignore. *Charlie.* Was he really in town or did Stacey just say he was here to dangle it in front of him like a carrot to a hungry rabbit?

Jack didn't remove Stacey's hand from his arm, although it was crawling at her touch.

"What about Charlie's father?" With the next statement, he was more honest than he thought he would be. "I won't do to another man, what you did to me?"

Stacey remembered that Jack was a stand-up kind of guy and she knew that some form of this question was coming.

"Jack, I wouldn't do that to Charlie." When she saw that Jack was starting to object, she jumped in. "We can work that all out," she paused, "later, when we figure everything out between us."

Jack didn't say anything. His thoughts were racing. For the last two years, he'd spent so much timing wondering if Charlie was really his and what he would do if he ever found him again. Yet, he couldn't ignore the horrible truth that Charlie might really be someone else's child and he would have no right to be with him. He wouldn't do that to his worst enemy. If that was true, he'd be left with only memories of a little boy that he had the pleasure of loving and raising for two, very short years.

The waitress came by to see if they needed anything else. Jack looked into his cup and noticed an almost full cup of coffee. They both told her that they didn't need anything.

As the silence grew with Jack's thoughts, Stacey knew she had to make her move now.

She slid her hand from his foreman and into his hand. She squeezed his hand gently. Jack looked up and they caught eyes.

"I know you have a lot of questions and I promise you that we'll work this all out. You'll have all the answers you deserve. I need you in my life again," another tear slide down her cheek, "and Charlie needs you too."

Jack's eyes never left hers.

Stacey continued. "I took a big risk coming here, to make it right." She stopped what she was saying, paused, and then she detonated the bomb she needed to set. "I even told Charlie that I was going to try my very best to make us a family again."

The rolling in Jack's stomach magnified and the shaking of his hands returned. He clasped the coffee cup tighter with his free hand in some false sense of security. His mind was racing once again and he was trying desperately to keep pace with everything that he was hearing and feeling. Finally, two things were clear in his head.

Jack squeezed Stacey's hand back to give her some reassurance. He looked her directly in the eye and smiled sweetly. "Before I even consider us getting back together, I need to see Charlie," he squeezed her hand a bit tighter, "then I need answers. Only then can we make it right."

Full of relief, Stacey's smile grew from ear to ear. "Of course, Jack. Charlie just needs you so much and I'll explain everything to you." Now it was her turn to squeeze his hand. "I really will. Then we'll fix us and we can be a happy little family again."

Realizing quickly that Jack might disagree with that statement, Stacey stroked Jack's hand and let her lip quiver slightly as she spoke, "we'll be even happier than before. I'm not the same woman that I was. I've changed. You'll see."

Jack didn't pull his hand away. Stacey was thrilled that everything was starting to fall into place, but she couldn't let her relief be too obvious. Liza had told her earlier today that sincerity and Charlie were the two keys that she needed to open the door. Then Jack would follow right behind.

"I have a great idea! Why don't the three of us meet at Pueblo Park tomorrow afternoon? You and Charlie can get to know each other again." Stacey leaned her head towards her shoulder and scanned Jack's face. "I hope it will be the start of many happy weekends together as a family."

Jack didn't even have to think about it. He knew without a shadow of doubt that he wanted to see Charlie again and as soon as possible.

Jack began, "We'll have time to figure that all out later about us being a family. You must understand that I never expected to see you again, so it's a lot to take in." Jack struggled with his words, but knew with certainty that he needed to see Charlie again.

"I think it's important for me and Charlie to spend a little quality time together," he looked directly at Stacey, "alone."

Stacey frowned. She hadn't expected that response. Jack sensed that she was worried that he might take Charlie from her and never return him, so he tried to reassure her, a kindness that she hadn't shown him, but he needed to see Charlie and that was all that mattered to him.

Jack looked at Stacey and spoke carefully. "You said you took a risk to come back here to make us a family." Stacey nodded in agreement as Jack continued to talk.

"Now, this is another risk you have to take, so that I have confidence in you that you're telling me the truth that Charlie is really here."

He could see Stacey listening closely and questions were evident in her eyes. Jack said what he needed to say to reassure her. "I'm not going to do anything stupid to lose this chance to see Charlie. I don't care if you stay in the car, parked at the park. You'll be able to see us the whole time."

Stacey was relieved that Jack had understood her fears. After all, if she didn't have Charlie, what leverage would she have with Jack to get her life back where she wanted it?

"Oh, Jack. I trust you. I'm just being a nervous mom, I guess. You two can have your guy time together." Jack's heart leaped in joy at the thought. Stacey saw the joy in his eyes and commended herself for getting what she wanted, once again. Jack was so easy!

They set up the meeting at the park for the next day at noon. Stacey took the car keys from her purse and looked at Jack tenderly. "I'm going to go now. I can't tell you how much it means to me to know that there's a chance for us."

She smiled at him sweetly. "The three of us had something special. I want us to have it back."

Jack didn't say anything, except that he would see her at the park the following day. Stacey left. Twenty seconds later, the trucker got up from his seat and walked out the front door.

Chapter Thirty-One

After he left the diner, Jon called Jack a little while later and Jack relayed to him everything Stacey had said. He bought her story as much as Jack did.

Jon reported that both he and his guys followed Stacey back and discovered she was staying at a local inn. Jack was nervous about her being there and wanted to go park out front himself, but Jon reassured him.

"You don't have to worry about it. I've got it covered. There's only one way in and one way out. Stacey, or more importantly, Charlie, won't get out without me knowing it."

Jack was more comfortable hearing that, but also concerned. "Jon, I know you have to go to work and sleep, you can't do it all."

Jon reassured him once again. "Jack, listen. I have time off coming. Between me and all my buddies in the department, we've got it covered. There won't be one second where we don't know where Stacey or Charlie's location is."

Jack let out a sigh of relief, but then remembered. "She'll find a way to fly out of there if she sees the boys in blue."

Jon interrupted. "Don't worry. She won't see a black and white outside or the guys in uniform. I have a commitment from several buddies to cover her day and night and they'll all be in plain clothes and in unmarked cars."

Finally Jack could breathe easier. On the other end, Jon was breathing easier too. He had lined up the men to help out. He had promised to pay them for their time, even if it took a while, but not one would accept the promise of any money. There was a code among cops, they were brothers, and they would be there for each other. Jon didn't have to worry about it. After all, he trusted them with his life. Besides, his buddies wanted to help Jack; they all knew his story. For Jon, that's all he'd wanted to do since Charlie turned up missing. Now, he had the chance to make it right.

Jack's second call of the night was to Cassie. He told her almost everything. He knew this unexpected situation would be so hard for her, but she encouraged him to find the answers he needed and to see Charlie. Finally, after talking for several minutes, he told her things would be crazy for a few days and there was a lot he had to do, but he promised to call her as soon as he could.

Now it was the next day. Jack hadn't slept a wink all night. He was already at the park and was a half hour early. He was like a kid on Christmas morning at the thought of seeing Charlie again. He'd told himself a hundred times that he couldn't pull Charlie into a long hug like he wanted to. That's all he needed, was to scare the dickens out of a little boy that probably didn't remember him at all. He'd have to remember that this was confusing for Charlie and he needed to keep him feeling comfortable the whole time.

Jack looked at the other kids playing in the park. There was a toy structure with slides and swings on the left, a large sand pit and a large grassy area on the right where kids were playing ball or some people were laying on blankets on the grass.

Jack was still confused. This was all so unexpected. He wasn't sure what to say to Charlie, but he just knew he needed to see him, make sure he was okay and to just spend time with him. His own mom had called him this morning, after hearing from Jon, and ended the phone call in tears, but simply told him "Charlie won't know that you're nervous. He'll just be happy to have fun. Just enjoy him." Jack agreed that was sage advice and he planned on doing just that -- enjoy being with Charlie. To see him again was the miracle he'd dreamed about for two years now!

Jack couldn't sit still any more. He got out of his truck and took a walk around the perimeter of the park. Sitting on one of the benches and reading a newspaper was one of the men from Jon's squad that Jack recognized. Jack didn't acknowledge him, but appreciated that the police were present. He knew there were other officers around too and felt secure with Jon's help.

He had to calm his nerves, but more than that, nothing could stop the excitement that was building inside him. He was going to see Charlie in a matter of minutes.

Jack walked back towards his truck and as he did, he noticed Stacey getting out of a car that was parked not too far away from his truck. She opened the back door of the car and Jack saw a mop of wavy brown hair. Jack speeded up his step and got to them just as Stacey and Charlie hit the sidewalk.

Jack's heart leaped into his throat. *There was Charlie!* He still had the same wavy brown hair, although a shade darker now, and Jack could see a few freckles across his nose. He was wearing denim jeans and sneakers and he had a green sweatshirt on with a dragon on the front of it.

Jack didn't know what to do and it was barely all he could do, to keep his hands to himself and not gather Charlie up and smother him in hugs and kisses. Instead he dropped to his knees right beside Charlie, so that he was much closer to being face to face with Charlie.

In a soft and friendly voice, he simply said. "Hi, Charlie."

Charlie had a finger on his lip and was tugging it nervously.

"Hi," he said shyly.

Stacey got down on her knees too. "Charlie, this is the man that I told you about."

Charlie looked at her and nodded. "Remember you guys are going to play here in the park for a while."

Charlie looked at Jack and Jack smiled at him. "Thanks for coming to the park today. I like playing here, but I don't have a little kid to play with me. I've known your Mom for a long time and she said it would be okay if you came to the park today."

Charlie quit tugging his lip with his finger and dropped his hand to his side. Jack continued, "I'm sure we'll have a good time together, but if you need to come over and see your Mom anytime, you just tell me and I'll bring you right back to the car."

Charlie looked at the car and then back to Jack. "Is that okay with you?" Charlie nodded his head yes and dropped his Mom's hand.

"I have some balls and stuff in my truck, right over there. I bet we could find some fun things to play with."

Stacey stood up and brushed off her knees. "You heard, Jack, pumpkin, you two go play and I'll be reading my magazine right here in the car."

Unexpectedly, Charlie reached up and took Jack's hand. Jack was overjoyed. The touch of that little hand was something he never thought he'd feel again. They got to the truck and Jack opened the tailgate. He then lifted Charlie into the back of the truck. Jack jumped in behind him.

All Charlie could see was a soccer ball, a baseball, a small plastic bat, two mitts, a regular bouncing ball and a kite. When Jack couldn't pace at his house any more this morning, he left for the sporting goods store.

Charlie looked in the back of the truck. "Wow, you have a lot of toys and stuff."

Jack chuckled. "I told you that I was excited to play with you. What would you like to play with first?"

Charlie looked around, "Mmm, I don't really know how to play soccer or baseball."

"That's okay. I can teach you."

Charlie looked up over the truck and looked at the play structure. "I like swings."

Jack patted him lightly on the back. "Swings it is then."

Jack jumped out of the truck and swung Charlie down. They headed towards the playground.

Charlie looked up at Jack and smiled. "I like to go high on the swings."

Jack pretended to be frightened. "Isn't it scary to go so high?"

Charlie chuckled this time and Jack's heart melted inside. "No, silly. You just have to pretend that you're a birdie."

Jack laughed. "So that's the secret. Maybe I won't be afraid to swing so high now. Do you think I could swing next to you?"

Charlie shrugged his shoulders. "I kinda need you to help me swing first. You have to push me on my back to make me go high."

Jack grabbed his heart. "Whew! What a relief. I was afraid I'd have to swing high like a birdie."

Charlie ran ahead and jumped on the swings. Jack stood in front of him on the swing. It was almost impossible to take his eyes off him.

"You have to push me from back there."

Reluctantly Jack walked around behind and started to push Charlie. Pretty soon, Charlie was flying high. Periodically, Jack would ask Charlie if he was going too high. "No, higher, higher."

After a while, Charlie decided he was done with the swings and they walked over to the slide. Charlie looked at the big, enclosed tube-like slide and peered up inside it. Jack sensed that he was nervous about going down the slide.

"Have you ever gone down a slide like this?"

Charlie turned his head from side to side. "No, I don't get to go to the park very much." Jack's heart broke in two. All kids should be able to spend countless hours playing in the park.

"I could take you down the slide." Charlie looked at him and Jack could see he was interested, but still unsure about it.

"We could climb to the top together. See over there," Jack pointed to the stairs and Charlie's eyes followed. "Then you could sit on my lap and we'll go down the slide together."

Charlie liked that idea and started running towards the stairs. Again, Jack was right behind him. When they were at the entrance of the tube, Jack sat down and reached over for Charlie and put him on his lap.

Jack told Charlie. "When we get to the bottom, we have to jump off the end and say something fun." Charlie nodded in agreement and turned his head and looked at Jack. "Let's go."

Jack pushed off and he used the heels of his shoes to slow them down a little bit. He didn't want Charlie frightened the first time on a slide. When they got to the bottom, Charlie jumped off his lap and turned around and faced Jack. His smile was from ear to ear.

"That was cool!"

Jack high-fived him. "That was awesome, little man!"

They went down the slide several more times. Charlie finally got his courage up to go down by himself. Jack promised to catch him. When Charlie got to the top, Jack pounded a loud drum roll with his hands on the slide. "Here comes the best slider ever. IIIIItttttt's Charlie!" He could hear Charlie giggle as he headed down. Jack caught him and threw him up in the air.

"You did it, Charlie." Charlie laughed out loud. "I did it." Charlie immediately ran to the stairs. "Again!"

About an hour later, Jack heard the faint sound of music and looked across the park. He pointed to the sound of the music. "Charlie, do you know what that is?" Charlie looked to where Jack was pointing, but he didn't know what he was pointing at.

"See the white truck over there and all the kids are standing by it?" Charlie nodded and Jack explained.

"That's the ice cream man." Charlie looked at Jack and his eyes lit up in delight. "Ice cream man?" Jack nodded.

Jack looked from the truck to Charlie. "I have an idea. How about we race over to the truck and I'll buy us an ice cream?"

"Okay, but I'm a pretty fast runner. I bet you can't catch me." Charlie started running for the ice cream truck and Jack was right behind him. If

Charlie would have turned around, he would have seen pure delight on Jack's face as he raced right behind him.

Jack and Charlie sat on the grass licking their melting ice cream. Jack had napkins in his pocket, but at the moment, he couldn't bring himself to wipe the ice cream off Charlie's face. He looked too cute with it melting down his chin and Charlie kept trying to lick it off his chin with his tongue.

"Are you having a good time today, Charlie?"

Charlie kept licking his ice cream but he nodded his head up and down several times. He'd been having a blast. This Jack guy was a lot of fun!

Jack asked gently, "Would you like to spend time together at the park again on another day?"

"Yeah, you're fun to play with." Charlie took another lick and then looked at Jack thoughtfully. "Mom said that you were my first dad."

Jack swallowed the lump in his throat. How in the hell was he supposed to answer that loaded question? He didn't want to lie to Charlie.

"I was at the hospital when you were born and a little tiny baby. You lived with me until you were two-years old."

Charlie's mouth dropped open. "You mean, you knew me, when I was this big?" Charlie held his hands about four inches apart.

Jack chuckled. "Well, a little bigger than that. You were about this long." Jack pointed to his own forearm.

"Did we go down the slide when I was a baby?"

"No, not when you were a little baby, but when you got a little bigger we were starting to go to the park sometimes."

Charlie asked what else they did together, so Jack piped up. "We liked to watch cartoons and play with your toy trucks in the backyard."

Charlie looked at Jack. "I still like cartoons!"

Jack laughed. "I do too!"

Jack remembered the picture hanging up at his parents' house; the one Cassie had seen. "We went fishing one time and went on a boat so early in the morning that it was still dark when we got there, and guess what happened?"

Charlie arched his eye brows and stopped licking his ice cream. "You caught a fish."

Charlie pointed to his own chest. "I did? I caught a real fish?"

Jack nodded. "You betcha. You know what was even cooler than that?" Charlie was listening closely. "When we went to clean it later, there was a whole other fish inside its tummy that it had swallowed, so you really caught two fish!"

Charlie thought that was hysterical and he fell back onto his back with laughter. When he sat up, he looked at Jack like he had a question for him, but he wasn't sure how to say it.

"Do you have something on your mind, Charlie?" Jack wiped his sticky face and took the ice creamer wrapper from Charlie.

Charlie waited for only a second before answering. "Mom said that we're going to be a family again and that I should be nice to you." He looked down and then with a worried look, he popped his head back up quickly. "I wasn't supposed to tell you that."

Jack looked at Charlie and the love that had been inside all along was still there. He was still crazy in love with this little boy, but there were so many unanswered questions. How could he explain all this to a four year- old?

Jack brushed a hair out of Charlie's eyes before answering him. "I'm not sure that we can all be a family together again."

Charlie looked sad. He liked this new person in his life. Never before had anyone spent so much time with him just playing. His Mom never spent *any* time with him, period. She always told him to leave her alone.

"Before I know the answer, I have a lot to talk to your Mom about a lot of grown-up stuff." Jack looked at Charlie tenderly and stroked his cheek. "But I tell you what. To me, you will always be my family and I'll always want to spend time with you and be a part of your life."

Charlie seemed to perk up. "You do?" Jack smiled and nodded. "Absolutely, Charlie!" More than you could possibly know, little one.

Charlie was very happy to hear that he would be able to spend more time with his new found friend. "I think we're going to live here now, so we can come back to the park again."

Jack gently prodded. "Of course, we can, but what makes you think you're going to live here again."

Charlie put his chin down to his chest until Jack reassured him that it was okay to tell Jack what was on his mind.

"I heard my other Dad tell my Mom that she was a shellfish and then they both started yelling, really loud at each other. I went in my room and covered my head with a pillow. I don't like it when they yell and they yell a lot!"

Jack felt sad for Charlie. "I don't like it when people yell either."

Charlie continued to confide in Jack now that he had an understanding listener. "When I woke up, I was in the car and Mom told me that we were coming back to live with my first dad."

Jack urged him to go on with his eyes. "We have to stay in a motel. Last night, Mom said she was coming to meet my first dad and that I had to stay at her friend from high school's house."

Suddenly Charlie wrinkled up his nose. "Mom's friend has a daughter, so I had to play with a girl."

Jack rolled his eyes and laughed. "Oh no, you had to play with a girl?"

Charlie followed suit and rolled his eyes. "Yuck, girls are gross. "

Jack patted him on the knee, "You know, Charlie, all girls aren't so gross."

Charlie shook his head no, he just didn't believe it.

The brief change of topic had been good for Jack. His heartstrings had been tugged at the mere mention of another dad, but he refused to react and confuse this little boy any more. He wasn't going to make a promise to Charlie that he couldn't keep, nor was he going to pretend it was all okay, when he just wasn't sure. He had already told Charlie the one truth that he knew for sure, and that was that he would always want him in his life. But in saying that, Jack knew that in his heart, there was no way he was ever letting him go again, even if he had to move heaven and earth to do it, but how he was going to accomplish this, he just wasn't sure.

Jack stood up and held out his hand for Charlie. Charlie took it. "How about I teach you how to kick the soccer ball now?" Charlie agreed.

Jack and Charlie started to walk back to his truck, hand in hand, but soon, Charlie felt his legs getting tired. He stopped and held up his arms to Jack and Jack scooped him up into his arms. Charlie put his arms around Jack's neck and rested his head against Jack's head.

"Thanks for the ice cream." Overcome with emotion by that one tiny act, Jack couldn't talk. He just squeezed Charlie and held him a little closer. His sweet Charlie boy was in his arms again.

Chapter Thirty-Two

Cassie sat on the couch with her legs curled up underneath her. She was looking at the window of her living room. It had been so hard to sleep again. Her mind was swirling with a thousand what-if's. She sat on the couch and looked up at the sky and it was bright blue. She thought it would be a beautiful day for Jack and Charlie to be in the park.

She turned and looked over at Abby. "I can't begin to tell you how much I wish I could be at the park today, somewhere off in the distance, where I could watch Jack and Charlie together."

Abby reached over and patted her on the leg. She had come to spend the day with Cassie. She didn't want her to be alone. She'd been worried about Cassie since Liza had made the announcement about Stacey's return. Cassie had told her about Jack's telephone call later that night, and it reassured Cassie on some level, but how reassured could she really be right now? It's as if all the cards had been thrown up in the air and no one knew how they were going to land.

Somewhere along the way, Cassie had started to feel that a silent promise had been made between her and Jack. Since the news of Stacey's return, Cassie felt that promise, real or imaged, quickly slipping away.

"Have you talked to Jack since your last phone call?"

Cassie continued to look out the window. "No, but I didn't expect too. There's so much going on and he wasn't sure when he could call next."

Cassie remembered that phone call with Jack so well. When they hung up, Cassie lay on her bed and cried, huge gut-wrenching sobs. As much as she tried, she couldn't stop the tears. She was overjoyed for Jack at the prospect of seeing Charlie and getting the answers that he so desperately needed, but she was scared too and she couldn't forget Liza's parting words, that Stacey wanted them to be a family again. She hadn't told Jack about Liza's parting words.

Being part of a family was a compelling thing and the pull to make it right, especially with a young child, was very powerful. Possibly more so for Jack, because losing the child he loved, had ended so abruptly and without any warning. Now, a miracle had happened and Jack was going to see that child again. What would it do to him?

Cassie admitted to herself, that she would be a fool to think that it wouldn't have an effect on his life, his plans, or his future. Jack had confirmed, at least to some degree, that Stacey had returned to make it right. What did that mean? Cassie wondered if she would lose the man that she loved, so that he could make his old life work again. How could she keep him from doing what he needed to do? The bottom line was that she couldn't, nor would she.

Cassie looked over at the clock hanging on the wall. "He should be meeting Charlie right about now."

A tear formed that traveled down Cassie's cheek, followed by another tear on the other side. "I really am so happy for Jack." She looked at Abby. "He's going to get to see Charlie again. Can you even begin to imagine what he's feeling at this very moment?"

"No, I really can't." Abby stared off into the sky herself. "We've all had terribly sad losses, but how many times does it happen where you get to recover that loss?"

Cassie didn't know the answer to that either. She hoped and prayed through the night that he would find the answers he needed and that somewhere, somehow there could be a happy ending in this for all of them. Her problem was that she wasn't entirely sure that she would be a part of that happy ending.

Cassie looked at her closest friend. "I'm in love with him."

Abby looked at her friend. "I know you are." She so desperately wanted to tell Cassie to believe that everything would work out for the best, but in her life, she'd learned that wasn't always the truth. Although she deeply hoped otherwise, she wouldn't lie to Cassie with false promises.

"I don't think Jack will make a stupid decision, Cassie." Cassie looked at her. "I can't imagine how he could. Look at what she did to him before."

"I can't imagine he would," but then she caught site of the various photographs of Brett in her living room, "but when a child is involved, it's a whole other story."

Cassie stopped and collected her thoughts before continuing. "I couldn't blame him if he wants to make it right so that he can be with Charlie again. He loves him and wants to protect him."

Cassie looked out at the clouds now billowing in the sky. "When you love a child, whether it's yours biologically or not, he or she belongs to you. There is almost nothing more powerful than how you love your child." Cassie looked up at Abby. "I won't take that away from him."

Abby knew there was nothing else that she could say to comfort her friend. All she could do was be there for her; that's what they'd always done for each other.

Soon they would all know Jack's decision. If Jack chose to try again with Stacey, Abby would be there for Cassie until her heart healed. The big question was 'would Cassie's heart heal after this?' Abby had never seen her love anyone else like she loved Jack.

Abby swatted her friend on the leg. "Come on. You can't just sit here staring out the window. I brought over a shrimp salad, let's go sit on the patio and eat."

Cassie looked at her and shook her head no. "Okay. Then let's go for a walk and get some fresh air." Again Cassie shook her head no.

Abby grabbed her hands and pulled Cassie up off the couch. "Come on. No arguing with me. You need food and you need fresh air."

Cassie groaned but didn't resist as Abby pulled her up from the couch and led her to the patio chair in the back yard.

"Okay, you take deep breaths and let the sun warm your face while I go get the salad. I'll be back in a minute."

After Abby brought out the salads, she tried to talk about her work, which normally Cassie loved, but today it wouldn't hold her attention. No surprise there. Cassie's mind was somewhere else.

Abby had eaten all of her salad and Cassie had only eaten a few bites of hers. Abby urged her to eat some more. "I can't really. Thanks for bringing it, but I just feel kind of nauseous. Literally, I think I'm just sick over all this worrying."

Abby leaned back in her chair. She was starting to have a funny little inkling in her head. She thought back over the last several days. Cassie had been hot and dizzy at the rehearsal and had to step out for air. Abby didn't think too much about it, until she walked in the theater and actually thought it was a little chilly in there with the air conditioner blasting. Cassie had mentioned feeling very tired several times. That wasn't like Cassie at all. She was normally energetic and full of get-up and go. She'd been in her line of work too long not to recognize certain symptoms.

"Cassie, can I ask you a silly question?"

Cassie still stared off at the sky, not really paying attention. "Sure."

"Have your breasts been tender lately."

Cassie reached to her breast and touched it slightly. "Actually, they have been. I noticed it when I rolled over them in bed the other night." Suddenly she looked at Abby, realizing how ridiculous that particular question seemed, in light of all the other things going on right now. "Why did you ask me that?"

Abby smiled, leaned towards her and took her hand. "I don't want to mislead you in any way," Abbey took in a deep breathe, "but I think there's a slight chance that you could be pregnant. Maybe."

Cassie pulled her hand away and covered her mouth with it. "No, Abs, no way."

Abby looked at her closely. "I could be wrong, and please forgive me if I am, but you have more than one symptom of being pregnant."

Cassie dropped her hand from her mouth. "Like what?"

"The sore boobs, exhaustion, dizziness, nausea, loss of appetite."

Cassie stared at Abby and then her eyes rimmed with tears. "Abs, how is it possible?"

Abby patted her hand and grinned at her. "Do we need to have a birds and bees talk?"

"No, of course not!" Cassie searched her mind for some sense of reality. "I mean, it's just not possible. Abby you know this." Cassie's mind was still searching for answers.

"I tried to get pregnant with another child for the last five years of marriage to Peter. Remember, I had that horrible, confusing diagnosis of 'undiagnosed fertility' that I was so frustrated by?"

Abby spoke softly. "That's kind of the point of undiagnosed fertility. They couldn't find a specific reason why you couldn't get pregnant again."

Cassie leaned back in her chair, feeling absolutely astonished. "I never even thought about birth control. First of all, Jack was my first lover in a very long time and secondly, I didn't think it was possible for me to get pregnant. Birth control didn't even cross my mind."

Abby pulled the car keys out of her pocket. "I think we need to run to the drug store and buy a pregnancy kit. Then we'll know for sure."

Although still stunned at Abby's suggestion, and as ridiculous as it sounded, suddenly Cassie couldn't wait for one more second. "Let's go."

A half hour later, they were back from Don's Pharmacy. Ironically, it was the very same pharmacy where they went to buy a pregnancy test kit twenty years early.

Cassie and Abby both read the packaging instructions a dozen times. Cassie had started to head into the bathroom several times, but then stopped herself. "Should I wait until the morning, when it's my first urine?"

Abby gently told her. "There are more hormones in your urine in the morning, but you can take the test now."

Cassie nodded. She knew that. She'd read it, but this whole day was so surreal. Instantly she realized she needed to know. In three minutes she would know one way or another. The stick would say 'pregnant' or 'not pregnant.'

Three minutes later, Abby and Cassie stood outside the closed bathroom door. The stick they were so anxiously waiting to see was lying on the bathroom counter.

Just like twenty years ago, Abby and Cassie nodded to each other for reassurance. Cassie turned the bathroom door knob and they both peered in at the stick that lay on the counter. *Pregnant.*

Cassie's breath caught in her throat and tears came to her eyes. Abby pulled her into a huge hug. Cassie looked at the stick again. It still said *Pregnant.*

"Congratulations, mama!"

Tears of joy rolled down Cassie's face. "After trying for so long, I would have never believed I'd get pregnant again." She had to sit on the side of the bathtub for a second. Her head and heart were both swirling with emotions.

Abby shrugged her shoulders. "It happens all the time." She lightly touched Cassie's belly. "But I'm so glad it happened to you."

Cassie touched her own tummy now and rubbed it tenderly. "Me too. I'm still in shock." She laughed. "I'm just thrilled, but stunned. Are we sure?" She looked at the testing stick again. *Pregnant.* "Look, Abs, it says pregnant!"

Suddenly Cassie stopped and looked at Abby. "Wasn't this whole scene kind of familiar?" Abby laughed. "Just a little."

They grabbed each other and held hands as they danced together in the bathroom.

Later on, when they were back outside on the patio and enjoying the sunshine, Abby asked Cassie when she was going to tell Jack about the pregnancy.

Cassie had been thinking that very question. "I am going to wait just a little bit. I'll go to the doctor on Monday morning and find out for sure."

Abby knew that pregnancy tests couldn't give a false positive, so she was convinced of the test results, but Cassie is a little older Mom and would need prenatal vitamins anyway, so she was happy she was going to the doctor.

Cassie continued her thought process. "I would never keep this child from Jack, but I don't want to influence whatever decision he's going to make because of it. If he is leaning towards staying with Stacey, I don't want to confuse him."

"What if he goes back to her?"

That would be the biggest hurt she'd ever have to get over. Peter's leaving was miniscule compared to Jack not being in her life.

"If he goes back to her, I'll tell him about the baby a little later. We'll make arrangements for him to see it often. This baby will know that Jack is his or her dad and I'll make sure they'll always have time together." Cassie would never sink to Stacey's level.

Cassie touched her tummy and stroked it gently. With tears in her eyes, she looked at Abby. "This baby was born out of love and I'll always be so grateful for it, no matter what decision Jack makes." Cassie's voice cracked. "Even if the decision he makes breaks my heart."

Chapter Thirty-Three

Stacey dropped Charlie off at her friend's house once again. Hopefully this would be the last time she had to leave Charlie there. Things were going better than expected and much quicker than expected too. When she called Jack this morning, he asked her if they could meet today. Alone. What could be better? Stacey was confident that once she could really be close to Jack, that she'd have him just where she wanted him and everything would fall into place.

Stacey dialed Liza's cell phone on the way over to Jack's house. If Liza picked up the phone, then Tom wasn't around and she could talk. Liza picked up on the second ring.

"Guess where I'm headed now?"

Liza could hear the excitement in her friend's voice. "Oh, do tell."

Stacey was hoping she could hold out and tease her for a little bit, but she just couldn't do it.

"Jack's house! He asked me to meet him, alone." Stacey practically purred out 'alone.'

Liza cheered and clapped her hands. "Perfect-o, Stacey. Wow, he was easier than we thought."

Stacey was supremely satisfied with herself. "I know. After all, how could he resist me?" She remembered the red silk bra and panties that she was wearing and she felt confident and sexy.

Liza chuckled. "Obviously, he can't."

The two of them talked a few minutes longer before hanging up.

Stacey sang along to the music on the radio as she drove to Jack's house. She had a new appreciation for the neighborhood he lived in. It wasn't as boring as living in the middle of the desert, besides, it was temporary. She would find another Richard soon. What is it they say? 'Three's a charm.' Yes, the next one would be her Prince Charming, who was rich and didn't want more children. Then Jack and Richard would be but a distant memory.

As she got closer to the house, she allowed herself to worry just a little bit. What if this didn't work? What would she do? She couldn't go back to Richard. What a nightmare that turned out to be.

Richard had his secretary forge Stacey's name on a medical authorization so that her medical records could be sent to the fertility specialist in San Francisco. Stacey thought there was some kind of doctor and patient privilege, but *no*, apparently not. The creep specialist informed Richard that Stacey had been on birth control the entire time.

Richard put two and two together and figured out that with her prescription birth control use, there was no way she could have had two miscarriages. Stacey begged for his forgiveness and pleaded with him to just teach Charlie the business when he was older, but Richard was furious and called Stacey every name in the book. He told her that he'd be filing for divorce the next day and that he wanted her and Charlie out of the house immediately. She packed up that night, took Charlie out of his bed and headed to the only place where she knew she could be secure for now and that was with Jack.

Even while she was driving back to California, she was pretty sure that Jack would take her back. Although she was normally confident in her ability to lure men, she still had a few concerns. Jack was a stand-up kind of guy and she knew that she'd hurt him deeply. She worried that it would be hard for him to forgive her.

Then all of her fears and concerns flew out the window when she remembered watching Jack and Charlie playing in the park. Those two were all smiles within a minute of reuniting. Jack's face lit up the second he saw Charlie and he grinned from ear to ear the entire time they were together.

Satisfied with this thought and remembering how crazy Jack had always been about Charlie, she was now confident in Jack taking her back. She would even tell him the truth, but only as a last resort, just to reassure him that she was sincere in being upfront with him and making a real effort at 'their marriage' and raising Charlie together. Stacey chuckled to herself, 'their marriage,' what a hoot! She needed to be in a real marriage like she needed another hole in her head.

Stacey pulled up in front of the house, touched up her hair and lipstick and said "show time" before getting out of the car.

Inside, Jack was pacing the floor. He'd been taking care of everything he could to clear up this mess and he rushed to get back home before Stacey arrived. He'd heard from Jon and knew where Charlie was. Jon was in an unmarked unit in front of that house and his buddy was positioned at back of that house. Charlie was safe, so he could breathe easier. Now it was time to play it all out with Stacey.

At Stacey's knock, Jack opened the door. True to form, Stacey's skirt was shorter this time and her blouse was unbuttoned just a little deeper. He saw a hint of red peeking out through the neckline of her blouse.

With a soft purr in her voice, Stacey began, "Hi Jack, can I come in?"

Jack opened the door wider. "Welcome."

Stacey looked around and didn't seem to notice that it was no longer empty. "Home sweet home."

Jack invited her to sit on the couch. She did and patted the seat right next to him. "I'm so glad you asked me to come over, Jack. It's been torture the last few days waiting for this moment."

Jack looked at her sweetly. "I'm sure it was, but you can only imagine how much I had to think about."

Stacey nodded. "I'm sure you did, but I just couldn't stop thinking about how much fun you and Charlie had at the park. It's all that Charlie talks about."

Jack couldn't help but to be sincere. "It was one of the best days of my life."

Stacey smiled knowingly and put her hand on Jack's leg. She left it there. "See! It's proof just how much we all belong together."

Jack stood up and turned to face her. He ran his fingers through his hair. "Stacey, before I make my final decision, I still need to know from you everything that happened, so that I can put it all behind me and move on."

Stacey hopped up and stood close to Jack. "Of course you do." Stacey was getting a little nervous and her earlier resolve was slipping away. She turned to the only thing she knew. She moved in closer to Jack and lifted her head towards his and her mouth was inches away from his. Jack seemed to lean in and then pulled away.

"There's time for that later. First we need to talk."

Whew! Stacey was relieved. He still wanted her and desired her. He didn't push her away. She reminded herself that she should have known that Jack would want to talk first.

Jack knew that he needed to get Stacey talking about herself. It was her favorite subject and it was the only way to get her to begin the conversation.

"So, Stacey, are you married to the guy that you've been living with?"

"Yes, but honey, you don't need to worry about that. It's easy to get a divorce nowadays."

Jack prodded her gently. "What about Charlie? Won't your husband, Charlie's Dad, want to see him?"

Stacey waved her hand away as if to push the mere thought out of his head. She inched herself closer to Jack again. "We don't need to worry about that."

Jack took her elbow. "But I do worry about that. I don't want the police breaking down the door when Charlie's father comes to get him."

Stacey looked down and away from Jack. She was searching for answers that would convince Jack that everything would be okay. She had practiced over and over at the motel, but she was starting to panic when Jack's questions were all racing in her head.

Jack continued on. "Stacey, you've just got to reassure me. I'm so worried about losing Charlie again."

Stacey couldn't seem to find the words. "Jack, honey, I told you we don't need to worry about it."

Jack stepped away from her, opened a drawer and pulled out the paternity test. He held it up in front of Stacey. "I'm not Charlie's father, Stacey. How can we really be comfortable in a new life together, when Charlie's dad could bolt through that door anytime?"

Stacey glanced at the paternity test, thought quickly and then looked into Jack's eyes. She knew that this time there was only one way to get back with Jack and that was with the truth.

Stacey forced herself to spring a little tear in her eyes, as she hoped the effect would soften Jack's heart. She batted her eyes softly and put an intentional tremble in her voice.

"If I tell you the whole truth, are you going to be mad at me?"

Jack shook his head no. "Of course not. No more secrets, okay? Then we can put this all behind us." Jack stroked her shoulder in an effort to reassure her.

Stacey reminded herself that the truth was the only way now. Jack wouldn't accept it otherwise, and then she'd be living on the streets. She managed to take three thousand dollars from Richard's safe when she left, but that was all she had and it was dwindling quickly. If she played her cards right, she could leave the Inn tonight.

Stacey walked back over to the couch and sat down. She patted the seat next to her once again and Jack joined her.

"Jack, honey," Stacey took in a deep breath, "You are Charlie's daddy."

Jack's heart leaped and he had to stop himself from jumping for joy off the couch. He had to physically force himself to stay sitting and hear out the rest of what Stacey had to say. He had to look away from her for a minute because he was overcome with emotion.

Charlie is my son!

Yet, he needed to hear the rest before he could truly celebrate.

Stacey could see the absolute joy in his eyes, so she knew it was all going to be okay. "I realize now that what I did was so wrong, but at the time, I was thinking about what was best for Charlie."

Jack practically gagged on her words. "How could Charlie being away from his father, be best?" Jack was furious at her suggestion and he was struggling to keep his anger inside.

Stacey rubbed his thigh up and down with her hand. "Just hear me out and I think you'll understand." Jack listened intently.

Stacey began. "I knew Richard before I met you. He came to San Francisco and Napa on business quite often. He was a nice man and liked to have a good time and he treated me nice." She looked at Jack. "It's before we were married, so it was okay."

Jack nodded and urged her to continue. Stacey looked directly into Jack's eyes and took herself back to meeting Richard again. "One night I was out with Liza and we were just having a harmless girls' night out." Jack didn't buy it for a second, but he wasn't going to let on.

"Well, that night Richard was back in town, but he was no longer the happy-go-lucky man that I used to have a good time with. He was the saddest man I'd ever seen."

Stacey looked at Jack tenderly. "It turns out that he was just distraught because his son had died in some kind of four-wheeler accident in the desert."

Even though this man was partially responsible for Charlie leaving somehow, Jack could feel sympathy for a person who had lost their child. It was something he could understand all too well.

"Richard is terribly wealthy. He has this large copper mine in Nevada and he'd worked all his life so that his son could take it over. He had daughters, but you know some of the older people, they don't see daughters the same way as they see their son."

Jack nodded in agreement, although he personally couldn't comprehend that.

Stacey looked at Jack and rubbed his thigh once again. "Now this is what will make you mad."

Jack braced himself. "I knew that you had been working so hard at work at being a dad to Charlie all the time that you were just exhausting yourself," Stacey watched him carefully and didn't see a reaction, so she continued. If she only knew how wrong she was and that Jack was ready to explode at her comment.

"I wrongly convinced myself that if I moved Charlie to Nevada, that Richard could teach him the business when he was older and Charlie would have a secure future. Charlie would be wealthy, have a business of his own and never have to worry about a thing. Life would be a little easier for you too." Stacey paused without realizing that Jack had started to shake.

"Liza and I gathered all the stuff and we drove to Nevada while you were gone." Jack thought his blood vessels were going to burst in his neck and it took every ounce of strength he had to control himself.

Stacey looked down and away, momentarily lost in her own thoughts. She honestly believed that Richard would grow to see Charlie as his son. After all, he would have a ready-made son already there. Unfortunately, Richard wanted his own son and he was insistent for two years that they have a child together. He saw a woman with a child and knew she could bear another one. Charlie wasn't even a consideration for him.

Stacey sighed. "I know it was a terrible mistake, but at the time, I was trying to do what was best for Charlie."

Jack could no longer control himself and he jumped off the couch, walked over to the fireplace and beat the mantel with his fist. "How in the hell could you possibly think it was best for Charlie?" Jack shook his head and held out his hands to stop Stacey from talking "Don't even try and answer me, Stacey. I already know the answer."

Stacey jumped up and headed towards him with a panic on her face. Jack stopped her again. "This had nothing," his jaw clenched as he spoke, "and I mean absolutely nothing, to do with Charlie. It had everything to do with you! You wanted a rich husband. Period. Doing something for Charlie had zero to do with it."

"Jack, honey, that's not true. I left with every intention of writing you and telling you the truth, but I needed Richard to get used to Charlie, and all Charlie did was cry for his daddy and that he wanted to go home. It just took more time than I thought."

Jack's heart broke once again for the frightened little boy who had no say about what his mother had done or that he was away from the one person he knew he could count on completely.

Jack was shaking violently inside and any kind of control was becoming increasingly difficult. His next words were angry, but he continued to struggle to keep from lashing out.

"Stacey, I will never forgive you for what you did to Charlie, or to me. I can't even begin to tell you how much it destroyed me to lose *my son!*" Jack pounded on the mantel again and Stacey jumped at the sound.

Jack paced in front of the fireplace and then stopped in front of Stacey. "Even if I could explain it to you, you could never understand. You care about Stacey and that's it; no one else."

Stacey stepped towards Jack and put her hands on his chest. "Jack, honey, that's just not true. I came back here to be with you. I brought Charlie back to you."

Jack laughed, "So getting kicked out of Richard's house had nothing to do with it at all?"

Stacey was stunned. How could he know? That dirty, rotten little rat Charlie must have told him. She was seeing her plan slip away and she had to do something quickly.

Stacey straightened her back, squared her shoulders and looked Jack directly in the eye. "Fine, then. If you can't forgive me, I'll just take Charlie away and we won't bother you anymore."

Now Stacey was angry. Here she was trying to get Charlie back into Jack's life and he was completely ungrateful. Leaving would certainly get his attention, although she silently prayed that he would beg her to stay once she got to the front door.

Jack walked over to the bookshelf and pulled out a large manila envelope and handed it to Stacey. "Here's a courtesy copy of a court Order for you Stacey. When you walk out the front door, a process server will hand you an official copy."

Stacey grabbed the envelope and started to open it. "What is this?" She looked at Jack in stunned surprise.

"It's a custody Order, Stacey. It grants full legal and physical custody of Charlie to me." Stacey quickly scanned it as Jack continued. "I got a court Order right after you left with Charlie and it was renewed in court this morning."

Jack pointed to another line in the Order. "As you can see, since you're a flight risk, you'll have supervised visitation with Charlie three times a week."

Stacey couldn't believe what she was reading. This just wasn't possible, was it? What in the hell was this legal nonsense? Supervised visitation? But I'm his mother.

Suddenly, she remembered her ace in the hole. The paternity test and she grabbed it off the coffee table.

Stacey waved it in front of Jack's face and stomped her foot. "I'll go see my lawyer right away and show him this. Here's all the proof I need. It says right here, that you are not Charlie's father."

Jack walked over to Stacey and looked down at the paternity test. With a cocky grin, he looked into her eyes. He pointed to a line on the paternity test and directed Stacey to it, "Look here, Stacey," Stacey's eyes followed Jack's finger, "you see, this dime store paternity test that you bought has tiny print right here at the bottom that reads that the samples were not collected according to the American Association of Blood Banks, and the laboratory cannot verify the origin of the DNA samples."

Jack carefully took the paternity test from her hands and stood reading it as if from a podium. "Gee, Stacey, my favorite line right below that says 'the test is non-legally binding.'"

Stacey looked up at him, clearly confused and Jack explained. "That means that the paternity test wasn't taken by an accredited laboratory, so the results are not legal."

Stacey looked at the writing on the DNA test and she was furious. She didn't notice that tiny print when she bought it. She just read the instructions on how to swab the cheek of the child and the proposed father. She remembered how easy it was. She swabbed Charlie's cheek while he was sleeping and just to make sure that she got a false reading, she swabbed Richard's cheek when he was passed out drunk.

Still, she wasn't ready to give up and hoped that Jack didn't believe her when she told him earlier that he was Charlie's father. Just a hint of self-doubt on Jack's part and the ball would be back in her court.

She lifted her chin in defiance and looked at Jack. "Fine, that's just fine, because I was lying to you when I told you that Charlie was your son, so I'll just go to court myself and demand that they do a legal paternity test on you." Stacey thought to herself, there I said it, maybe now Jack will come to his senses and this could all be over with.

Jack looked at her and cocked his head to one side. Then a smile grew on his face. "For once in my life, Stacey, I do believe you. I really do believe you. You told me the truth when you said that Charlie was my son."

Stacey continued to be defiant and stood there looking directly at Jack with her arms crossed in front of her chest.

Jack continued, "Even if I didn't believe you, *which I do*, the court can't require me to take a blood test to determine paternity."

Stacey looked at him and raised her eyebrows in surprise. Jack shook his head. "Nope, Stacey, they can't. That's another thing you might want to check on with that lawyer of yours."

Jack leaned in close to Stacey's ear. "You see, there's a little law here in this state that when a child is born during the course of marriage, there's an automatic presumption of paternity."

Stacey was even more confused and Jack could read it on her face. Her voice trembled. "An automatic what?"

Jack filled in the blanks for her. "What that means, is that since Charlie was born while we were married, the court automatically assumes that I am Charlie's dad and they can't force me to take a paternity test."

Stacey's breath was taken away. How did this all happen? She'd just lost everything. Her money would be gone soon. What was she going to do? She felt weak in the knees and had to sit down on the couch again.

Jack looked at Stacey and told her one final thing. As angry as he was with her, he had to think about Charlie first.

"Unlike you, I won't turn my son's world upside down by keeping you completely out of his life." Jack knew it would be extremely difficult, but he would never hurt Charlie by keeping his mother away. The hardest thing he'd ever done was lose his son, but keeping him physically and emotionally safe would be easy.

"I'll get a therapist for Charlie so that he understands everything that has happened to him, and I hope you'll work with the therapist too to help Charlie through this." Jack pointed to the legal papers again. "On the court Order is the address and phone number for the place where you'll have supervised visits with Charlie. I'll have him there tomorrow at noon for your first visit."

Stacey stammered and stuttered and started to stand up, "But, Jack, I have Charlie in my custody. I have to go pick him up," she stood up, "now."

Jack looked at her and shook his head no. "No, Stacey, Charlie is in my care now. Jon and another officer picked him up at your friend's house a few minutes ago."

Chapter Thirty-Four

Tom Beardsley's secretary buzzed him. He told her he wasn't to be disturbed this afternoon. He had too many things to do and too much on his mind.

"Sorry to bother you, but Jack Shaw is here and he said that it's urgent that he talk to you."

Tom was confused. Jack Shaw. What did he want? He'd done business with him in the past and he had a reliable reputation and did good work, but Tom couldn't think of a project that was going on right now. Fine, he could use a quick break from the pile on his desk anyway. "Send him in."

Jack walked in and closed the door behind him. Tom stood up and shook Jack's hand.

"What can I do for you, Shaw?"

Jack wasn't angry at Tom Beardsley, but he had a bone to pick with his wife, Liza. Since she would never listen to reason, Jack had no choice but to go through her husband. It was crucial that Jack do everything he could to protect Charlie from here on out.

Jack stood with his hands on his hips and faced Tom. "I don't know if you know much about my history, but my ex-wife is Stacey," he paused, "who happens to be good friends with your wife."

Tom Beardsley was immediately disgusted. "Christ, Shaw. We're grown men. We don't need to get into any crap that has to do with wives and ex-wives." Lord have mercy, after having two ex-wives, one thing that Tom Beardsley knew for certain, was not to get involved with matters related to ex-wives.

Jack didn't back down. "Normally, I would agree with you a hundred perfect, except that I have a problem with your wife."

What did she do now? Tom raised his voice slightly, "What about my wife?"

Jack continued. "The long and the short of the story is that I just got custody of my son." Tom was unimpressed. His kids were grown and they were still pain in the ass most the time.

Jack looked him in the eye. "As you may or may not know, when my ex-wife left, she took our son away. Basically kidnapped him; I didn't see him for over two years."

Tom was getting more curious. What the hell did this have to do with his wife?

Jack continued. "Apparently, your wife helped her do that."

He caught Tom's surprised looked and went on. "Liza helped Stacey take a minor child across the state line." Tom grew a little pale as Jack brought him up to date.

Jack's hands remained on his hips. "My son is back and that's all I care about personally, but I've heard through a good source at the Sheriff's department that the District Attorney is interested in charging Liza with accessory to kidnapping charges. That's their call though. You'll have to deal with that."

Tom was furious now, although it wasn't with Jack Shaw. In some strange way, he respected the man for coming directly to him.

Jack went on. "Normally, I wouldn't give a crap what your wife does, but I was pretty upset after I found out about her involvement in taking my son away."

Tom had no doubt about that. "Why are you telling me this now, Shaw?" Jack was worried that Tom Beardsley would try and buy Liza out of the legal mess.

"Apparently your wife and Stacey were in San Francisco recently and they hatched this plan to have Stacey come back to town." Jack's grip from his hips loosened, but he forced himself to keep his fists at his side.

"Once again, Beardsley, I don't give a hairy rat's ass what your wife does, but if she's continuing to be involved in something that affects my son, I want it stopped *now*!" Jack pounded his fist on Beardsley's desk.

Tom yelled to Jack. "I get your fuckin' point." He took in a deep breath and then calmed down a little. "Don't worry, Shaw, I'll make sure she's not a problem to your boy again."

Jack was calmer now too. "I appreciate it. I hope you can understand that I have to protect my son." Tom nodded in understanding. Although his kids were a pain most of the time, he'd still do anything to protect them.

Jack left and Tom sat back down in his chair with a sigh. For days now, he'd been struggling with the information he'd learned from the private investigator that had followed Liza to San Francisco.

When Liza asked to go to San Francisco alone, something in his gut told him that two and two didn't add up. When he happened to see the credit card charge for the Rolex watch on his online credit card statement a few days after Liza begged him to go alone, and before she'd even left for San Francisco, he knew Liza wasn't shopping for his birthday gift. When he saw that credit card statement, he called his investigator to discreetly follow her.

Tom opened his desk drawer and an envelope with the compromising pictures were still sitting in there. Most of the pictures weren't extremely clear, but it was obvious that Liza was dressed to kill. So was the woman with her and their companions were sitting mighty close to them and stroking their legs. Now he knew that the other woman was Stacey. The investigator's report indicated that each couple went into a private room. He thought he'd made it clear when they got married that that door was closed. Apparently, Liza opened it again.

Tom sighed again. *Dammit.* When he married Liza, he'd already taken a ton of heat from friends he'd had for years, not to mention his kids. No one was happy when he married her. There's no fool, like an old fool he thought to himself. He winced at his own stupidity.

Now, Liza was possibly facing some kind of kidnapping charge. Tom shook his head from side to side. That wasn't a battle he was willing to fight.

Tom picked up his phone and buzzed his secretary. "Get my lawyer on the phone."

"Your corporate lawyer, sir?"

"No. My divorce lawyer."

Chapter Thirty-Five

Cassie locked the door to Cassie's Closet behind Dani. She was the last one to leave for the evening. Before she turned off the lights, she took a look around. All the plastic partitions were down now. She had a completely new kitchen area, living room area, baby and toddler area and new dressing rooms. She smiled at the completed work. She was so proud that the dream that she'd had for this place for so many years, was now complete. It was stunning and tomorrow she would have her staff assemble all the appliances, furniture and everything else properly. Then she'd have the grand reveal and the party that she'd been promising everyone.

As happy as Cassie was to see the final result of her dream, it was sad that Jack wasn't here. Somewhere along the line, she'd envisioned that he would be by her side for the reveal. This was his project, his baby too. At the thought of a baby, Cassie grinned and touched her stomach lightly. The doctor had taken a blood test and confirmed that she was pregnant. She was getting over the shock and found herself more and more excited each day. She'd thought to herself over the last few days, what an incredible gift she'd been given. She was going to have another child, Jack's child.

Cassie hadn't heard from Jack for days. As anxious as she was to hear from him now, she knew that eventually she would. He needed time to consider everything and make his decision. Now that she'd gone to the doctor and confirmed her pregnancy, she would call him in a couple of weeks if he hadn't called her before then. Besides, if he hadn't called by then, it would be pretty obvious that he'd made his decision. Cassie's shoulders slumped at the thought.

Cassie turned around and started to walk back to her office. It was time to close up shop and head home. From behind her, she heard the soft tap of a knock on the door. She wondered if someone hadn't noticed that the "open" sign had been turned off. She turned back towards the door and started to call out that they were closed when she immediately caught sight of a familiar figure in the doorway. Her heart leaped.

It was Jack!

Cassie was pretty sure she sprinted to the door so that she could unlock it and let him in. She couldn't believe he was really there.

Cassie couldn't help herself. A smile broke out a mile wide across her face. Just seeing him standing there made her heart do a little flip.

"Hi." Cassie said softly.

Jack stepped closer to her. "Hi, yourself." God, but if she wasn't a sight for sore eyes, Jack thought to himself.

Cassie didn't know if she should hug him or not. All she knew was that she couldn't take her eyes off him.

Jack's eyes were shining brightly. Cassie wasn't sure, but it seemed like he was as happy to see her as she was to see him.

Jack couldn't stop himself. He went right to her and took her face in his hands. His lips touched hers and all the agony of the last several days started to leave his body. When they pulled apart, a tear was in Cassie's eyes and she sought Jack's eyes for answers.

Jack stood back, but kept both of her hands held tightly in his own hands. As he faced her, he thought she was the most beautiful woman he'd ever seen. He knew he'd missed her the last several days, but his heart pounded when he kissed her and he was reminded just how much he truly needed her.

Jack looked into Cassie's eyes. "I have so much to tell you." Cassie wanted to hear every single word of it too.

Jack looked at Cassie tenderly. "I found out that Charlie is my son. I mean, he's really my son." Cassie was so thrilled for him. She couldn't stop herself; she pulled him back towards her and held him tightly.

"Oh Jack, I'm so happy for you!" She genuinely was.

Jack broke the hug just long enough to look into Cassie's eyes. "I'll tell you all the details later, but he's mine and he's back with me."

There was just about nothing else that Cassie wanted to hear more, but she needed to know Jack's decision about Stacey. That decision affected the rest of her life; one way or another.

"What about Charlie's mom?"

Jack knew what she was really asking. "Stacey is going to be a part of my life." Cassie's heart dropped but then Jack looked deeply in her eyes, "but only because she's Charlie mom." Now Cassie's heart soared.

Jack continued to hold both of Cassie's hands. He looked into her eyes and he could see all the love that he always wanted, but never thought he'd find. Cassie had been able to look into his eyes even when there was pain, and somehow find a way to get beyond that pain and breathe life back into his heart and soul.

Jack now looked past Cassie and around the store. He could see that all the work was done and that it looked beautiful. Then he looked back into Cassie's eyes. He spoke softly. "It had to be here, at Cassie's Closet, where I came to tell you that this is where I fell in love with you." A tear escaped Cassie's eye.

"From the first moment I walked in and saw you, my heart skipped a beat. From that moment on, I never stopped thinking about you, not for one second." Jack smiled and wiped away Cassie's tear.

"You brought me back to life Cassie."

Jack dropped to his knee. "I want to spend the rest of my life with you. Jack stopped talking and now on bended knee, he squeezed both of Cassie's hands, "but before you answer me, you have to know that I'm a package deal, Sweetheart. I hope to God you'll say yes, because I can't imagine you not being in my life."

This time, Jack kissed both of her hands. "I need you. I need us. Will you marry me?"

Cassie started laughing and crying. She was shaking and tears of joy were flowing down her cheeks. She looked down at Jack, still on his knees, and smiled, "I'm a package deal too, my love."

Jack was a little confused. "Of course, Brett will always be a part of our family..." His voice trailed off, as Cassie let go of one of his hands and touched her belly softly.

He looked up at her in stunned surprise as the realization kicked in. "A baby?" Cassie nodded.

Jack let out a loud whoop and stood up to kiss Cassie full on the mouth. Then he kissed her again. And again. When he pulled back, he looked at her. "Are you sure?"

She nodded her head yes and laughed. "I'm sure. So is the doctor." Jack dropped to his knees and kissed her belly. "We're going to have a baby!"

Jack popped back up, facing Cassie. He was beyond thrilled and excited. He was going to have a child with his love, Cassie.

Cassie pulled Jack into her arms, she was so excited. She couldn't remember if she'd answered him yet or not, but every fiber of her being knew the answer. She shouted out "yes, yes, yes" to the marriage proposal and to their life together.

Jack picked her up and twirled her around. When he sat her back down on her feet, he kissed her over and over again and promised her that he'd never stop loving her. She promised him that there would never be a day when he wouldn't know how much she loved him.

Jack knew that was a promise he could believe in.

Epilogue

They say that we have snapshot memories, a memory that is simply so clear, that we'll remember every detail of it the rest of our lives, just like a photograph had been taken. Today was one of those days for Cassie.

Cassie sat upright in her hospital bed. To the right of her were Jack's parents, her parents, Jon, Jeremy, Kevin, Colleen and a somewhat exhausted looking Abby. All of them were happily chattering away and pushing away the floating balloons that seemed to fill the air. Among the happy chatter, Cassie heard someone mention getting a snack in the cafeteria downstairs. All of them blew kisses or leaned over and hugged her, with a promise to be back soon.

After they left, Cassie looked down to the foot of the bed and there stood Jack, Brett and Charlie. Brett lifted Charlie into his arms so that he could see the tightly wrapped bundle that Jack held in his arms.

As he peered over to the baby, Charlie started giggling and glanced at Jack. "Dad, dad, look."

Jack looked over at Charlie with a smile. "Yeah, buddy?"

Charlie giggled again. "The baby has one eye open and one eye closed. Ah, that's so cute." Jack looked down at the baby and then back to Charlie. "You used to do that when you were a baby. You'd yawn and one eye would stay open for a minute afterwards."

Charlie looked up in amazement. "I did?"

Jack leaned over and kissed the top of Charlie's head. "Yep, the baby is just like you."

Jack and Cassie were both so happy about Charlie's progress the last several months. He had adjusted to living with them quickly and easily and was so excited to be a big brother. It was almost scary how easily it all happened, but Charlie's therapist reminded them that Charlie had basically been starved for love and attention for the last two years, so he was going to respond to all that love and affection quickly.

Cassie and Jack made a point to give Charlie all the love he could handle every day and then some. There wasn't a quiet second in their house with all of Charlie's stories and incessant chatter, but it was nothing short of music to their ears.

Charlie followed Jack everywhere. When Jack got custody, he explained to Charlie that he was his real dad and some of what happened, but he told him at a level that a four-year could understand. The rest would come later. All Charlie knew was that he was loved and cherished by his dad and Cassie. Now he was thriving.

Cassie heard Charlie calling Jack "dad" dozens of times a day. It never got old and sometimes she could still see the emotion on Jack's face when he heard that simple, precious word from his son.

Charlie accepted Cassie quickly too. She won him over easily the first night they met, when she brought chocolate chip cookies and board games. Charlie wasn't used to having a woman play with him, so he thought she was pretty cool. After the three of them laughed their way through Charlie's winning streak, Cassie knew that she was in love with Charlie and his cute freckled-face nose. How could she not? He was precious, loveable and made their lives full, but more than anything else, he made his father very, very happy.

One night about four months after they got married, Jack and Cassie were both tucking Charlie into bed, which they always did together. They took turns telling him a good night story and pulled the blanket up to his chin. Charlie looked at both of them and asked if he could ask a question. They both said of course.

"You said I get to live with you guys forever right?"

They told him absolutely yes and Jack rubbed his chest. "Why, Charlie?"

"Because I love you both so much, I don't ever want to leave."

With their reassurance that he would always be with them, Charlie was asleep within a few seconds, completely unaware that Jack and Cassie continued to sit on his bed and watch him sleep, both in awe of the child they loved so much, and who had now told them that he loved them too.

Stacey showed up for the supervised visitations for less than a week. Then she was a no show. They hadn't heard from her for several months now and she was likely on the run. Charlie hadn't asked about her in as many months. Jack and Cassie both understood that a day would come when Charlie was older and he'd ask questions about his Mom's abandonment. Ultimately those answers were Stacey's cross to bear, but Jack and Cassie were just going to make him feel very loved and wanted by them. Hopefully, he would have that solid foundation from them and Stacey's betrayal of him, wouldn't affect his life in a negative way.

The District Attorney filed kidnapping charges against Stacey, but with Stacey on the run, there was little they could do. They'd heard through Jon's contacts that the State of Nevada was also going to pursue charges for bigamy against Stacey. Although not normally done in most states, Stacey's husband Richard found a loophole. If a person married you with the intention of financial gain, then the courts could pursue the bigamy charges. Apparently, he had influence in the state and was determined to have her tried criminally. It was yet to be seen what would happen, but Cassie's money was on a scorned husband finding Stacey and the State of Nevada.

From her hospital bed, Cassie felt Jack's eyes upon her and he stood much closer to her now. She looked at him holding the baby. Jack had a twinkle in his eye as he broke his eye hold from Cassie and looked down at the tiny pink bundle in his arms.

Jack and Cassie's daughter, Sydney Lauren Shaw, lay in his arms. He lifted her up to give her a soft kiss on the cheek before gently laying

Sydney into Cassie's arms. As he did so, he gave his wife a kiss. "She's so beautiful, just like her Mom."

Cassie's heart filled with emotion. Cassie couldn't believe that she had been given such special gifts in her life. She felt like the luckiest woman in the world.

Jack knew what she was thinking. He had so much love and laughter in his life now. Most days, he pinched himself to make sure he was really awake and not dreaming, but it was all true. He had an amazing son and step-son, and now a beautiful daughter. Most of all, he had Cassie. She was the love of his life and the one that made it all possible. She was his dream come true.

Jack leaned over and kissed her. His lips lingered close to her lips. "You've made me a very happy man, Mrs. Shaw."

Cassie smiled, leaned in closer and touched her lips to his. "And you've made me a very happy woman, Mr. Shaw."

Better With Time

Visit *www.brendabutlerauthor.com* for announcements about the second book in the Shaw Brothers' series, anticipated for release in the Fall 2013.